A Most Unlikely Wedding

Marry Me series
Wedding of the Century
The Unexpected Wedding Guest
A Most Unlikely Wedding
Baby Blues and Wedding Bells

More romance by Patricia McLinn

The Wedding Series
Prelude to a Wedding
Wedding Party
Grady's Wedding
The Runaway Bride
The Christmas Princess
Hoops (prequel to The Surprise Princess)
The Surprise Princess
Not a Family Man (prequel to The Forgotten Prince)
The Forgotten Prince

Seasons in a Small Town
What Are Friends For? (Spring)
The Right Brother (Summer)
Falling for Her (Autumn)
Warm Front (Winter)

Wyoming Wildflowers Series
Wyoming Wildflowers: The Beginning (prequel)
Almost a Bride
Match Made in Wyoming
My Heart Remembers
A New World (prequel to Jack's Heart)
Jack's Heart
Rodeo Nights (prequel to Where Love Lives)
Where Love Lives
A Cowboy Wedding

A Place Called Home series
Lost and Found Groom
At the Heart's Command
Hidden in a Heartbeat

A Most Unlikely Wedding

Marry Me Series
Book 3

Patricia McLinn

This book is dedicated to those
who helped me cover the continent:
Patience Smith and Cheryl Kushner in New York,
Mary Louis Schwartz (a k a Lulu) in Hollywood,
Pam Johnson (again?) in Wisconsin

CHAPTER ONE

"I NEED A man. Right now."

In full knowledge that she was unlikely to get what she needed, Kay Aaronson drove her hands through her cropped hair—yet another mistake, getting it chopped off last winter. At first, she'd tried to grow it out, but exasperation had gotten the better of that effort. So she'd cut it shorter to something with a modicum of style, which, her mother had relentlessly pointed out, it had lacked after the initial shearing.

Come to think of it, last winter's impulsive dive into a chain salon—"A chain? A *chain*?!" her mother had cried—also had been because of a man.

So was the fact that she would be homeless when she returned to New York in a couple of days.

Men—they were nothing but trouble.

Kay cupped her hands over her face, wishing the world would go away. At least the male half of it.

"What kind of man would you like, dear?"

The cultured voice, with a twang of Wisconsin, made Kay drop her hands and open her eyes.

Trudi Bliss—"call me Miss Trudi, dear"—looked back at her with a faint smile deepening the lines of her seventy-plus years and with patient eyes, rather like those of an excellent waiter poised to take Kay's order for a man.

One *homo sapiens*, male, please. Reasonably attractive, mentally stable, unattached yet capable of attachment, served in a thick sauce of humor. Better make it to go, since she'd be returning to New York as soon as she got this last phase of filming done.

If she got this last phase of filming done, which brought her back to her current problem. And the reason she truly did need a man.

Well, not exactly a man. An actor.

"One to replace the jerk who just walked out," she told Miss Trudi. "That's what I need."

As if there were spare actors littering the wide, tree-roofed streets of Tobias.

In the forty-eight hours since she'd arrived here, Kay had seen plenty of strange sights, but nothing that resembled an actor, except the ones she'd imported from New York.

God, she should have listened to that little voice in the back of her head two days ago. The little voice that had a hissy fit when the well-appointed mini-bus she'd hired at Chicago's O'Hare Airport had headed northwest into the wilds of Wisconsin.

Better yet, she shouldn't have listened to Dora in the first place.

Why on earth had she accepted the idea of doing this shoot in her grandmother's hometown?

Dora had talked about Tobias so often when Kay was little that she had dreamed about the lake, the woods, the house where her grandmother had grown up. But Dora had never gotten around to bringing her only grandchild here before the rift between Dora and Kay's father had separated Kay from her grandmother.

For sixteen years she hadn't talked to Dora, not until a few months ago.

"Yes, I gathered that a replacement would be required," Miss Trudi said. "Although I must say, no other member of the company appears distressed by his departure."

No other member of the company's career hung in the balance, Kay thought.

Well, career was a little strong.

Better make it: No other member of the company's shot at *possibly* opening the door to *beginning* what could *someday* turn out to be a career hung in the balance.

"No one's going to miss Brice's personality," she agreed. "But without him, we can't finish. I can just hear me telling Serge, Oops, sorry, I can't give you B roll on an 1899 wedding after all. Even though you're counting on it for pop diva Donna Ravelle's next music video. Even though you gambled on an unknown. Even though this is an opportunity of a lifetime. Even though it's the first step in my plan. Even though I promised…"

"Nonsense, Kay. There is no benefit in looking at the most dire outcome. You said you require a man, so you must have a contingency plan that will allow you to proceed. What is most essential in a replacement man?"

As if this sweet elderly lady who'd been her grandmother's first art teacher could do anything about replacing the jackass actor who had stomped off the shoot moments ago.

"One who'd fit in Brice's wardrobe," she said.

He had waited until they had sunk so much time and money into the project with him playing the groom that starting over was impossible. And then he'd tried to stick her up for more money.

She should have folded. Should have forgotten how much she abhorred blackmail and extortion, and said yes. She would have found the money somewhere, even if she'd had to—no, she wouldn't borrow from her parents. The strings attached to such a loan would tie her up tighter than the Lilliputians strapped down Gulliver.

"Anything else?" Miss Trudi asked as she absently reeled in a length of peach chiffon scarf that had fluttered loose.

What the hell, Kay thought, she might as well dream big.

"To fit the wardrobe, he'd have to be about Brice's size and build. Same coloring would be good, though we could dye his hair and there's always makeup. We're only going to see him from the back. And as long as I'm wishing for the moon, if he could act, even a little, it would be a big improvement on Brice."

"I make no representation about his acting, but I know someone who fits your other requirements, dear."

Kay blinked. The woman sounded sane. And certain.

On the other hand, Miss Trudi was the one who had gotten them to come to Tobias, Wisconsin in the first place.

No, not the *one*, Kay corrected herself. One of the two.

Dora had been absolutely certain that Bliss House provided the best backdrop for Kay's film shoot. Dora had explained that Miss Trudi's family home was being converted to a crafts center to draw visitors to Tobias. Not only did the house provide an ideal background for an 1899 wedding but including it in a video might give business a boost when the center opened this fall.

Hating to risk the tenuous bond she'd been renewing with her grandmother, Kay had agreed to bring the shoot here.

It had been a pain to get the cast and crew to Wisconsin, but Bliss House *was* perfect—as long as they avoided scaffolding, power tools and construction workers.

With Bliss House as the background, she knew they had great footage. All she needed were a few over-the groom's shoulder shots, and she would have a piece of work that would start her on her new career path. Sure, she'd started on a number of other careers in the past, but this time she had a plan.

Just a few more shots…

"You find the right man, Miss Trudi," Kay said, "and I'll do any-thing you want."

"Anything, my dear?"

"Anything."

Whatever this sweet old lady wanted would be a snap.

"OH, ROB, YOU should do it," Fran said. "It'll be good for you."

Rob Dalton looked from his younger sister to Miss Trudi. They'd both lost their minds.

"Good for me? How on earth is being in a music video good for me?"

He'd been digging post holes for a compost bin behind the garage when Fran called from the back porch that he had a visitor. When he'd seen Miss Trudi sitting in one of the wicker chairs, he'd hesitated.

Not because he didn't like Miss Trudi, but because he resented being yanked from the mind-numbing, energy-draining physical labor that almost made him forget.

Good manners won over self-preservation.

Fran opened the porch door and handed him a towel. He scrubbed his face, then the back of his neck.

It stung, burned slightly from today's sun and yesterday's sailing, despite the farmer's tan gained in weeks of helping Max Trevetti's construction crew catch up after a tornado damaged Bliss House.

If he'd been in Chicago, with tomorrow a work day, he'd be in for an uncomfortable time with shirt-collar, tie, and suit coat. But tomorrow would be just like today. No collar, no tie, no suit.

No answers.

Fran sat near the door with that look of concern she'd tried to hide all summer. Good thing he was better at hiding things than she was.

"I mean meeting new people, doing something different—all that will be good for you, Rob," Fran said.

Him, in a video. It was nuts.

"I want to finish the compost bin and—"

"Rob, I truly appreciate your work around the house." Fran had moved back into their childhood home when their father became ill, and stayed on after he died almost two years ago. "But I told you before, it's not necessary. You should be doing fun things. That's why you took this summer off."

Not exactly.

"I'm not sure a music video qualifies." His dry tone won a smile from his sister.

"There is no actual music at this point, you understand, Rob," inserted Miss Trudi, as if that might be a drawback. "So there is no need for you to dance in this segment of the production."

Dance?

Rob closed his eyes. Building a compost bin looked awfully good.

"The director requires someone to stand in for an actor who departed precipitously in a dispute over pay. The primary need is to have a figure to aid filming close-ups of the young woman who plays the bride."

"Miss Trudi, I'm sure there are dozens of guys in town who would be thrilled to—"

"Oh, but it must be you, Rob. You see, it requires someone of similar physique and appearance to the departed actor."

"Still, there must be regulations about this sort of thing. Rules to—"

"I am quite certain that Kay will manage all that. I haven't had the opportunity to speak with her in depth as I had hoped, however, I can assure you that she is an amazing young woman to have arranged and carried out this entire enterprise."

Miss Trudi speaking in depth with someone involved with making a music video boggled his mind.

"Let me think about this."

"Time is too short, Rob. I fear that if filming cannot resume immediately, Kay will be forced to take the production elsewhere, and you know we are counting not only on the fee for the Bliss House budget, but to capitalize on the publicity."

The fee wasn't much. But then again, neither was the Bliss House budget, especially for publicity. Miss Trudi was right, they needed this. If that meant he stood in for an actor, what could it hurt?

"All right."

"Excellent. If it's convenient, may I ride with you to Bliss House?"

"Sure. I'll take a shower, and then we can go."

"Or you could ride with me, Miss Trudi," Fran said.

He frowned at his sister. "You're going to Bliss House?

"Are you kidding? I wouldn't miss this for the world."

"PERFECT! ABSOLUTELY PERFECT!"

The quick-moving woman dressed in black with the dark, feathery hair circled him like he was a cow carcass and she was a butcher deciding where to make the first cut.

At least she didn't have a knife handy. But Rob wondered how much damage those polished nails of hers could do.

"Kay, this is Rob Dalton," Miss Trudi said. "He's a member of the Bliss House committee, and he's agreed to help you complete rolling B."

Still circling, the young woman murmured, "B roll."

"Ah," Miss Trudi said. "Your camera operator explained that to me earlier. Rob, this is Kay Aaronson, director of this project."

"How do you do." He put out his hand, but she was behind him now.

He looked over his shoulder. Through Bliss House's open front door he saw his sister greeting Steve and Annette Corbett. The couple had instigated Bliss House's renovation last winter—and Steve was town manager—so it made sense for them to be on hand.

He had the uncomfortable feeling, though, that sense hadn't brought them here. Especially when he considered Steve's big grin and the fact that they'd arrived just in time for Rob to make a fool of himself.

He wished he were back digging post holes. Better yet, he wished he had a good pen in his hand and a fresh white-papered legal pad in front of him to write out exactly what steps to take next—steps to essentially dismantle the career he'd worked so hard to build.

On the other hand, he'd tried sitting on the roof with a good pen and a legal page this morning and got nowhere. That's what had moved digging post holes to the top of his to-do list for the day.

"Turn around." Kay Aaronson waved one long-fingered hand as she squinted at him. "I want to see the back of your head."

He complied, and studied the chaos in Bliss House's renovated front hall and stairwell. Cameras, lights, toolboxes, mysterious electronic black boxes, enough wires to reach Minnesota, chairs, rolling cloth-covered wardrobe racks, paper coffee cups from empty to brimming, bottled water, reflector stands, and crumpled papers. It looked as if another tornado had hit.

"Uh-huh. Good. Good."

"Ms. Aaronson, there are practical considerations before I agree to—"

"You're right. We'll have to style your hair." She reached up and brushed her fingers into his hair.

It felt as if a shock jumped between them. But it was a very peculiar shock. Not the concentrated, intense burst from scuffing across carpet in a winter-dry house. Instead, it seemed to spread swelling heat across the base of his neck.

But it *must* be an electrical shock. It was the only logical explanation.

Apparently she'd felt it, too, because she snatched her hand back, though she kept talking.

"Not sure if we'll have to dye it. It might be a little lighter than Brice the Rat Fink's. We'll need makeup on the neck to tone down that red. Jeff!"

"Dye? My *hair?*" Rob demanded. He heard laughter from behind him.

But Kay had spun away. "Miss Trudi, you are a miracle-worker and a savior. You've rescued me and I can't tell you how grateful I am. I never thought you could do it, but you have. He's perfect."

"Ms. Aaronson—" Rob started.

"Call me Kay."

"Fine. Kay, there must be rules about filling in for an actor."

"Rules?" she repeated as if she'd never heard the word. And then she had her arm around a wiry man of about thirty who had hurried up with a large plastic contraption resembling a tackle box. "Jeff, you know Brice's hair—I want Rob's cut like it. You make the call on the color."

"Got it, Kay. Chair! Table! Light!"

Just like that, a folding chair was slid behind Rob, chopping against the back of his knees to strongly encourage him to sit. The man named Jeff opened his tackle box on a table that materialized and opened it.

No self-respecting fish would go after these hairy, fuzzy, and multicolored lures.

A plastic bib was wrapped around Rob, and he heard scissors going at the back of his head before he could react. His hair would grow back. But there were some sacrifices he wasn't willing to make for Bliss House.

"Ms. Aaronson—Kay. You are *not* going to dye my hair."

She flitted in front of him again, squinting in concentration.

She kept circling. The movement made the wispy ends of her dark hair flutter. Her hair smoothly followed the shape of her skull until it reached those feathery ends.

"The color's fine, Kay," Jeff said between snips. "Now that I'm taking off where the sun lightened it."

"Better than fine," she said with a nod as she came back into view. "Especially since this won't be in color. If the suit fits as well, he's going to be perfect. Absolutely perfect."

A smile spread across her face. Not only her mouth, though that was clearly made for smiling. But over her cheeks, into her eyes. Hell, it seemed to sparkle in the wispy ends of her hair.

Rob didn't know how long he'd been staring at her before he realized she was staring back. He didn't know what color her eyes were. Only that they had a depth that could pull him in and never let him surface.

And then she pivoted away, calling out, "Wardrobe! Get that suit ready! Ready to go in ten, everyone! Ten!"

CHAPTER TWO

ROB DALTON WASN'T sure how much more of this he could stand. Kay Aaronson kept touching him.

Tweaking the back of his hair, smoothing the lapel of the ancient suit they'd put him in, patting his arm or his back. Everywhere those narrow, light, quick hands touched he had that shimmering electrical sensation. Was the woman ever still?

Oh, hell. Maybe it was this suit making him feel like a stuffed ... well, a stuffed suit. And literally hot under the high, stiff collar.

He wanted to get this over and done with. He wished to hell he was back with the compost bin. But he'd do his part for Bliss House by standing around in an itchy suit.

His personal cheering section had expanded to include Max Trevetti and Suz Grant, the other two prime movers behind Bliss House.

The construction company Max had founded and Suz had joined as his partner had nearly completed Miss Trudi's new quarters and was renovating Bliss House in record time. They had every right to be here. Rob just wished they weren't.

He wasn't concerned about them or Annette razzing him much, at least not in public. Fran wouldn't either. In fact, sometimes he wished ... But that was another matter.

But Steve...

They'd grown up next door to each other, and sometimes they reverted to the level of kids. So if Steve let loose, it was sure to impress the hell out of this woman from New York.

Not that he was particularly interested in impressing her. He just wanted to get this over with.

"We're shooting the wedding of Donna Ravelle's great-great grandparents," Kay said to him. "It's a time when weddings were simple, when marriages were made from love and would last—at least that's the view in her music video. Her song's about her marriage breaking up after a fancy wedding. She's looking at pictures from her wedding, and then family photos from this wedding—her ancestors' wedding. She's seeing how different they are. And then there're photos from her great-great grandparents' happy married life. So this wedding is simple, but the marriage endures. And—"

"Excuse me. Why are you telling me this?"

"So you know your character, get the motivation."

He felt the corners of his mouth twitch. That was different. Not that he didn't smile. It was just that, lately, it had taken conscious effort.

"I am not an actor, Kay."

"No, I know that, but ... everyone fantasizes about being pulled out of a crowd and stuck in front of a camera."

"Not everyone. Do you?" He had no idea what made him ask that.

"No." She seemed horrified at the idea of being on the other side of the camera.

God, her face was like a pane of glass.

He was *not* going to stand here staring into her.

"I have no lines, isn't that right?"

She nodded. "We're shooting M.O.S.—*mit out sound* is what it's called."

"And I understand I'm basically a prop," he continued. "That all I have to do is stand with my back to the camera while I wear this get-up. So, tell me where to stand and where to face."

She tipped her head. "What did you say you do for a living?"

"I was a financial analyst. And I learned that time is definitely money."

"Ah." She nodded. "Well, Rob Dalton, who was a financial analyst, you have a good point. Just don't ever say I denied you your chance at an Oscar."

There came that twitch at the corners of his mouth again. "I never will, Kay Aaronson."

"IS SOMETHING WRONG, Rob?" Kay asked as they set up for the last sequence.

"Sorry." He stepped off his mark and shimmied his broad shoulders, drawing attention to the suit coat's snugness there. "This suit itches."

Once they'd gotten past the delay—Rob had insisted she check out the legalities and technicalities of having him step in—things had gone great. He'd been standing perfectly for hours, even with spectators clumped by the front door.

Friends and relatives of Rob's, she'd surmised when they showed up. Kay guessed they formed two couples with one extra woman. Kay had wondered if the solo woman, who was very pretty in an understated way, might form another couple with Rob.

She hadn't had to guess at the connections long. Miss Trudi had murmured explanations of family trees and a wedding this summer. She'd also said that the woman on her own was Rob's sister. And Rob didn't have any romantic attachments.

Which mattered to Kay only because a girlfriend's presence could ruin his concentration. Which had been perfect.

Until now.

The last few minutes he'd been twitchy. And she'd noticed every movement.

Simply because he was so vital to the shoot. And it was such a relief that he filled out that suit so well. Especially through the shoulders. And the chest. And his rear end. And those long legs. And his neck, especially his neck. The high shirt collar had made Brice look as if his head sat directly on his shoulders, but Rob had the right proportions to carry it off.

Who knew they grew financial analysts built like this in Wisconsin. Her parents' financial consultant was a sweetheart, but he had more chins than hair and a bottom-heavy physique built for creaking back in leather chairs.

"I *told* you it scratches." Laura, the actress playing the bride, said with gloomy satisfaction. "Whenever Brice touched me, I came out all over in hives, because that thing scratches like crazy."

Laura *had* said something about hives, but Kay had thought she was complaining about Brice, not the suit.

Before Kay could respond, Miss Trudi appeared in a swirl of chiffon, and took Laura firmly by the elbow, leading her away. "Now, Ms. Ontorio, I'm certain you were taught that what you felt was an itch, while the action in response to an itch is a scratch."

"Huh?" Laura muttered.

Kay should be ordering Miss Trudi to return her leading lady right now, but she was too glad to be spared a moment to get her stop-gap leading man back on track.

That was the only reason.

As Miss Trudi and Laura rounded the corner to the kitchen, Kay heard the older woman say, "Furthermore, one does not contract hives from material."

They'd made great progress, filling in close-ups of Laura from over Rob's shoulder, or with only the back of his head showing. All they had left was having the bride come down the front stairway and practically fall into her new husband's arms before they left on their honeymoon.

Kay turned back to Rob, prepared to address his comment about the suit as if there had been no interruption. She'd gotten better at that in these past three hours. At the start, any little interruption and her attention would skip to something else. Like how thick and dark the lashes around his serious eyes were and—

Uh-oh.

No, no, no, no, no. Absolutely not.

"Wool," she blurted out.

The seriousness in his eyes eased a couple degrees. "Is that filmmaking slang? Or the latest New York buzzword?"

"No. I mean the suit." Did he have any clue how delicious he looked in that old-fashioned suit? "It's wool. Are you allergic?"

"Not allergic, just blessed with nerve endings. How did the other guy stand this get-up?"

Get up. No, no her mind would *not* go there.

"He had special silk underwear—sort of trouser liners. Had that written into his contract."

And Brice hadn't been shy about prancing around in the liners. She'd bet her return ticket to New York that a serious, solid man like Rob Dalton would never flaunt himself in his underwear. Well, except maybe for an interested audience of one.

Boxers or briefs?

With some guys it was obvious, but Rob she could see going either way. Boxers' solid tradition and roominess would suit him. But then so would the athletic spareness of briefs.

Sometimes you could see a line that told the story. And you could see other things that told a different story, though with this old-fashioned suit...

Kay sucked in a breath, jerked her gaze away from his wool-covered crotch, and looked directly into his eyes. He knew exactly where she'd been looking, and had probably read her every thought.

Oh, lord, please not *every* thought...

"In his contract, huh. He must have worn costumes like this suit before," Rob said.

He'd had her. Flopping around on the riverbank. Ready to be thrown into the frying pan. And he'd let her off the hook.

"I'm sorry," she said. And she saw from a glint in his eyes that he knew the apology extended beyond an itchy wool suit. "They wore more underwear back then. If long-underwear would help, maybe we can scare some up."

"Thanks, but you said we're nearly done. And it'll be better for your filming to have me itching—as long as I don't scratch anywhere, uh, inappropriate—than having me sweating like a horse."

"You're right." No, no she would not imagine him sweaty. And inappropriate spots to scratch were totally off the mental menu. "Sorry for the discomfort."

She looked away from him … and right at his friends. Who were all looking back at her with intense interest. They looked like nice people. Not the kind to guess how she'd been envisioning their friend and brother.

What was the matter with her? She did not like this type at all. She liked them dark and dangerous, or blond and artsy, or red-haired and intense, or…

But never controlled and solid citizen and calm. A financial analyst for heaven's sake!

No, wait. He'd said he *was* a financial analyst. As in *used to be*. So what was he now?

Not that it mattered. She was leaving tomorrow, never to return to Tobias. Better—much better—to keep her mind on her work and her plan.

"Not your fault," he said. "Shall we get started on this shot?"

"Of course." She grabbed onto that idea with both hands, ignoring his friends, ignoring him and—most of all—ignoring herself, while she got busy corralling Laura and the crew.

"Okay," she said to Rob and Laura when everything was ready to go. "The bride and groom are about to go off on their wedding trip. The bride comes down the stairs in her traveling dress, the groom is waiting. Rob, put one foot on the bottom step and extend your hand—you're so eager to touch her, you can't wait for her to come to you. And then pull her into your arms. And the bride, Laura—you go right to him. The kiss during the ceremony was solemn and formal, but this kiss is the two of you truly starting the love affair your marriage will be. Okay? Got it?"

"Yeah," Laura said with little interest.

"Yes," Rob said.

"Okay, let's do it."

It was a waste of tape. Laura could have been on her way to a life sentence. And Rob bore a remarkable similarity to a hunk of cast iron.

"Laura, this is your chance to shine. The camera will be all on you, as if it were your lover. Give it something to love back. Let's try it again."

The second time was worse.

Oh, Rob did okay, stepping up and reaching toward his bride as instructed. Laura looked suitably passionate this time, but she looked past Rob, as if she wanted to lock lips with the camera. When she did connect with Rob, it was a pathetic keep-as-much-of-my-face-in-the-frame, don't-mess-up-my-makeup-or-hair smooch.

"No! No! Did you hear me at all?"

Laura jumped back from Rob. She wasn't used to Kay snapping—none of them were. But for heaven's sake, they were so close to being finished, and to mess it up so badly...

She took Laura's hand, drew her aside. "Stand here, and watch."

She dashed up the stairs to Laura's mark, spun around and found the actress studying her nails. "Laura!" She waited until the younger woman looked up, then pinned her with her eyes. "Watch. Because next time I want you to do it exactly like this."

She drew in a breath, set the mood in her head, and only then did she look at Rob.

He looked up at her. His face was serious, but there was something so alive in his eyes she couldn't look anywhere else.

He had extraordinary eyelashes. In an utterly masculine face, they were thick and lush and dark, both top and bottom, so from a distance they gave the impression his eyes were dark, almost smudgy. But at this distance, and especially with his eyes trained on her so intently, between the dark, dense fringe shone silvery eyes flecked with green and brown.

Unending eyes.

She started down the steps to him. Not because her timing dictated the move, but because she wanted to see those eyes closer. When he stepped up and held out a hand to her, her pace quickened. One more step—

And then she was there, in his arms, He drew her in. She wound her arms around his neck. Their mouths met.

And Kay Aaronson burst into flames.

CHAPTER THREE

Rob Dalton had decided against becoming a rocket scientist in fifth grade, the moment the homemade gunpowder he'd created to fuel a homemade rocket blew up in his face.

His parents had come thundering down the basement steps in response to his yowl, his father trying to hold back his mother—to protect her in case it was the worst—and his mother refusing to be held back. The expressions on his parents' faces made more of an impression than the explosive flash.

His mother had checked him for major damage, waving her hand to dispel the smoke. His father had stamped out the smoldering remains of his rocket. He'd gone to school for two weeks with singed eyebrows to the merciless delight of his classmates.

Although that project went up in smoke, its lessons stuck with him.

Plan. Prepare. Check. Then recheck. Pay close attention to timing—if he'd waited another minute before bending over the mixture he wouldn't have forfeited his eyebrows.

And don't mess around with chemicals, which can be perfectly benign individually but explosive together.

Now, he'd broken that rule but good. All it took was a kiss. And the chemicals packed in the restless frame of one woman.

A stranger. Edgy, nervous, never still. Jumping from thought to thought. Talk about volatile chemicals. A filmmaker for God's sake. A New Yorker about to return there. And the woman who'd jumped back from him as if there really had been an explosion.

All-around, he'd forgotten every element of that childhood lesson.

Along with messing with volatile chemicals, he hadn't planned, prepared, or checked, much less rechecked. And the timing—it couldn't be worse.

"Laura, let's go! This is it—no more rehearsal. We're going to shoot this time. Let's wrap this up. Jeff! Cameron! Let's go, let's go!"

Kay whirled in among crew and support staff like the rotators of a blender. She hadn't looked at him once.

"Wow! That was something."

Steve arrived, with the rest of them right behind. Steve and Max grinned. Annette and Suz looked at each other, then from him to where Kay had disappeared. Fran looked only at him, and she looked worried.

"That was, uh," Steve paused, "quite a performance." Rob saw the devilment in his friend's face. He'd been the prime tormenter about the singed eyebrows, too.

"Yeah, it was. A performance," he replied. "I think I'm getting the hang of this acting."

"Acting? If that was acting—"

"Steve, come on, we're in the way." Annette tucked her hand into her husband's arm. "They're trying to finish."

"All right, all right. See you later, Rob."

Max and Suz looked interested, but they, too, retreated to the doorway. That left his sister.

"Rob? Are you okay?"

"Sure, Fran." He turned away from her concerned eyes, and toward the actress Laura. The woman he needed to kiss for the camera. "Let's get this finished."

And he hoped to God his metaphorical eyebrows would grow back fast this time.

"WHAT THE HELL is going on here?"

Brice projected his voice down the hallway, drawing every eye to his outraged stance. Sure, *this* role he got into.

But under her irritation, Kay felt a trickle of relief.

The actor's return provided a distraction. Though not enough to wipe out the memory of Rob Dalton's eyes as she came down the stairs. Not enough to wipe out flames still popping through her bloodstream from the touch of his lips. And definitely not enough to wipe out the sensation of his mouth on hers.

"I'll tell you what's going on, Brice. We're finishing this shoot. Without you. Despite your best efforts to torpedo this project, we're just fine thanks to great help from a stand-in."

"Stand-in? You can't do that. I have a contract."

"A contract you broke. Anyone who turns his back on his colleagues that way—"

"I'm SAG. All I have to do is turn you in to the union and you'll never work in this town again no matter how much money your family has!"

His threat lacked bite since they were in Tobias, Wisconsin, not exactly a hotbed of film production. But she got the gist.

"You want to talk about not working again? I already checked—"

"You can't do this. There are rules—"

"*I* can't do it? *You* can't do it! There are a million things more important than rules. Like loyalty. Nobody likes a snitch, Brice, and that's what you are at heart—a weasely, turncoat snitch. Besides, I contacted SAG and they told me how to keep this official. There was an email in your agent's inbox before we started."

Bless Rob Dalton for insisting she do all that. He'd also signed a statement waiving any pay or credit. She half-turned to smile at him. He was staring at her, his face blank, his eyes narrow.

She might have liked time to consider that expression but Brice broke his superior stance and hurried toward her.

"You need me. Nobody can stand in for me. I'm the only one on this shoot who's a real pro. Not some rich girl wannabe who only got a job because her daddy's buddies with somebody."

There it was, the all too familiar slam. If she had an opportunity, she must have bought it one way or another. It followed her no matter how hard she worked.

Although the idea that her father helped her get a job almost made it laughable. Almost.

"We'll do just fine without you, Brice."

"I was in a feature film!"

Hands on hips, she stood her ground. "You had two words. *It's time.*"

"I can't help it some damned editor left the best part on the cutting room floor."

He was still projecting, and the volume was giving her a headache.

"Look, Brice, when you get back to New York talk to your agent." Who'd muttered a few choice things about Brice when Kay called him. "Right now, we have to finish and get these folks out of here."

"I get it." He raised his hands in mock surrender. "Like I said, I'm a pro. And I'll take your word that you'll make good on what I should have gotten. So I'll get in costume and we can finish this piece of—"

"No."

That ego of his was like blinders. A niggle of something familiar scratched at her consciousness, but she had too much else to handle at the moment to let it in.

"You walked away, and I won't have you back, Brice," she said without heat. "We're going to finish with Rob. So go. Leave."

She saw the light of understanding hit his eyes, immediately followed by anger.

"You can't do that to me. I'll make you pay. And all your money won't—"

Rob stepped between them. Nothing flashy, nothing flagrant, but suddenly he was there between Brice and her. She hadn't even been aware of him moving from the base of the stairs where he'd seemed rooted since The Kiss.

She pushed at Rob's arm, to make him turn, so she could edge in front of him. He didn't budge.

"I was thinking the same thing about you," he said to Brice.

"Wha—?"

"That you would pay."

She stepped around Rob. She might have grabbed the conversational reins at the point. But she had to admit to curiosity about his approach.

"Yeah?" Brice pushed his face forward. Kay would have been tempted to slug him. Rob apparently wasn't as easily tempted. He simply held his ground. "Who's going to make me pay?"

"Whoever you signed a contract with," Rob said. "Not only should you not be paid, you should be sued for failure to perform and—"

"I performed. I performed plenty."

"Failure to perform in the legal sense. Failure to fulfill your contract."

The prompt reply seemed to flummox Brice. "You some kind of lawyer?"

"No. However—"

"I figured. And let me tell you, buddy, there'da been no trouble with me finishing if it hadn'ta taken so damned long." Brice's native accent reasserted itself. "That's from amateur directing. Only a stupid rich bitch amateur woulda dragged us out to God knows where, woulda put together a crappy crew and woulda used a no-name broad for the supporting role. I'm—"

"Supporting!" Laura squawked from the background. "The bride's the *lead*!"

"—the only thing goin' for this damned mess—"

"Yet you withdrew support when you felt this would impede the project irrevocably." Rob shook his head in sorrow, and to Kay's mind it was the best piece of acting she'd seen all day. "That's another problem. In fact, Bliss House should look into suing you for alienation of income, since your failure to perform could prevent the receipt of monies expected by the organization. The town of Tobias could have a claim against you on that basis, too."

"Hey, you said you weren't a lawyer."

"I'm not, but I have dealt with similar cases from the financial end, and I am on the Bliss House steering committee, so…"

"And I'm Tobias's town manager." One of Rob's friends, the man in chinos and a blue oxford cloth shirt, stepped forward, the one Miss Trudi had said married dark-haired Annette earlier this summer. "As well as on the committee."

"The Bliss House committee will certainly consider the damage you've done to its prospects," said the woman with the sun-streaked hair. Suz, according to Miss Trudi. The big guy in jeans, looked around like he dared anyone to disagree with her. That was Max Trevetti. "And Rob has a point there about damage to Tobias, don't you agree, Steve?"

"Absolutely. In the meantime, since we have the Bliss House committee here—" Steve gestured to the others. "—we can start that now."

They chorused agreement.

Brice looked to the crew, apparently seeking support.

Unfortunately for him, they did not have short-term memory loss, and recalled his *crappy crew* comment. He swore savagely.

"I'm getting out of this hick town," he snapped. Ah, but he couldn't resist an exit flourish. "Come find me in New York when you discover you can't do this without me."

He'd barely cleared the doorframe when Kay called out to the crew. "Take ten to set up and then we're going to finish this. Let's go!"

While Jeff and the makeup person fussed around Laura and the technical types got busy, Kay faced the Tobias group.

"Was any of that for real?"

"Not a word." Rob's eyes were bright, but his expression remained solemn.

"I don't know. There were some good words in there," Steve Corbett said, grinning. "But alienation of income, Dalton? That was brilliant."

Kay laughed with them. "Well, thank you." With a conscious effort, she widened her appreciation beyond Rob. "Thank you all."

"Glad to do our part to keep that location fee," said Annette Corbett.

"Speaking of which, we should let you get ready," Rob said.

She thanked them again. But before she could move to check on the crew's progress, Miss Trudi tucked a hand in her arm.

"You gave that young man quite a stern talking to, Kay."

Seemed to Kay the sternest talking had come from Rob. "He deserved it. Deserter. He betrayed all of us."

"Yes, you were quite clear in your opinion of his loyalty."

"What loyalty? He couldn't wait to try to snitch."

Miss Trudi wasn't looking at her anymore. Kay traced the woman's gaze to Rob, who turned away, but not quite fast enough. Kay was certain he'd been looking at her, a certainty that had nothing to do with vanity.

It wasn't that kind of look.

Which was irksome considering her hormones hadn't yet pulled into the garage and turned off the ignition after their kiss. Nope, they were still revving their engines like cabbies who'd actually stopped at a red light.

Miss Trudi patted her hand. "This is all so interesting," she said before floating off in a waft of chiffon.

"Ready when you are, Kay," the cameraman called.

She jerked her shoulders straight. "Ready."

CHAPTER FOUR

T HE CAST, THE crew, and the bulk of the equipment were packed off for their return to New York, and the shoot was completed.

Successfully completed, if a little unorthodoxly.

A lot unorthodoxly, if you counted the director and the stand-in actor wrapped in one another's arms and their mouths—

No, she'd be gone soon, and whatever *that* had been would stay here in Wisconsin.

So, all she had to do was fulfill whatever Miss Trudi wanted as a quid pro quo for finding Rob, and she could be on her way home … Well, back to Manhattan, anyway, since she no longer had a home.

She couldn't move back to her parents', that was for sure. Not when they were still distraught that she'd broken her engagement to Barry last winter. Distraught? How about ticked, outraged, and horrified?

She straightened from zipping a tote bag. After she'd packed the equipment and people into the rented bus for the return to O'Hare, she'd gone through Bliss House and gathered everything left behind, bringing it to the patio to sort in the waning daylight.

Two tote bags, a sweater, three hair brushes, a roll of heavy-duty extension cord, enough magazines to stock a newsstand, two books, and a phone. Along with her tote, she would have a hefty load when she walked to the motel, since the departure of the bus left her without wheels. But it hadn't seemed that far, and carrying this stuff might be good practice for being a vagrant when she got back to New York.

Even with her trust fund income increasing her options, finding an apartment was not going to happen in an afternoon.

Any of a half dozen friends would take her in. But then they'd tell her how stupid she was for letting Barry take over the apartment now that he'd returned from six months in Argentina.

"You have nothing to feel guilty about in calling off the wedding. Even if you did, that apartment is way, way too much to assuage any guilt, especially over Barry. Giving up a place in a great building in the Upper East Side—that's crazy!" her friend, Gail, had said, encapsulating the argument that came from all her friends.

They didn't understand that, yes, she did have reason to feel guilty and, no, the apartment wasn't too much. Especially since she'd never particularly liked the place her parents had picked out. She would have preferred a brownstone in Hell's Kitchen.

But she couldn't tell them that, either.

No, she wouldn't go to her friends and she couldn't go to her parents. That left…

Dora.

But this talking again with Dora was too tentative. Their relationship might not ever deepen beyond what it was now … whatever it was. Plus, if she moved in with Dora she couldn't tell her parents where she was living. Ever.

She'd just have to find another solution to her homelessness. After all, she had a couple hours drive to O'Hare and a couple hours in flight, not to mention airport time. Surely she'd come up with a solution by then.

But, first, she'd deal with this little matter of repaying Miss Trudi for finding Rob Dalton to step in.

Step in … The way he had stepped in to kiss her.

And there it was, the heat sweeping back through her like someone had turned on a blast furnace.

She felt as she had as a kid watching the fire in the fireplace in Dora's studio. Watching it and wanting to reach for it—knowing it could burn, yet that knowledge never dimming the glow or the fascination of endlessly changing flames.

That's what kissing Rob had felt like. Fascinating. And endless.

Well, as endless as a single public kiss—in front of an audience, no less—could be. Actually it had felt short. It was what it *promised* that was endless.

He'd followed her direction and advanced one step to take her hand, but from there their movements had been ad lib. Using his hold on her hand to draw her in to his embrace—like she'd needed any drawing—and guiding her hand around his neck—like she'd needed any guiding.

He'd bent a little, and she'd stretched up. But when their mouths met, it was a perfect fit.

So perfect that it had been entirely natural to part her lips.

His tongue immediately possessed her mouth, sensations shooting into her breasts and low in her stomach that were unmistakable. If the onlookers hadn't made enough noise to penetrate the buzz of desire, she would have had him out of that suit and—

"Kay?"

She jumped and spun around.

Rob held his hands up in surrender, but didn't retreat. "Sorry to scare you. I should've realized you'd be jumpy after that run-in with Brice."

"It's okay." She didn't disabuse him of the notion that she'd jumped because she'd thought it was Brice. She'd jumped because she knew it was Rob. "What's up?"

She'd half expected not to see him again. During the remainder of the shoot he'd been cooperative, professional, and distant.

"I wanted to say good-bye. Wasn't sure when you're leaving."

"Not until an 8 a.m. airport shuttle, so that's another—" She checked her watch. "—twelve hours."

"Your timing's off. It's nearly thirteen hours until eight. You're probably still on East Coast time." He stepped toward her. Did that look mean that her hormones hadn't been doing the samba alone? "Listen, about that scene. Showing how to play it. And—"

"Guess I got too much into the role, huh?"

The blaze from the setting sun hit the right side of his face like an overexposed key light, making it almost as hard to see his expression there as on the deeply shadowed side. It also highlighted the strength of his neck, which looked even better in a t-shirt than it had in the costume.

Damn. Why did this happen when she had only one night.

Although ... that might make this the perfect situation. No emotions, just sexual chemistry. No complications, no expectations, no chance of disappointing him. Less chance, anyway.

Oh, what the hell...

"That was a lie. It wasn't the role," she said. *Ca-ching!* Was that her heart? She never remembered it doing this *ba-BAM* percussion before. She sucked in a breath. "Listen, I'm heading back to New York in the morning, and it's not like we're going to see each other again, and maybe some of it was because I hadn't been kissed in ... well, months. Not since my fiancé—"

He stepped back. "Fiancé?"

"Yes. Fiancé." *Don't slow me up with details.* She'd been working toward saying she wouldn't mind spending her last hours in Tobias doing a few re-runs of that kiss, and he was burning time by harping on Barry?

"You're engaged."

She heard the flatness of disappointment in his words, and her spirits lifted.

"No, no." She waved one hand. The left one, bare of rings. "I'm not engaged. Not anymore."

"Not anymore."

Damn, they didn't have all that much time. She didn't want to waste any of it dismantling this hurdle when they could sail over it.

"It's simple," she said. "I *was* engaged at the time I was telling you about—the last time I was kissed. Since then, the engagement ended."

"I'm sorry."

"Oh. It's not—I mean, I wasn't heartbroken or ... I don't deserve sympathy—my parents would certainly tell you that. I was the one who called it off." She dropped her head to dig in her tote for a bottled water. "My parents ... they love Barry."

She wished he'd say something. Instead, he waited. It wasn't a good waiting, like he hung on every word. It was more like he'd braced himself for what came next.

"Barry's a great guy," she concluded. "Really great."

"Then why did you break off the engagement?"

"Hmm? Oh. Uh." She shrugged. "Because if I hadn't, we would have been married in twelve days."

"You dumped him less than two weeks before your wedding?"

Okay, that was not a good tone to that question at all. This was going downhill fast. What had happened to their easy-going camaraderie from earlier today?

"I was incredibly stupid about the whole thing. If I'd called it off sooner, I would have spared everyone a lot of trouble and embarrassment, not to mention money." She waved a hand. The one with the water bottle in it. Some slopped over. "Non-refundable deposits all over the place. Not that calling if off earlier would have satisfied my parents. They were all for me marrying Barry. He's a great guy. Just not the right guy for me."

Which she should have realized far earlier. Barry was the same guy he'd always been—unobjectionable, pleasant, and as communicative as a blank wall.

She backtracked mentally, to how they'd gotten on the topic of Barry. Oh, yeah. "To tell the truth, there wasn't a lot of kissing going on before my engagement ended, either. So maybe that was part of it, when you—when we kissed. I mean, maybe it was just me, but ... Well, it was one hell of a kiss."

She waited.

Nothing.

"Ohhh-kay." She manufactured a smile. "I guess it was just me. Time for me to exit left and—"

"It wasn't just you."

And that was it. Full stop.

She felt a shiver of I-*knew*-it joy. It was short-lived, because he did not appear to have any intention of repeating the activity anytime soon. And *soon* was all she had.

She sure could use another line or two of dialogue to figure out this guy. Apparently she was going to have to drag it out of him.

"Then, what—?"

"Kay? Oh, my dear, I am so relieved that you have not left yet." Trudi Bliss came hurrying up, a satchel of books weighing down one shoulder. She was accompanied by a blonde girl with a strong-willed mouth who carried an armload of books.

"I do so enjoy the fine prospect that Bliss House offers from this hilltop, although the price of our superb view is that one must climb to reach it from any direction. And with these volumes … Oh, thank you, Rob," Miss Trudi added as he took the heavy satchel from her. "You are so kind."

"Come sit down, Miss Trudi." Kay guided her to the bench tucked into the new brick wall that defined the patio.

"Nell spotted your shuttle bus departing as we exited the library, and I feared you had departed as well. Kay, this is Nell Corbett, she is Steve and Annette's daughter. Nell, this is Kay Aaronson."

"The movie lady?" The child's eyes brightened.

"Yes," Miss Trudi said at the same time Kay said, "Trying to be."

"I'm going to win Oscars," Nell said.

"Which one? Acting or directing or—?"

"Not just one. Lots of different kinds."

"Nell has varied ambitions," Rob said in a low voice.

Kay bit on the inside of her cheeks to control her grin.

"But they wouldn't let me watch the movie being made." Nell's tone lodged the complaint.

"Weren't you at day camp?" Rob asked.

Nell shrugged. "I can already swim. But I haven't made a movie and now it's all done and the movie lady's leaving."

"Not until the morning." Kay turned to Miss Trudi. "And I wouldn't have left without saying good-bye and thank you. Especially not since I owe you a huge favor. If there's anything I can send you or arrange for—"

"No, no, my dear. However, there is something I request in return for arranging for Rob to complete your video."

"Beware Miss Trudi the headhunter," Rob murmured.

An excellent headhunter, since she'd bagged the perfect head—his.

"Nell, my dear, will you excuse us for few moments of private conversation. No, Rob, please stay." He stopped, while Nell went to the back steps and opened a book. "Kay, dear, I am pleased to have assisted you, as I am pleased that you have expressed a willingness now to assist me."

"Of course. What can I do for you, Miss Trudi?" Kay asked, keeping her gaze off Rob's perfect head.

"Oh, my dear, it is not for me, at least not directly. It is for Bliss House, which in turn will benefit Tobias and I shall benefit in seeing both those entities benefit." She smiled. "Your grandmother has told me of your great successes, not only artistically, but in promoting tours. We should like you to use your talents to promote the opening of Bliss House in its new incarnation."

Oh, my God. When Rob had said beware Miss Trudi the headhunter, he'd meant she was hunting *her* head.

"I spoke with your grandmother, and she very much hopes you will agree. We know that with your creativity and energy the opening shall draw many more visitors and much greater attention than it would without your assistance."

A tingle of interest climbed Kay's spine. She had enjoyed promoting those artistic tours, and Bliss House was a fantastic place...

Then another thought hit Kay.

"But ... but Bliss House isn't opening for weeks."

The older woman nodded. "Our opening is set for the weekend of October fifteen, which is eight weeks from now."

"Eight weeks. But ... you mean you want me to stay here *eight weeks?*"

"Yes." Miss Trudi beamed. "We will find you somewhere comfortable to live—"

"Miss Trudi, she has to go back to New York and edit what she shot here," Rob interrupted. "Filming is just part of the job."

"Actually, I don't have to edit." Was it Kay's imagination, or was he eager to hurry her out of town? "Serge—the producer—wants all the raw footage. He said he doesn't know what he wants to use until he sees it. But I suspect he wants to see what sort of work I do before it's edited."

Miss Trudi's beam, momentarily dimmed, returned to full wattage. "That is wise of him, as well as fortunate for us, since it means you can stay in Tobias."

"But I don't know anything about promoting a crafts center."

On the other hand, she *had* made a promise.

You find the man, Miss Trudi, and I'll do anything you want.

"That's okay," Rob said. "Nobody could expect you to survive eight weeks in the wilds of Wisconsin."

She knew when someone agreeing with her did not qualify as a compliment. "I'll do better than survive. I'll do a great job."

"You agree to help us?" Chiffon and all, Miss Trudi lifted in hope.

It would take time for the video to get into the pipeline and even longer to get noticed. She couldn't land another assignment even if she were in New York. So, staying in Tobias should barely budge her Plan's schedule.

And there was another benefit to staying here. A big one.

We will find you somewhere comfortable to live…

She wouldn't have to worry about the jungle of Manhattan real estate quite yet. Without rent to pay, she could save most of the trust fund income for two months and build up her nest egg, which had been nearly sucked dry when she'd paid all the expenses of the elaborate wedding her mother had planned. It had only seemed fair, since she'd canceled the wedding.

She would agree to this for those practical reasons.

"Yes."

"How wonderful," Miss Trudi said. "Now, here's what I've planned…"

As for Rob, she could take a hint. He wasn't interested in pursuing The Kiss. Not for thirteen hours, certainly not for eight weeks. She might have liked the thirteen hours, but longer? No way. She would steer well clear of him.

Lost in thought, Kay had missed something, because Rob now held the tote bags.

"Wait—What—?"

With two bags slung over one shoulder and the other in an easy grasp, he gestured for her to precede him down the drive toward the street.

"Miss Trudi pointed out you don't have a car," he said, "and the motel's too far for you to walk, especially with all this, so Nell and I are giving you a lift on our way home."

It occurred to Kay then that steering clear of someone might not be quite as easy in Tobias, Wisconsin as it was in Manhattan.

CHAPTER FIVE

ROB ANALYZED ODDS, calculated risks and weighed decisions as a profession. He was good at it, with a natural ability polished under the mentoring of Mitchell Gordon, leading to a meteoric rise in the Chicago financial community.

Although Rob knew of no formula to quantify this situation, he did know the chance of a relationship between him and Kay Aaronson being anything other than a disaster.

Zero.

Start with the obvious differences in backgrounds. Add her blithe dumping of her fiancé and how she'd described Brice—a weasely snitch with no loyalty. That had fit Brice, but she'd said one more crucial line:

There are a million things more important things than rules.

Then there was the timing.

Even if he'd been looking for a relationship, even if he'd considered one with someone who had no regard for rules, he wasn't idiot enough to start one now.

"…and after I write the books that are even more popular than Harry Potter, I'm going to make them into movies myself," Nell was saying when he tuned in to her chatter. She'd been talking non-stop from the time they left Bliss House, dropped off Kay at the motel, and headed here. "So it's a good thing Kay's staying, so I can learn about movies from her."

"Uh-huh."

Nell needed no more encouragement to elaborate on her movie-making career-to-be and how she would graciously thank everyone when she accepted her unspecified Academy Award.

He turned on to Kelly Street, which ran behind the block-deep yard of the house where he and Fran grew up, a solid, spacious home, but nowhere near as grand as its next door neighbor, Corbett House. That's where Steve and his younger brother, Zach, had grown up, and where their mother, Lana Corbett, now lived alone.

Kitty-corner across Kelly Street from the back of Corbett House and directly behind the Dalton's house was the much more modest home where Steve and Annette and Nell lived.

Nell said thank-you for the ride and hopped out with her books. In the rearview mirror, Rob saw Steve crossing the street toward him. Steve stopped to say something to Nell, before she scurried home.

As soon as Rob opened the car door, Steve pounced. "So, what's the story with that video director and the way you two locked lips?"

"You waited out here to give me grief, Corbett?"

"I was taking the garbage out," Steve lied cheerfully, then sobered. "I've never seen you so, uh, involved in a kiss, and I was at your wedding."

"It was acting."

"Bull." He said it with no heat, as if he didn't need heat to make his point. "It's about time you got back in the game."

"Yeah, like you did such a great job at that before Annette came back."

"So learn from my mistakes. I know Janice did a number on you, but getting back on your feet is what you came home for this summer, isn't it?"

Not exactly.

"It's a shame this video director's leaving in the morning," Steve continued, "so you won't have the chance to get to know each other."

Rob said nothing.

With the ease of a lifelong friend, Steve read the quality of that silence and whistled. "She's not leaving?"

"Apparently not right away," Rob acknowledged. "Miss Trudi has asked her to remain in town and help promote the Bliss House opening. Of course, the committee could withhold approval and—"

"No way. That's a great idea. Unless—what are the financial arrangements?"

"No salary. We're supposed to find her a place to stay."

"I like this idea more and more. What I don't understand is why you're not dancing in the streets. In fact, there're plenty of guest rooms in that big house of Fran's—" He tipped his head toward it. "—even with you taking up one."

"I don't think that would be a good idea," Rob said dryly.

"That's your trouble, Rob, you think too much."

"You're not exactly a wild and crazy guy yourself, Steve."

"Just wild and crazy enough," Steve said, his attention still on the news about Kay. "And I have a feeling this one's going to drive you wild or crazy or both."

"She's not my type."

"Then rethink your type, buddy. Judging from that kiss—"

"She dumped her fiancé twelve days before the wedding." Not to mention the other factors—literally not to mention them, because he wasn't telling Steve any of that.

"And that's supposed to convince me she's irredeemable? You do remember my history with Annette, don't you?" he asked. Annette had walked out of their first wedding eight years ago. She and Steve did a lot of maturing before they were ready for their second wedding, and a marriage that worked.

"Kay dismissed it like an everyday occurrence. After Janice … No, thanks. I'm not going near someone prone to walking out. If that makes me less than wild and crazy, that's the way it is."

"You always were too stubborn for your own good," Steve grumbled. Then he grinned. "You know, all this talk about wild and crazy reminds me … it's time to go home to my wife."

KAY SAT ON the wall whose gentle curve enclosed Bliss House's patio, her fingers feeling the brick's shaded coolness, her head tipped back and her eyes closed, absorbing the pleasant breeze and ignoring the sounds of construction on the far side of the building.

She could swear Miss Trudi had said eleven-fifteen, but Kay seemed to be the only one here.

And then she knew she wasn't alone. Not only that, but she had the strongest suspicion she knew who was here.

It felt like the heat of the sun abruptly cranked up.

She cracked her eyes open.

Rob Dalton.

A dozen feet away, eyeing her as if wondering if he could back away without her knowing he'd been here.

She opened her eyes wide and sat straighter. "Good morning."

"Good morning." His version sounded nearly as wary as it was polite. "Are you here for the meeting?"

"Miss Trudi called and asked me to officially meet the Bliss House committee. Eleven-fifteen—Central Time." She'd changed her watch last night as soon as Rob closed the door to her motel room, having deposited the tote bags. As if being in the right time zone might prove something to him. "But the door's locked, and nobody answered."

He checked his watch. "Eleven-sixteen. It's not like the others to be late. So, how'd you get here?"

"Walked."

"That's a couple miles."

She shrugged. "Twenty blocks." She walked a lot in the city. Which drove her parents nearly as crazy as her propensity for taking the subway. What had slowed her this morning were all the people saying "good morning." She kept stopping, believing she'd run across one of the handful of Tobias citizens she'd met, but they were all strangers. "I'm tougher than I look."

And that was the end of that topic.

As silence stretched out like bubble gum on a hot sidewalk, she tried to remember what they'd talked about yesterday before they'd kissed and everything changed. Mostly the shoot, but she had nothing more to say about that.

But there had been that *I* was *a financial analyst* thing.

"You said you *were* a financial analyst, so what are you doing now?" Her words came out abrupt and a little ragged.

He turned away, scanning Bliss House. "I took the summer off. Leave of absence."

"Oh. So you'll be going back to financial analyzing in—Chicago wasn't it?—after Labor Day?"

"Chicago," he confirmed. "What about you? Have you always wanted to make music videos?"

She slanted a look at him. "Hey, don't make it sound better than it is," she said with minimal sarcasm. He said it like she'd taken up fan-dancing and was skipping the fans. "Second-unit director, that's what I am."

"Second-unit director. Is that what you want to do?"

"This week." She tried on a grin.

"This week," he repeated, his tone flat. Her grin died an awkward death. "And next week?"

She shrugged. "Sure. I'm on a roll. I suppose you knew you wanted to be a financial analyst from your first breath. I have a lot of interests, so I had to eliminate some possibilities."

"Like a possible husband."

She ignored that. "It's taken a while to sort out my options for a career, but now I have a plan. The music video's just a start."

"What did you eliminate?"

She waved a hand. "A few things."

"Like?"

"Sculpting. After decoupage and mobile-making. I taught, too."

"Which? Sculpting or mobile-making?"

Kay was not a touchy person. She knew she wasn't. But the particular tone this particular man used for those particular words felt like someone had raked a comb over sunburned skin. It was that intonation of *he-should-have-known-she'd-do-something-flaky* like sculpting or mobile making. The oral equivalent of rolling his eyes.

"Both. I've done a lot of jobs." She made sure he couldn't miss what her tone said right back at him: *Want to make something of it, buster?*

His mouth opened, as if to respond. Instead, he turned his head, and in a second she heard what had caught his attention—voices of several people walking this way from the parking area. The same group who'd watched filming yesterday.

In a flurry of introductions, she cemented names and faces. They all welcomed her warmly, though Fran, Rob's sister, was quieter than the rest.

"Why're you out here?" Steve Corbett asked.

"Kay said the door's locked."

"Really?" That was Annette Corbett. "It shouldn't be. Miss Trudi's usually the first one here and has things set up."

"It should work," Annette's brother, Max Trevetti, said. "The old door handle stuck, but I replaced it."

Suz Grant sighed. "I miss that old door handle."

The look Max gave Suz should have combusted the woman on the spot, instead, she smiled at him, wide and promising. It didn't take a detective to figure out something had happened between the two of them involving the now-replaced door handle, and whatever it had been was a powerful memory. Powerful and private.

Kay looked away and right into the eyes of Rob Dalton.

That's what she got for respecting Max and Suz's privacy.

Rob apparently had come to the same conclusion about Max and Suz's exchange, because the recognition of sexual heat in the vicinity was right at the surface of his eyes. And then she could swear it combined with a memory of the way their mouths had fit together. Or was she projecting her own memories, her own heat—?

"The door's not locked."

Max's bemused announcement dragged Kay's head around, away from Rob.

Sure enough the door swung open under Max's push.

"I swear that door was locked."

Her protest was lost as they filed inside. At that moment Miss Trudi came bustling around from the front of the house, apologizing for keeping everyone waiting and asking who would like tea.

Kay went to wash up after her walk. When she returned, one opening remained at the table for her. Right next to Rob. Oh goody.

"As I believe all of you know, Kay has agreed, as a favor to us, to apply her skill and imagination to the task of drawing the public's attention to the opening of Bliss House in October, as Miss Trudi said."

"Sorry for a tacky question," Suz said, "but with the budget so tight, especially after the tornado, how can we afford any—?"

"Oh, there will be no expense to Bliss House," Miss Trudi said. "If my new guest room were complete, I would be delighted to have Kay stay with me. As it happens, however, Grita Holland left this morning for a two-month visit to her grandchildren in Kentucky. So, Kay is going to housesit."

"That's quite a coincidence," Steve said.

Kay didn't see it. People went on trips all the time and needed someone to look after their house, yet Steve looked at sweet Trudi Bliss as if she were a Times Square three-card monte operator trying to get him to put down cash.

"And abrupt," added Annette. "Two days ago she said she wouldn't see those grandchildren until Christmas."

Now they were *all* eyeing Miss Trudi. Geez, and people said New Yorkers were suspicious.

"It is wonderful how it worked out. In addition, a donation has arrived that will defray Kay's other expenses. But that is a matter to discuss in executive session," Miss Trudi added quickly, as a number of mouths opened. "At the moment, I believe we should welcome Kay, and give her—"

"Wait a minute, Miss Trudi," Rob interrupted. "We don't know anything about Ms. Aaronson. No offense," he added to her.

She didn't say, "None taken." It would have been a lie. He did, too, know things about her.

You got to know someone damned fast under the sort of pressure they'd dealt with yesterday. She knew that he was calm, reliable, unintimidated, serious but not without humor and that he could kiss her backbone into jelly.

What she did say was, "May I?" as she touched the legal pad beside his tablet displaying number-filled spreadsheets.

He looked unsettled, which pleased her greatly, but murmured, "Of course."

"Goodness. Rob," Miss Trudi started, and she clearly didn't appreciate his comment, either. "Kay's family settled here shortly after Tobias Corbett himself, and I have known Dora Aaronson all her life. As for Kay, we need know no more than what we have seen—that she is a talented, lovely young woman."

Twin vertical furrows creased Rob's forehead just above his nose.

"We should know her work history." He rubbed at the furrows with two fingers. "It's a sensible precaution."

Kay leaned forward, plastering on a smile.

"I will email my job history as soon as this meeting's over." Then her triumph took a left turn. "Well, not as soon as it's over. I have to check out of the motel before two."

"How will you move your luggage, dear?" Miss Trudi asked.

"I'll call a taxi and—"

"Oh, dear!" Talk about mixed signals—Miss Trudi's voice sounded distressed, but the light in her eyes said the opposite. "Tobias does not offer taxicab service. I would drive you myself if I possessed a car."

"Or a driver's license," Max muttered, then added in his normal voice, "Sorry we can't help, Kay, but Suz and I've got a meeting with the state guys in Madison that we should leave for in twenty minutes."

"I've got to give Steve a lift back to town hall," Annette said, "but then—oh, no, I'm in charge of snacks for Nell's camp today. I'll be there the rest of the day. But if you drive with me to drop off Steve, we can pick up the snacks and you can drop me off at the camp. It's on the other side of the lake, but then you can have the car, as long as you're back by three-ten—"

"Surely there is a less complicated solution." Miss Trudi seemed to be looking at Rob.

"There is," Fran said. "Rob drives Kay and me back to the house, and we get my car and then—"

"I'll do it," Rob said. And didn't he sound thrilled? "Fran, you ride home with Annette. I'll take Kay to the motel and get her things to the Hollands'."

"Much simpler," Miss Trudi said with approval. "Now, shall we present our reports to give Kay an overview of what Bliss House will offer?"

CHAPTER SIX

*E*LEVEN-FIFTEEN, HIS ASS.

If he'd gotten a decent night's sleep he might have been sharper when Miss Trudi called this morning and told him the meeting had been moved up to eleven-fifteen.

He'd said Fran had already left to run errands, and wouldn't be there until eleven-thirty, the original starting time.

In retrospect, her airy, "That will be quite all right," should have alerted him to a set-up.

Miss Trudi Bliss had ideas about throwing him and Kay together.

Bad ideas.

Very bad, considering he'd felt as if he'd been hit in the gut when he came around the corner and saw Kay sitting there, a breeze ruffling the fluffy ends of her hair, the way his hand might if he were...

But he wasn't.

In a few weeks, Kay would be back in New York and he would have changed his life, returning to Tobias for good. Not even the strongest chemicals could interact half a continent apart.

"For historical accuracy, I started with the original garden plans we found in one of Miss Trudi's scrapbooks," Fran was saying.

Rob had argued that Kay could be filled in one-on-one. Miss Trudi had insisted everyone could use an update so it was more efficient to do both together now, over sandwiches.

Max and Suz had led off with a construction update, followed by Annette on the craftspeople who would display their goods and Steve on the town's cooperative efforts concerning parking, lighting, and other services. Rob had opened a new document to make notes on all this, since Kay had appropriated his legal pad.

"We also need to appeal to modern tastes," Fran continued, "so the gardens contribute to an overall atmosphere that opens the wallets of our customers."

Chuckles came from all around.

"Color is vital. My aim is to have the color change with the seasons, to encourage customers to return frequently to see the garden—and of course stop inside and purchase crafts."

"Perfect, Fran!" said Suz.

As Fran talked with enthusiasm about the gardens, Rob became aware of a solidifying concern for his sister.

Fran had been building her own life in Madison when their father became ill. She'd given that up and returned "temporarily" to nurse him. Temporarily had turned into years. Would she leave if she'd planted her heart and soul along with these roses and daylilies and peonies she was talking about for the Bliss House gardens?

Plus, every time she said "heritage" or "antique," he felt the Bliss House budget cringe.

Then there was the matter of labor. This didn't sound like a few volunteers throwing petunias in the ground.

Somebody should start reeling in the string on her kite, gently bring her back to earth.

He looked around the table. Steve smiled and nodded. Max took notes on coordinating construction with Fran's plans, Annette and Suz looked rapt, and Miss Trudi had tears in her eyes. Tears of joy.

He cut a look toward Kay, to his right, with her chair pushed back a little, her head bent over his legal pad. Then he saw her hand moving in quick strokes.

Sketching.

It took another instant to realize she was sketching what Fran described. She was on her third sketch of the same area—the main garden off the south side of the house—and each sketch different. Winter, spring, and summer.

Clear as day, they reflected the descriptions Fran gave of how the gardens would vary by season. How on earth did Kay capture those differences with only a pen? Every line was blue, yet he could swear he distinguished colors. And not solely from what Fran had said. Something in the way Kay made the shapes conveyed color. Amazing.

The tightening in his gut unfurled like one of those buds opening.

If Fran's gardens were half as wonderful as these sketches, there was no question they would have to buy them and get them put in the ground. After that he'd encourage Fran to open her wings—and he'd give the Bliss House budget CPR.

Then Rob looked beyond the marvel of what she was creating to Kay.

Other than her hand, she was utterly still. Almost as if all the energy and intensity that usually shot out of her had concentrated into a single beam that channeled through her hand onto the paper.

"Rob?"

He looked up to find everyone else watching him watch Kay.

"The budget report?" prompted Fran.

As he reminded them all of the budget realities, he saw from the corner of his eye Kay flip his pad to a new page. No longer drawing, she waggled the pen between her fingers, bounced her foot, and chewed her lip.

"Once I see the details on this timely grant Miss Trudi produced—" Trudi smiled serenely at his words. "—I'll know if we're covered on Kay's expenses. But unless Miss Trudi finds more miraculous money, the budget remains as tight as ever."

That left one person at the table who hadn't said anything.

"So, Kay," Rob said, "what's your plan?"

"Plan?"

"Yes. Your goal for promoting Bliss House's opening and the steps that will get us there."

She smiled. It was a little too bright. "I don't have a shred of a plan."

"Of course she doesn't have a plan yet," Suz said. "She hasn't even had a chance to unpack."

Murmured comments about giving Kay time flowed around the table.

"We don't have time. We need a plan fast," Rob said flatly. "In fact, we need a plan that's fast, good, and cheap."

THEIR SECOND DRIVE to the motel was even more heavily silent than the first one. But yesterday they'd had Nell to mask it.

"I'll be back in an hour," Rob said in front of Room 17. "That'll give you time to pack. Leave anything heavy for me."

Swinging her legs out of the car, Kay shot a look over her shoulder. "I'll do that."

As he watched her unlock and enter the room, he debated whether she had slammed the car door or just closed it firmly.

Now, an hour later, standing in the doorway of her motel room, he knew she had slammed it.

That became clear when she opened the door to his knock, took one look at him, said "Oh, it's you," then turned and headed for the round table in the corner that held a laptop, mini-printer and other electronic gear.

"Ready?" he asked, eyeing an empty suitcase on the bed and clothes hanging in the open closet.

"No." She returned and handed him papers. "I printed these for you, in addition to sending them by email, and here's your legal pad back."

As soon as he took possession of them, she went to the far side of the bed and began piling items into the suitcase.

He sat in the worn tweed chair next to the table. He looked at the legal pad first. She'd torn off the pages with her sketches, curls of leftover paper indicating she'd jerked them loose, possibly in anger. He checked the trash can nearby, but it was empty.

The six printed sheets she'd given him had five to seven blocks of information on each. He riffled the pages, catching phrases about sketching at children's parties, portrait sketches of tourists, managing a do-it-yourself ceramics outfit, docent at various art museums, website design, arranging, coordinating, and promoting art-themed tours for New York visitors, working at a frame shop, a degree in film, movie gopher.

Good lord, and he probably hadn't seen half of it.

"This could have waited until after you'd settled in," he said.

"If you didn't find it satisfactory, how could I know I was going to stay? I don't recall all the contact numbers, but you should find enough people I worked with who will assure you I'm not an embezzler or some other kind of criminal."

"There's no guarantee," he said under his breath. She frowned but before she could say anything, he added, "Thank you."

"You're welcome."

"You're angry."

"Yes, I'm angry."

But as she said the words he knew they weren't entirely true. She wasn't only angry, she was hurt. And he'd done the hurting.

That didn't mean he'd feel guilty. He'd acted reasonably and responsibly.

"I have an obligation to Bliss House," he said. "This was a small precaution in an unusual situation."

She gave a disbelieving grunt. "I'm not going to hurt Bliss House, for heaven's sake. And somehow this doesn't feel like it's about Bliss House. It feels like it's about me and—"

She stopped as abruptly as if someone had jabbed her pause button. Lips parted, eyes wide, the only movement her chest rising and falling. That was plenty. The movement brushed the curve of her breast against the black fabric of her top, catching the slanting light so it outlined, almost as if he could feel—

Oh, no, he wasn't letting his mind go there. At least not while he was awake and had control of it. Last night's dreams he couldn't do anything about, but conscious, he would keep control.

She blinked and gave a fine shudder.

"Are you okay?" he asked.

"Just fine. It was one of those moments … You know, when you're talking along, not watching what you're saying and suddenly the words coming out of your mouth open vistas and reveal insights and precipitate epiphanies." She looked at him expectantly.

He looked back.

"You don't have moments like that?" she persisted.

"No. I think before I speak."

"Always?"

"Always."

"Too bad." She sounded genuinely sorrowful. "Well, I'll share this one with you. I was talking about how I'm no threat to Bliss House and your distrusting me feels like it's about me, and I was about to say *I don't get it*, when suddenly I did. Get it, I mean. And I'm flattered."

He rubbed his forehead. "Flattered?"

"It *is* about me. Specifically, it's about kissing me. And I'm flattered that you think I'm such a femme fatale that I could push you into bad judgment. And all from one innocent kiss."

He wouldn't put innocent and that kiss in the same sentence.

Another man might have tried to deny or at least delay. But lying went against the grain, and delaying … well, he'd had his fill of delay this summer.

"You're probably right."

She arched one eyebrow, unsatisfied. She wanted her pound of flesh … and if he didn't watch it, a certain part of him was going to feel like considerably more than a pound of flesh.

"You're right." He dropped the qualifier. "It was partly about that. I won't forget my responsibilities because of one hot kiss. Under the circumstances it would be bad judgment for there to be any more between us."

"I wasn't asking for more," she shot back.

He wanted to argue. Wanted to say her eyes had asked for just that when he'd found her on the patio last night. Wanted to say the asking hadn't been entirely gone when they met this morning. Wanted to say she would kiss him back if he kissed her. And he'd be willing to test that right now.

Not a good idea. Not the saying and not the testing.

"Kay, you're an incredibly appealing woman and I..." Better not to get into how she appealed to him. He cleared his throat. "It doesn't make sense to pursue it. We're from different worlds. And the timing couldn't be worse."

"Because I'm leaving later or because I'm staying now?"

She'd cut to the bone with one slice.

He didn't know if that made him fear her or admire her more. But he couldn't give her anything less than an honest answer.

"Both."

She tipped her head, studying him. "Fine."

She folded a dark gray t-shirt into the suitcase.

"Fine?" he repeated.

"Yeah. We forget the kiss. It's not like we won't be able to keep our hands off each other for the eight weeks I'm here."

He could tell her he'd be gone before she was, and by the time he finished dealing with what he'd left behind in Chicago and returned to Tobias for good, she'd be gone.

"So, we work together as colleagues," Kay said, and the moment was past. Crazy to think about opening that topic with her anyway. If he told anyone, it wouldn't be a stranger.

"Colleagues," he repeated.

"Sure. And the first thing I want to know so I can do a good job," she said briskly, "is more background on Bliss House being turned into a craft center. When my grandmother recommended it for the shoot, she only told me about it being Miss Trudi's family home."

He told her about Miss Trudi's dwindling financial resources and how the Victorian mansion had been crumbling until Steve and Annette arrived at this solution. Miss Trudi donated the seventeen-room house and grounds to Tobias. A cozy, modern apartment was built for her in one corner of the property. The rest became the craft center to give Tobias's craftspeople a retail outlet and to attract visitors.

Damage from a tornado last month had set back the schedule, but they'd adjusted and were on track for the opening in mid-October.

All through his speech, she peppered him with questions.

"So the kitchen's being made into a tearoom with the patio accommodating more customers in the summer, but what about the—"

She'd moved on to the last of her hanging clothes, when he interrupted. "You do know it's summer, don't you?"

She followed his gaze to the top she held. "It's sleeveless."

"It's also black. That suitcase looks like the inside of a cave."

"Black goes with everything, it's always appropriate, and it's a great backdrop for other colors."

"What other colors? Most people wear light colors in the summer, you know. To stay cool."

"Black is good for the city."

"Doesn't show the smog?"

"I heard you've lived in a high rise in Chicago for years. Not exactly down on the farm."

He surrendered with a gesture. "Okay, okay. Just don't blame me if you're hot."

She opened her mouth, then closed it. But the second meaning for his words had clicked in his head before her reaction. What worried him was whether that meaning had clicked in his head *before* he spoke the words.

"Well, isn't that an interesting comment—" Her eyes widened with the least convincing rendition of innocence he'd ever seen. "—from the man who thinks before he speaks?"

He stood. "I'll wait in the car."

CHAPTER SEVEN

K AY AARONSON LOOKED around the kitchen of the Hollands' house.

She hadn't had a chance to do that during the whirlwind tour Rob gave before leaving as fast as his long legs could carry him.

As he'd said, they were from different worlds. As different as this kitchen was from the gleaming, stainless-steel-appliance-ridden kitchen her parents recently gutted without a qualm. Her mother had declared the stainless look "pedestrian, now that everyone's doing it."

But this kitchen … It looked like a real home. There were yellow paper napkins in a wooden holder on the table, a cookie jar decorated with a green and gold Green Bay Packers logo atop the refrigerator, and a piece of white legal pad paper on the table addressed to her.

Kay,

You'll find the basics in the fridge and the second drawer between the fridge and the sink. Miss Trudi said to feel free to help yourself to whatever else you need.

Rob

So this was what he'd done between dropping her off at the motel and returning to pick her up. She opened the fridge. Lettuce, eggs, carrots, tomatoes, cheese—naturally—butter, orange juice, milk, coffee, blueberries, and a half-dozen fresh peaches.

She took a peach, washed it and dried it with a paper towel while she looked in the drawer. Bread, crackers, a tin of mixed nuts, and a generic bran cereal. Not bad.

That didn't change that Rob was not her type.

She bit into the cool peach.

Sure, he was good-looking. Broad shoulders, dark blond hair. Clear, intelligent eyes. That neck. And there was chemistry.

But clearly chemistry didn't sway Rob Dalton.

And that was *good* news.

Barry wasn't her first relationship wreck. Really, had any of her relationships been successful? She was *glad* he wanted to forget kissing her.

Okay, she was a little hurt, too.

I won't forget my responsibilities because of one hot kiss.

Couldn't get much plainer than that. She knew exactly where she stood with him—nowhere.

Which was another way he wasn't her type. She preferred a man with some mystery.

She climbed the stairs to the guest room where Rob had deposited her suitcase before departing as if the tornado that had hit Tobias last month had scooped him up.

The room had a white bedspread on a double bed with a yellow and white quilt folded at the foot. Dormer windows looked to a neat back yard. A dresser and bookcase were tucked into an alcove.

Someone who challenged her intellectually, that's what she wanted. Barry's idea of communicating was small talk at a cocktail party.

She went to the tiny adjoining bathroom to wash peach juice off her hands. She opened the narrow closet, enjoyed a waft of cedar, then got busy.

Interesting that Rob was involved in finance—or had been—yet he didn't boast about his killings on Wall Street the way Barry had.

Remembering comments around the Bliss House committee table she wondered, did she have that right? The others seemed to believe he remained a financial analyst. That was a bit of a mystery…

Oh, God. She'd just thought she wanted *a man with some mystery.*

She shook her head and forced a laugh. Yeah, but she hadn't meant a mystery about his job status.

Besides, the last thing she needed was a romance in the middle of the country. A career in films meant New York, LA. Not Wisconsin.

Beyond career considerations, what did she know about life in a place like this, a home like this?

She arranged a cotton top on a hanger. In the closet, three black tops lined up next to four pairs of black pants.

Maybe Rob was right, maybe she did need more color.

That didn't mean he was right for her. Far from it. The chemistry was a fluke.

She supposed it was admirable of him not to have taken advantage of her willingness. He was like the kitchen. Straightforward, comfortable, and well-built. So ... so *Midwestern*.

Only as she stowed the empty suitcase in the closet did a question hit her.

What did it say about *her* that a man who was good looking, intelligent, thoughtful, a gentleman, and kissed like she'd never been kissed before was not her type?

"GOOD EVENING, ROB. How pleasant to see you."

Miss Trudi welcomed him to her new apartment as warmly as if she hadn't been sidestepping him all afternoon.

He'd looked for her here, at Bliss House, the library, and two of her friends' houses. Each place he was told she'd just left.

"I have a few questions for you, Miss Trudi."

"Of course, you do." She led him to a couch. "You want to know about Kay, and who can blame you—such a lovely young woman."

"I do not—"

"I know you would not ask me to betray confidences." She patted his arm. "I do appreciate that quality in you. But I can tell you that Kay had an upbringing sadly lacking in many aspects. She did not want for material goods, even when her father—Ah, we shall not speak of that. Her parents—"

"Miss Trudi."

"—have devoted themselves to their position among the social elite of New York City, leaving far too little for Kay. Despite that and certain, ah, strains in the family, Kay has grown up to be a remarkable—"

"So remarkable she dumped her fiancé."

"She called off her engagement two weeks before the wedding, yes."

"Twelve days." He sat back. "I'm not saying she's a bad person, but look at all those jobs. She clearly can't settle to anything. Not a job, not a relationship."

"Settling is not always a good thing, Rob."

He ignored that. "Kay's not the person to help with Bliss House. What does she know about Tobias? She's from a different world."

"Nonsense. The human heart is the same anywhere it beats. Consider Kay's grandmother, Dora Aaronson. A famous artist, you know."

"I know who Dora Aaronson is." She was Tobias's only claim to fame. "You already told us that she was involved in having the video shot here."

"The point I am establishing is that Dora was raised and educated here in Tobias before moving to New York, entering what many would call an entirely different world. Yet the heart of the woman now feted as an American treasure is the same heart as the girl to whom I taught art."

"If you say so."

"Indeed I do. Despite the sorrows of her life, including this terrible estrangement from Kay, I know that her heart is the same."

He was tempted by the worm Miss Trudi dangled—*this terrible estrangement from Kay*—but he saw the hook, too.

"It's so sad when two people who have loved each other grow apart, or are cut apart," she continued. "A sadness you should empathize with, having recently suffered the end of your marriage."

The hook suddenly looked more appealing than the alternative—a discussion of his divorce.

"What happened? With Kay and her grandmother," he clarified.

"Ah, who can know what happens between two people?" Miss Trudi asked.

"The two people," he said.

She gave him a peculiar look. Sad and twinkling at the same time. "You are a dear man, Rob."

"Uh, thank you."

"I do wish, however, that you would rid yourself of the notion that the human heart adds, subtracts, and multiplies by the same rules that govern mathematics."

"I don't—"

"Of course you do, dear. Although it is not a conscious act, I do concede that."

He'd let this conversation get way off track. "Miss Trudi. I came here to ask you about the money. Where's this supposed donation that's covering Kay's expenses coming from? Bliss House cannot afford any expenditure not already in the budget."

"It is so fortunate that you reminded me. I have carried the check right here in order to give it to you as soon as I saw you—no, not that pocket. It must be ... Perhaps I left it in my smock."

Oh, no, she didn't. No delays. "Miss Trudi—"

"No! Here it is."

Miss Trudi Bliss placed a check in his hand. He saw the name of a well-known bank, a foundation he'd never heard of, and a dollar amount with five figures to the left of the decimal point.

A GOOD NIGHT'S sleep put everything back in perspective for Kay.

Nothing had changed, she realized as she walked toward Bliss House.

While she waited for the producer to work with her footage, then for the video to come out in a few months, she would do her best to help Miss Trudi and Bliss House. Also, she would ask friends for recommendations of an agent to find an apartment. Her life would be in perfect order when she returned to New York.

But first came paying back Miss Trudi.

From across the street she contemplated the entrance to Bliss House's grounds. It appeared like "before" and "after" photos spliced together. On the left was the "after," with the brick wall freshly repointed and the wrought iron atop it sparkling. On the other side was "before," with rust, crumbling mortar and weeds. She'd wanted a two-shot of Brice and Laura at the gate, but no matter how she'd framed it, "before" showed.

A sound made her look up.

Trotting down the under-construction walkway right toward her was a huge, hairy beast. A dog. It had to be a dog. But it looked as far from her mother's pampered little toys as an animal could be.

"Good dog. Good dog," she said with desperate hope. The tail kept wagging and the dirty beast kept coming. "Sit!"

The dog sat.

Kay stared in amazement. How about that?

The animal had a broad head that narrowed to a black-button nose. Not a cute button, more like an elevator button. This close, she could see, under a coating of dust and dirt, paler fur around its neck. The ears tipped at the ends. They moved around like a radar dish trying to pick up a signal.

"Good dog."

The ears zeroed in on her, and she could swear the mouth grinned.

"Well, time to get to work," she told the dog as she pulled her phone from her tote and clicked for the video recording app, "and get acquainted with this place."

The dog started to get up, and she said, "Sit!"

It sat. This was one smart dog.

She edged past him, trying not to step in Fran Dalton's flowerbeds, and headed toward the house. She'd gone maybe three yards when she became aware of the dog trotting behind.

She started up the stairs, and heard what must be toenails on the steps behind her. She turned around, and there it was.

"Oh, no you don't, buster. You can't come in." The dog backed down, not looking the least crestfallen. *Buster* didn't quite fit. Another name came to mind, the name bestowed on an injured robin fledgling she and Dora had nursed back to health one spring and watched fly off the windowsill to its own life. "I'm busy, so you're on your own, Chester."

The dog stood at the bottom of the steps and watched her, head tipped, mouth grinning.

KAY FELT FOR the light level adjustment on the app on her phone as she panned the tearoom. A pale blur blotted out everything else in the viewfinder. Kay jolted her head back.

"Hello, dear. How are you today?"

"Oh. Miss Trudi." She had stepped in front of the camera. "Hi."

"Would you like a cup of tea? Max and his gentlemen are at work at my lovely new home, so I am using the facilities here today."

"No thanks." She spotted a box on the high counter that divided the work area. "Are these doughnuts yours, Miss Trudi?"

"No, dear. Suz brings them for everyone—she is very fond of baked goods. Please, do help yourself."

"It's not for me. There's a dog outside and he might be hungry and thirsty."

Miss Trudi plucked two plain doughnuts and placed them on a napkin. "Of course you must take these, as well as water, to the poor creature."

They found a container for water and carried it to the front porch. The dog still sat there. His tail thumped when he saw them, then picked up speed when he caught a whiff of the doughnuts.

Kay broke up half of one and put the pieces down. The dog inhaled them. Poor thing.

Miss Trudi spread her arms, a damp breeze fluttering the loose sleeves of her tunic. "What miracles our dear Fran is working with these gardens. She has such talent. Her mother would be so proud."

The doughnut's second half disappeared as fast.

"The Daltons were always such a nice family. So sad that Dennis and Vicki passed away at such young ages. Vicki was so finely attuned to her children's emotions that they lost a great deal with her death, particularly coming as it did at turning points in their lives, as Rob departed for college and Fran entered tenth grade. Dennis felt his own grief so keenly that he did not aid them to the extent he might have."

The dog looked hopefully at the other doughnut. Kay nudged the container of water with her toe. The dog sighed, dropped its head and drank. Not all the water got in the dog's mouth. Kay quickly pulled her toe back.

"In their losses, Rob and Fran are most fortunate to have each other. But that should not blind one to their individual strengths."

Kay put down the pieces of another half a doughnut.

"I have seen a number of people misjudge Rob Dalton," Miss Trudi said, "believing that because he is reliable and sensible that there is no spirit to him. I know you wouldn't make that error."

"Nope," Kay said, deliberately flip. "I wouldn't. He's got plenty of spirit—mean spirit."

With the last bit of doughnut gone, the dog licked its chops and drank again.

"Oh, no, you mistake him, I can assure you. Rob—"

"You heard him going on about needing my work history."

"Yes, indeed, I did, and found it most interesting."

"Interesting? He took delight in needling me about having a lot of jobs."

"Are you quite certain of that, my dear?"

"Sure. And what's so wrong with diversity, huh?"

"A diversity of experience can be beneficial," Miss Trudi agreed. "As can diversity in people involved in a relationship, say, theoretically, a romance."

Kay wasn't in the mood to discuss romance, even theoretical romance.

"Thanks for the doughnuts, Miss Trudi. I need to get back to work."

CHAPTER EIGHT

TWENTY MINUTES LATER, Kay used her hand to shade the phone's screen as she exited Bliss House's back door, concentrating on what it was showing her.

Backing up step by careful step, she panned from right to left. Across the gardens-in-the-making, along the wall that marked Miss Trudi's current domain, to the drive, the low brick wall that enclosed the patio, and a figure sitting on the wall.

Rob.

The panning stopped. When the zoom zeroed in on his mouth with no conscious effort on her part, she quickly lowered the phone.

He sat just to her left. If she'd backed up a few more steps she would have been in his lap.

"Hi." He sounded as wary as he looked.

"Relax, Rob. I'm not going to jump you."

"I didn't think you were."

Liar.

Why else would he have run out of her motel room and practically thrown her belongings in the Hollands' house?

"Yeah, well … Good. Because I got the message. So…" The moment called for bright and sunny, so she pulled out her brightest and sunniest voice. "What brings you here?"

"I gave Fran a ride. Now I'm waiting for papers Max needs run over for Steve's signature. Could you please turn that off?"

"Sure." She put the phone in her tote. "I was recording Bliss House."

His hands curved around the edge of the wall at either side of his hips. The morning sun hit his left hand—just right to see the pale band of skin at the base of his ring finger.

"What's the matter?" He looked around, trying to see what had made her jaw drop.

She had never looked for a ring. A ring he'd recently taken off, judging by that band of white.

"You're married? You got all righteous about my broken engagement when all the time you're—"

"I'm divorced."

Two crisp words instantly iced her anger. They were two jabs from a boxer—*one-two, I'm-divorced*. Yet this boxer aimed the blows at himself.

"In the process or—?"

"Divorced. Papers signed. Legalities completed. No longer married."

Only recently, judging from the ring mark. Was that what he'd meant about the timing being bad? Was that why he was so wary of her?

"I'm sorry. That's ... I'm sorry. Well, guess I'll find Fran and ask, uh, about the gardens."

She gave a sort of wave, turned, and tripped over something warm and solid at knee level. What an exit—a pratfall.

Except she didn't go down, because Rob's long arm wrapped around her and pulled her back.

It should have been a nice, neat save. But instead of leaving her upright, the reversed momentum landed her hard against his chest.

He'd half-risen from the wall to grab her and now her contact knocked him back to his seat. He hadn't let go of her, so she came with, collapsing into a heap with her top half sprawled across his chest, her butt slamming against his thigh and the rest of her flailing around like one of those crash dummies who'd forgotten his seat belt.

And what all those sprawling and slamming and flailing parts wanted to do was wrap around him and hold on.

"So, who's your friend?" His question fluttered the hair by her ear.

With a leer, it could have been a come-on, especially since she had a suspicion that the part of him next to her hip was growing more friendly every second. But the question was spoken with amusement beneath straight-forward curiosity.

"Huh?"

Not exactly witty repartee, but the best she could do while she fought to banish that wrapping-and-holding urge at the same time she searched for the ability to breathe normally.

"Your friend. The shadow you nearly took a header over who's trying his best to apologize."

Enough oxygen had reported for duty that she levered herself up by pushing against his chest. He grunted.

"Sorry."

"No problem."

His voice belied the words.

She had caused him a problem.

She hoped the kind that had to do with his increasingly friendly anatomy, and not that she'd bruised or broken anything.

"Thank you for saving me from—Oh!" She got her first look at what had tripped her up. "You know, whoever's dog this is shouldn't let it wander around loose on a construction site. It's dangerous."

"For the dog and people." Rob muttered. Then he added in a regular tone, "Do you know him?"

"No. But Chester's been following me around all morning."

"Chester? You said you didn't know him."

"I don't. But I couldn't call him Hey You, so I'm calling him Chester. He was here when I arrived, and every time I come out, there he is."

"Sounds like he knows you, even if you don't know him—or is it a her?"

"I haven't asked."

Rob grinned. "City girl, huh?"

"Polite," she shot back.

Still grinning, he leaned over, extending his hand. "C'mere, fella."

The dog sidestepped closer to Kay.

"The owner is definitely negligent," she said. "He was incredibly thirsty."

Rob looked at her from under his brows. "You gave him water—anything else?"

"Doughnuts. He was starving, the way he wolfed them down. What are you laughing at?"

"Me? Not a thing. Huh. I usually have good luck with dogs. We had dogs when I was a kid, and they always obeyed me. Come, Chester."

The dog didn't react. Who could blame him? Who'd want to respond to such a liar?

Not laughing at me, my eye.

"He doesn't seem to know commands," Rob said.

"He does too. Watch. Chester, sit."

The dog sat. She gave Rob a smug look, and he laughed.

"You know what they say about dogs resembling their owners? Well you two gave me the identical look."

Kay felt something rising in her, like when she could hear a subway train pulling in, and she was at the top of the stairs but she had to catch *that* train or she'd be late, late, late…

"That's ridiculous. This dog clearly belongs to someone else. If you'll excuse me, I have more work to do."

KAY HAD REFUSED offers from Max and Suz and Annette for a ride to the meeting being held the next afternoon at Town Hall to accommodate Steve's tight schedule. She'd wanted the walk to rehearse her ideas.

Rob hadn't offered her a ride.

No surprise. Sure they'd had a fairly pleasant conversation about the dog. But that didn't change his position.

Inside the well-tended Town Hall, she found the elevator behind the stairs. The doors began to close in slow-motion. A long-fingered, tanned hand wrapped around one edge to halt them.

Rob appeared. "What are you doing?"

"Going to the meeting."

"You'd entrust your life to this antique? Most people take the stairs. Besides, the meeting's on this floor."

She'd gone for the elevator out of habit. Buildings without elevators were in the same class as those without indoor plumbing as far as her parents were concerned. She'd have to keep that in mind when she called a real estate agent. Tonight, definitely tonight.

"I asked Max to check, and that dog—Chester—doesn't belong to any of his guys." Rob directed her down a hallway. "Apparently they're fond of it because only Nell and this dog have kept Miss Trudi's cat Squid from terrorizing them full-time. But it hasn't been real friendly until it started following you. And he's going to keep following you since you're constantly feeding him."

"I just fed him a leftover cheeseburger I happened to have yesterday."

Her shoulder bumped his arm as he reached ahead in the narrow hallway to open the door. A polite gesture, but it didn't leave much room for her to get by.

"Leftovers you happened to have, huh? Guess leftovers happen when you buy three cheeseburgers for lunch."

She stopped, turned. "How did you—?"

His face was about a breath away from hers, and that made his mouth so close she could taste it.

She jerked herself into motion again as he said, his voice huskier than usual, "Welcome to small town life. Not even your lunch order is private."

"YOU NEED TO get big attention, so you need to go big." Kay sat forward, her expressive hands sketching *big*. "I propose a gala. A gala like Tobias has never before seen."

Rob had the strangest feeling now that her hands imparted that shimmering sensation he'd experienced during the shoot without even touching him.

Or maybe it was memory. From when he'd caught her from tripping over that dog at Bliss House, or just now, when she'd passed so close he could see the flecks of light in her eyes.

"Tobias has never seen *any* galas." Kay didn't seem to hear his mutter.

"Picture this: a floating orchestra on a raft playing for VIP guests as they are brought across the lake on a multi-decked sight-seeing boat. As they approach the pier at twilight, a blaze of lights line the path to Bliss House.

"At Bliss House there's another orchestra playing, with soft spots bathing the façade and fairy lights in the gardens. There'll be dancing, and at the stroke of midnight, the doors ceremoniously open. The guests are welcomed inside for a buffet supper. Salmon, and—What?"

Glances shot around the table like a pinball machine gone mad.

"I expect tweaking as we go along. I'm open to suggestions," Kay said.

"Well, dear," started Miss Trudi, "one or two things occur to me."

"Try a dozen," Rob muttered.

"Twelve? My, my," Kay said in a brittle tone. "Don't hold back to spare me. Name them."

"There are no multi-level sight-seeing boats on Lake Tobias. In fact, no sight-seeing boats at all." He held up one finger. "Bringing VIP guests from *where*? Presuming we have VIP guests. The resort across the lake isn't going to let us crowd hypothetical VIP guests down their pier to this non-existent boat for nothing." Second finger went up. "A floating orchestra? Where are you going to get a raft that big?" Third finger. "And—."

"It doesn't have to be a full orchestra."

"And," he resumed, "how will you keep them from freezing? It's darned cold on that lake at night in October, even if the weather's good." Fourth finger. "How are these people getting up the hill to Bliss House? It's a long climb. And if you're thinking of driving them up, in what? Think of trying to get people off the boat and into cars, then out of cars at Bliss House. How are you going to entertain these VIPs while they wait?" Fifth and sixth finger. "You're going to keep these people outside at Bliss House where it's cold, in gardens that won't have much blooming because it's October in Wisconsin." Fingers seven, and eight. "Dancing? Outside? Where? And at the risk of repeating myself, this orchestra will also be freezing its, uh, fingers off. But I'll wrap that in with the dancing and only count it as one." Ninth finger.

"And leaving them outside until midnight? Most of Tobias is asleep by midnight. Those who are awake are not thinking about eating salmon." Ten, and cycling back to his left thumb, eleven.

Then, emphatically, he raised his left index finger for a second time. "We cannot afford this. Not the boat, not the orchestra—no, two orchestras—not the buffet supper, not the salmon and not the VIPs."

Silence.

The kind of silence that made your ears ring, your head pound, and your heart wonder if your mouth had lost its mind.

"Well, that was quite thorough. I certainly can't complain that you held back." Kay flashed a grin that twisted something inside him.

Sure her ideas were as impractical as having Tobias host the Olympics, but that didn't mean he had to savage them ... savage her.

All because she'd electrified the air.

"Sorry, I—"

She waved off his apology. "If you're right there's no reason to be sorry—and from the expressions around the table you are right. My ideas suck."

"Oh, now—" Annette started.

Rob stopped her. "You're right. These ideas suck."

"I suppose you can take the woman out of the city, but you can't make her fit in the town. I'm sorry to disappoint you all." Sounds of protest came from Annette and Suz. "I'll be out of your hair in—"

"Nonsense." Miss Trudi's crisp voice silenced the room as effectively as clapped hands in a well-trained classroom. "One does not achieve success by abandoning an enterprise at the first obstacle. Kay has brought us creative and exciting ideas. Yet they do not suit Tobias. We cannot, unfortunately, allow her time to discover naturally what elements are best suited to Tobias."

"I know how the project started, I poked around the house," Kay objected.

"That provides an introduction on which to build. Now we must provide a broader and more detailed understanding of Bliss House and of Tobias."

"That's a great idea, Miss Trudi," Suz said. "Sort of a crash course."

Miss Trudi nodded. "I can imagine nothing I would more enjoy than serving as guide and teacher for Dora's granddaughter. Alas, lacking the ability to drive, I must forgo that pleasure. Suz, perhaps you—oh, but you are new-come to Tobias."

"Right. What you need is a native," Suz said.

She got a beaming smile from Miss Trudi. "An excellent insight. We need a native to guide Kay in her exploration of Tobias."

Looks zinged around the table. Suddenly edgy, Rob planted his feet.

"Steve, who could know Tobias better than you?"

"Too busy with work, Miss Trudi. Otherwise I'd be honored."

"Of course, and with a new wife and your efforts on behalf of Bliss House it would be entirely too much to ask of you. Annette, you have even more duties for Bliss House, not to mention our dear Nell."

"I might be able to give Kay a morning or two. But—"

"Thank you for that generous offer. Although it does seem that continuity would benefit Kay. Perhaps, Fran...?"

"I'm in the same category as Annette. I have a few mornings, but negotiating with suppliers and scheduling planting takes most of my days."

"Oh, I know, Fran. We couldn't ask more of you. And dear Max, you and your men labor to all hours, however, if you have time...?"

Max shook his head. "No way, Miss Trudi. Sorry."

"But we need a native to show her around," Suz said, a glint in her eye.

This was a set-up. A scam. A conspiracy.

"Alas, since Rob is engrossed in a project—"

"A compost bin," said Steve, the traitor.

"I nominate Rob as Kay's guide," Suz said.

"An excellent suggestion," said Miss Trudi, as if it had never occurred to her.

"We don't get along," Kay protested.

Miss Trudi talked over the scoffing snort that came from Steve's direction. "I am certain that for the sake of Bliss House you will overcome that and see the benefits of this arrangement. Rob knows Tobias, is familiar with the workings of Bliss House, and has a finger firmly on the financial pulse of our endeavor."

"I haven't lived here in years. I—"

"I second the nomination of Rob." Steve overrode him. "All in favor?"

He didn't vote, but the enthusiasm of the others made up for it.

"Aye!" This group had never agreed on anything faster.

"Opposed?"

Every pair of eyes came to Rob. Including Kay's.

He kept his mouth shut.

CHAPTER NINE

"DO YOU WANT to start your in-depth Tobias tour now or tomorrow? You took off before we could talk."

Rob spoke from the car he'd pulled alongside her. Cobalt blue. Nice lines, more reserved than flashy. Sort of like him.

She'd love to send both of them into a demolition derby.

Kay kept walking, leaning into the warm headwind. Another half block to Bliss House. "You'll hold up traffic."

His car rolled, keeping pace. "What traffic?"

He was right. Not another car in sight. It was eerie. She faced him.

"I'll spare you and find information about Tobias and Bliss House myself."

"Then Miss Trudi would come up with another scheme. Besides, the committee voted and the idea has merit."

His reasonable tone made her want to throw something at him.

"Look, we both know there's this—this *thing* between us. A *thing* you want nothing to do with, as you've made very clear. You don't want to do this, and I don't either. Especially not since you consider me an idiot." Okay, so her ideas hadn't fit. He didn't have to hit her over the head—twelve times—to say she didn't belong here. "So we tell them you showed me all over Tobias, but we go our separate ways. They're happy and we're happier."

"It doesn't matter if we're happier. The committee gave me a job, I'm doing it. I'll meet you at Bliss House." He drove on.

She had half a block left to walk off a good thirty-block mad.

Why did he have to be determined to fulfill the obligation the committee thrust on him? Who knew a do-the-right-thing mentality could be so damned inconvenient?

She came around the corner of the wall that provided Miss Trudi's quarters privacy, and there was Rob, leaning against his car.

No financial analyst, past or present, had the right to look like that. Arms crossed over his chest emphasized its breadth. Rolled back sleeves showed the power of his forearms. One foot crossed over the other drew attention to the long, sleek jeans-clad legs as well as where they met and—

She shook her head to erase the image.

"Get this straight," he said. "I do not think you're an idiot. I do think your proposals sucked. But I'm confident that when you're educated—"

She snorted inelegantly.

"—about Tobias and Bliss House that you'll have great ideas. I watched you at the shoot, and you've got more ideas than you know what to do with."

Nothing like a compliment to deflate righteous anger to an airless balloon.

"It's actually a sensible idea when you think about it," Rob said, "and they made a good case that I'm the logical person to show you around."

Just what every girl wanted to hear—a guy was going to spend time with her because it was sensible and logical.

"You should get to know the lakeside area," he continued, "the restaurants, the lay of the land, how people in Tobias live. We'll visit Town Hall, the hospital, and library. I'll make an agenda, so you'll know what—"

"No agenda."

The trouble with that protest, she realized after she voiced it, was that she hadn't refused the entire idea, just the notion of an agenda.

"We'll start with a walk around town. That can't hurt. And it looks like we have a volunteer to join us."

Chester trotted toward them.

"He's still here." Kay didn't know if she was disappointed the dog hadn't found his way home or happy to see him.

"Hey, Chester," Rob said in a low croon. "Here, boy."

The dog didn't even look at him, but sat in front of her, clearing a half moon of dust and leaves with his wagging tail. "Hi, Chester."

"Since you're clearly this dog's favorite person, why don't you check his collar for tags? He might be lost, and getting confused by the new name."

She'd assumed yesterday that the dog belonged to a worker, and responded because he liked her. But if it was hungry, she'd bought Chester's affection with doughnuts and cheeseburgers, and then—admit it—had been pleased the dog preferred her to Rob. How pathetic was that?

"All right," Rob said, "I'll do the dirty work. You keep him distracted."

He'd clearly misread her silence as hesitation to touch the dog.

"Hey, Chester, can you believe he insulted you like that? Yeah, you're right. He isn't very bright. You're not dirty. You're well-traveled." The dog's soft brown eyes studied her as if translating the words into its own language. "Did some moron desert you?"

Rob was doing more than removing the collar; he patted the dog's wind-ruffled fur and peered in areas not remotely near the neck.

Kay kept talking to the dog. "No wonder you're looking for handouts. It's the *logical* and *sensible* thing to do. But I don't have any cheeseburgers or doughnuts right now. Maybe somebody else—"

"Hey, don't encourage him to run away, not with the collar off. Chester, stay." The dog gave him a disdainful over-the-shoulder glance. Rob sighed. "You better make it official."

"Chester, lie down." He did. "Stay."

"There's a number." Rob tipped the tag to the light. "Got your phone? Try 262-555-2891."

She punched in the numbers. Her breath came out in a whoosh as a recording kicked in.

"What is it?" Rob asked.

She held out the phone so he could hear. Instead of taking it, he placed one large hand over hers and guided the phone to his ear. She extended her arm full length. It wasn't enough. His warmth seeped into her.

"Disconnected." His tone seemed to carry more strain than the words warranted, but that must be her imagination, since anything else wouldn't fit his agenda.

She clicked the phone off. "That was useless."

"There is one piece of information we've added."

"What? There's no name. No other tags to give us a lead to his—"

"That's the new information. Under all that matted fur, this is a her."

"Are you sure? Why didn't you notice before? You said you had dogs when you were a kid."

"A gentleman doesn't question a lady about the sex of her dog. And Chester's coat is such a mess it's hard to tell anything. Guess you'll have to stop calling her Chester. Unless it's short of Chesterina or Chesterette."

"She's Chester. Like Glenn Close."

He chuckled. "If anyone could train her to an Oscar performance, I have a feeling it's you."

"Not me."

She didn't know what he found in those two syllables to make him look at her that way. She opened her tote and checked that she'd put the phone where it belonged. She had.

"I don't know how to take care of a dog," she admitted, just to get Rob to stop staring.

"Your family never had pets?"

"My mother's had dogs. Little ones. But taking care of them, no, the housekeepers do that. Feed them, take them out." Whatever else people did for dogs. "Besides I can't have dogs in my…"

She'd been about to say *in my building*. But she didn't have a building anymore. Tomorrow, she would call tomorrow.

"I will not be pushed into adopting a dog," she said. She'd simply given a creature food and water, and earned its gratitude. "If we're going on this walking tour, let's go. Chester, sit. Stay."

She refused to look at the dog as she walked away.

ROB LOOKED BACK. The dog sat where Kay had left her.

He should take out his phone and use its camera. A picture of Chester's heartbroken yet expectant expression should be a surefire inoculation against getting involved with this woman. Chester had let herself get attached. He wasn't going to make that mistake.

Yet there was something about the way Kay looked at that animal … She was smitten all right, but she was wary.

"You could see more if you slow down," he said as he caught up with her. She was recording on her phone again while the breeze tousled her hair.

"I'm used to New York walking."

"You also could see more, if you didn't keep your eye glued to that thing."

"I want a record of what I'm seeing instead of just my impressions. So tell me the history of Tobias," she ordered.

"The town was founded by Tobias Corbett," he started. He glanced back at Chester, still sitting, still watching Kay.

As ROB TOOK Kay on a zig-zag path from Bliss House's hill to the revitalized waterfront, he filled her in on Tobias Corbett and his descendants.

The Corbetts had produced worthy, prominent citizens who built Corbett House on one hill and the Blisses had produced one-of-a-kind eccentrics who built Bliss House on another.

"You love it here, don't you?" Kay asked unexpectedly.

"Yeah, I do."

"But you stayed away for a long time. Why?" She made it a challenge.

"I had my life mapped out. Returning to Tobias didn't come until later."

"How come a guy so career-driven that his schedule kept him from someplace he loves is on a leave of absence?" She aimed the phone's recorder at the library as they approached.

"The divorce."

She looked up. "Is that all?"

"There's no *that's all* about divorce."

"I meant is that the only thing, and you knew that. If you want to tell me it's none of my business, fine, but something's gnawing at you."

"On a day like this? Sunshine, a breeze—"

"The big thing—the big thing that's bothering you."

"Not a thing." She'd made a lucky guess. No one else suspected anything beyond the divorce. "Janice, my ex, used to say I was the original WYSIWYG—what you see is what you get. An ordinary guy from a nice town in Wisconsin, had a normal family, did okay in school and got a good job."

"She was an idiot."

He grinned, surprising himself. "Because she let me go?"

"Because she didn't really see you. You've got your demons, just like everybody."

She looked him over again. Not the way she had when she'd catalogued how well he would fill Brice's spot. This was a different look entirely. Like she was looking inside him.

"Hey!" Nell, coming from the library, skirted raised flowerbeds to reach them.

"Hi, Nell." Kay clicked off the recorder. "You sure must like books—didn't you get a stack from the library a few days ago?"

"Finished those. Can I ask you somethin'?"

"Sure," Kay said before Rob could decide whether to warn her that Nell's *somethin'*s could be lethal.

"Miss Trudi says your grandmother taught you to paint, and that she has a whole big studio you got to use when you were a kid."

"That's right. It's a great place."

The girl tilted her head. "You loved it, huh."

He wouldn't have made that leap. Yet he recognized the truth of it. Sometimes Nell Corbett was scary.

"I loved it," Kay said. "It was like Disneyland and Willy Wonka's Chocolate Factory—literally. Dora always had chocolate. She said she didn't know how anyone could create without chocolate. And she was almost as particular about her chocolate as she was about her painting. The smell of paint still makes my mouth water."

Nell heaved a giant sigh.

"I wish I had a grandmother I could paint with. I've only got one grandmother and she doesn't like anything fun. Hey! *You* can paint with me at Fran's day after tomorrow. There's no camp that morning. You could come paint with me and we'll see who's better."

"It's not a competition, and I'm working and—"

"Painting's work. That's how your grandmother got famous, right?"

"Yes, but—"

"And she's made a gazillion dollars." An SUV horn honked. Nell stepped toward it. "Rob, you bring her to Fran's house day after tomorrow."

"But—"

There were no buts, because Nell had gone.

Laughter brightened her eyes, but Kay said with a fake shudder, "Competitive painting. Why do I have the feeling I'm the underdog."

Being around Kay gave his grinning muscles a workout.

"Because you are," he said. "Make no mistake about it."

DURING THE CLIMB back to Bliss House, Kay pretended great absorption in the view on the phone's video screen.

Actually, she'd been absorbed with the man beside her. Close beside her. Sidewalks in Tobias made walking cozy. In crowded Manhattan everyone knew it was nothing personal if you bumped shoulders. Here, when their shoulders bumped, she jolted and hoped he didn't notice.

Why did she react this way to him? He wanted nothing to do with her. He was a budget freak. He talked about how hot their kiss was with one breath and in the next he cited sense, different backgrounds, and bad timing to overrule the attraction. And ... and he made agendas for heaven's sake. She was the least agenda-ized person in the world. They cramped the soul, not to mention making you squint.

Although he showed no sign of a squint, and those muscles had to be too well behaved to cramp.

"Looks like there's a problem," Rob said as they turned the corner beside Bliss House's grounds. "What the heck...?"

A half dozen of Max's men knotted in front of a bright yellow machine used for moving dirt. The driver took his hat off and wiped his brow. She could see the men looking at something on the sidewalk directly in the path of the idling machine. The group shifted.

Kay broke into a run. "Excuse me, excuse me." She wormed between two men to where Chester was lying where she had left her.

A plastic bowl of water and a hamburger on an opened wrapper were just out of the dog's reach. She drooled and sniffed hard in the vicinity of the hamburger, but she didn't move.

"Oh, Chester." Kay blinked at the burning behind her eyes as she bundled the phone into her tote. "I'm sorry. I'm so sorry."

The tail *thwap-thwapped* against the sidewalk.

"Lady, is this your dog?"

"No," she said. "Chester, okay."

The dog bounced up and immediately went to the food. Every face in the circle looked at her.

"If that ain't your dog, lady, you should go on TV with that act," said one gray-haired, burly man. "We've been trying to get that danged dog to move the last twenty minutes so we can get the Bobcat across. Tried bribing him with water and food, and stubborn cuss won't move an inch."

"I'm sorry. It's my fault. Don't blame Chester." She picked up the bowl and the licked-clean wrapper. "We'll get out of your way. Chester, come."

Chester padded beside her into a maple's filtered shade and out of the path of the machine, which roared to life. Shaking their heads, glancing at the dog, and passing comments, the men returned to work.

Rob stood to one side as she put the bowl down to let Chester drink. "Guess the logical thing now is to call animal welfare to pick hi—her up."

"Animal welfare? The pound?" Her voice climbed. "Don't you read the stories? Don't you know what can happen to animals there?"

"Kay, shelters do their best to adopt out the dogs and cats."

"Their best? But not all get adopted. And then—No. Absolutely not."

He looked at her as if she were a column of figures that kept adding up differently. "In that case, Kay, I think you've got yourself a dog. If she stays loose, someone else will call the pound. And even if they didn't, if she doesn't listen to anybody but you, it's not safe for her out here."

He was right. What if those men hadn't been so patient?

"I can't take a dog to the Hollands' house."

"Sure you can. They love dogs, have two they take everywhere. Besides," Rob continued, "you haven't adopted her. She's adopted you."

"She must be desperate," she muttered.

Without answering, he opened the back door of his car and said to the dog, "Do you want to come home with me?"

Chester didn't budge.

"Do you want to go home with Kay?"

The dog hopped in the car. The two faces—one female canine, one male human—looked at her expectantly.

"This is temporary," she said.

"Sure," Rob said. The dog sank onto the leather car seat with a sigh.

Serve him right if he had toenail marks all over the seat.

"If I do things wrong, you can lump it," she told Chester. "And I don't want any lectures from you," she added to Rob.

He raised his hands. "Not a word."

"Good, because everybody should remember this is short-term. I'm going to post notices, run an ad. The owner will claim her. This is to keep her out of the pound. Nobody's going to get attached."

"AS LONG AS Chester's already in the car, I'll be happy to give you a lift to the Hollands'," Rob offered.

"You better be happy to give me a lift to more than that, since I don't have a car and you engineered this whole thing."

Some of her anger had worn off during their walk, but the asperity remained. He liked it.

"Me?" He pled innocence with one hand to his chest.

"You. Let's start with a pet store for food, a leash and, uh, stuff."

"I'll call and ask where Steve and Annette get supplies for Pansy, Nell's puppy. They got her a couple weeks ago."

"Good news," he announced when he hung up. "There's a pet superstore on the highway that Annette says even has on-the-spot grooming. And you'll get your first introduction to Tobias retail."

As they drove, he refused to feel guilty for not telling her the Tobias Animal Welfare Center had a no-kill policy, with dedicated volunteers placing adoptable animals and caring for the rest. Something about these two—woman and dog—made him sure they should be together. Almost as sure as Chester appeared to be.

"You'll still need to call animal welfare," he told Kay. "Somebody could have reported her missing. And it's the law."

"The law? The law has no heart. People come first, not stupid rules and regulations. People and animals."

They'd reached the superstore so he tucked reaction—overreaction—away for future consideration.

Nearly two hours later, they emerged with an overflowing shopping cart, a tag with Kay's phone number on it and a half-dozen books. Chester had been groomed, her matted lumps from ears to tail replaced by fluffy fur.

"I need to find a vet for her," Kay said once they were in the car.

"Everyone takes their animals to Allison Maclaine. She was a couple years ahead of Steve and me in school."

Kay's thanks were muffled. He turned and saw that she was twisted in the seat, facing the back, where Chester lay serenely.

"Stop worrying," he said. "It looks like she's a good traveler."

"I wasn't worrying exactly. I was wondering if she's regretting this."

"Are you kidding? She's thrilled—as long as she's with you."

"God, doesn't she know she can't go around giving out trust that way."

She'd clearly meant the comment to be light, maybe even funny. She'd failed.

CHAPTER TEN

"WHY ARE WE stopping here?"

Here was a structure of brick, frame and stucco cobbled together, with a three-quarters full parking lot and a sign proclaiming "The Toby."

"It's a must-see stop on the Tobias tour. Besides, with all the attention we've paid to this dog's diet, you and I haven't gotten dinner. The Toby isn't haute cuisine, but it'll keep us from starving."

"You mean leave Chester in the car? Alone? She'll feel deserted. It's too soon. And she could get heat-stroke. Or—"

"Relax. I'll get takeout, you stay with Chester. There's a picnic table."

Sitting on the bench while Chester sniffed under the table, Kay admitted this was a good idea. Trees held off the slanting sun with long, cool shadows, while the light turned golden.

This had never been her favorite time of day. As a kid it was when her parents prepared to go out. After daylight, before nightlife ignited. Catching a sunset in Manhattan wasn't impossible, but usually required planning to be where the western view wasn't blocked. A sunset was a goal, an occasion. Here it was part of everyday life. She liked that.

She slipped off her sandals and wiggled her toes in the warm grass.

"Hey, Kay, look who I found inside."

Rob strode toward her. For a flash, it was like the moment she'd come down the stairs at Bliss House. All she could see was him, all she could feel—

No. She forced her focus wider. Behind him walked Annette and Steve, also carrying a bag, and Suz and Max.

"We were in line when Rob told us you rescued a dog," Annette said.

"Oh, I didn't—"

"And we're waiting to be served," added Suz. "So we had to come see this girl named Chester."

Chester wagged her tail, but pressed against Kay's knees.

"She must not have been out on her own that long," Max said. "She's got a bit of a gut on her."

"That's fur," Kay said indignantly.

"Along with doughnuts and cheeseburgers," Rob murmured.

She shot him a glare. "You can feel her ribs. She's skin and bones."

"And fur," Max said. "Looks like she's a golden retriever-collie mix. She's a beauty."

"That's what the groomer said," Kay told him, almost ready to forgive his "gut" comment.

"Oh, she's a love," Suz crooned, and had her hand licked.

"With those bloodlines she'll be a people-pleaser," Max added.

"She found the person she wants to please, that's for sure," Rob said.

"And with those bloodlines she'll shed like crazy."

"Yeah, like that bothers you, Annette," Steve said. "Who was that I heard singing love songs to Pansy while you vacuumed this morning?"

"Fur doesn't bother me," Annette said with dignity. "I said it so Kay would know in case it bothers her, so she wouldn't get too attached."

"Too late," Rob said. "Chester picked her and there's no going back."

Kay shook her head. "I'm going to put up notices to find the owner. Finding her owner would be the best-case scenario."

Even looking into the sun's glare, she saw that none of them believed her.

JANICE HAD CALLED. According to Fran's note on the counter, Janice had said to call her whenever he got in. Fran had underlined *whenever*.

Rob found the note when he returned home after dropping off Kay, Chester. and all the new paraphernalia at the Hollands'. Before he'd left, he'd told Kay what she should be sure to see in Tobias tomorrow. When Kay said she could get a rental car, he'd said he might as well drive her around because he could add Tobias commentary as they went.

God, what was he thinking?

Could it possibly be what everyone seemed to be accusing him of thinking?

When he'd married Janice, he'd had reasons to believe their future would follow their chosen track. Janice had been focused and steady, where Kay was scattered and changeable.

If he got involved with Kay it would be like leaning over so the mule that had kicked him in the teeth could get a clear shot at his ass.

With that image in mind, he was half tempted to ignore Janice's message. It was no accident he hadn't given her his new cell number. But he wouldn't put it past his ex to call again in the middle of the night and he didn't want Fran disturbed.

Strange how little he missed Janice. He supposed because they hadn't really been part of one another's lives for a long time.

He settled in the family room with a beer and turned on the TV to the all-business channel, took a swig and punched in Janice's number.

"Rob. I was about to give up hope. I can't imagine what you could find to do in that tiny town until this hour."

He resisted the temptation to make a crack that people in small towns had sex, too. But that would just prolong the preliminaries before they got to what she wanted. Besides, he wasn't having sex, and he sure as hell didn't want to discuss that with her.

"I'm here now, Janice. What's the problem?"

"I don't know why you would assume it was a problem."

He held his silence.

Impatience sharpened her next words. "The problem is what you could be doing to yourself."

"I'm fine."

"No, you're not. If you're even considering throwing away your career over some technicalities, you are far, far from fine. If you've pulled out your trusty legal pad and done a pro and con assessment, you have to see I'm right, Rob. Do you *want* to ruin your career?"

If she knew how many times he'd sat with a legal pad and hadn't been able to write down a thing, she'd never let this go.

"No."

"Well then, that's your answer."

"No, it's not. There's more to consider than my career."

She pounced. "That's right. The future of a company that's been good to you, the welfare of its stockholders, and the careers of people you've worked with and liked."

As if he hadn't thought of all that.

"If the company comes clean—"

"Oh, please. Like that would do any good. You know that in a situation like this, if there's simply the appearance of irregularities, the regulators, the politicians, and the media will be out for blood. They know how to get the big headlines—bring down a respected company. They'll tear apart a profitable company for nothing, when—"

"Mitchell told you to call."

Damn, damn, damn. Even now he'd hoped his mentor and friend would make things right, as he'd said he would. This call was proof that Mitchell was following another path.

"I don't know what you—"

"Mitchell Gordon called you into his office and fed you all this and told you to get me to promise to be quiet."

"So what if he did contact me? He thought you'd listen to sense, that even though we're divorced that you'd respect my judgment. He's concerned for your welfare, you know. And you owe that man, Rob. He gave you your start, he boosted you all the way along."

Yes, he did.

As if she'd heard his response, she said, "Don't you have any gratitude, Rob? Or loyalty? My God, Mitchell was your champion, and now you're going to stab him—and yourself—in the back for technicalities?"

Nothing like pitting gratitude and loyalty against integrity.

"They're not technicalities, Janice. Those laws are there for a reason. They protect people's incomes, their ability to live their lives."

"What about the incomes of all your fellow employees? What about their lives? You're willing to sacrifice them for a bunch of strangers?"

For strangers and a principle.

"Even if you don't have any feeling for Mitchell or the company, how about having the smarts to protect yourself?"

"If my career goes—"

"If?" She laughed. "Oh, your career will go, all right. It's your freedom that could be in jeopardy. Staying out of jail."

"I had no hand in any of the company's wrongdoing." And he had copies of the records to prove it. He wasn't entirely naïve. As much as he'd hoped Mitchell would do the right thing, he'd documented what was going on and his own lack of involvement before approaching his boss.

"How about withholding evidence for months? You could go to jail for that, you know."

Yes, he knew. The lawyer he'd consulted in June had wanted him to turn over everything he'd had right then.

But he'd promised Mitchell. He'd wondered if Mitchell knew the position Rob was in when he'd begged for this summer to "set things right."

Now he had his answer.

Because Janice wouldn't have thought about that twist on her own, it wasn't her brand of manipulation. Mitchell must have handed it to her.

"What's your interest in this, Janice?"

"I still care about you, Rob. I hate to see the career I helped you build—

"What's you're real interest?"

She gave a throaty laugh. It was meant to be sexy. He knew it was mostly to mask that she was pissed that he wasn't cooperating.

"I don't know why you would think—"

But her stalling had given him time to work it out. "Mitchell promised to give you part of the advertising account if you persuade me to come back into the fold."

"That account is one hell of a coup," she purred.

"It would be if you got it."

"Oh, I'm not putting all my eggs in the Rob Dalton basket. I've worked up ideas for a campaign to offset anything you might say to the media."

"Mitchell was making you a promise he can't keep, Janice. Torenson makes the decisions about advertising."

"So, I'll win him over. Mitchell will take me in, introduce me, and—"

"That's the first difficulty. Mitchell and Torenson hate each other. Second, Torenson vacations every year with the top brass from the company he's using now."

"I'll win him over," she snapped.

"Janice, Mitchell's playing you. Using your ambition to get you to do his dirty work."

"Screw you!"

She hung up on him.

Everything he'd told Janice was true. Unfortunately, everything she'd said was true, too.

An investigation could do irreparable harm to the firm and to the careers of many innocent employees. And, yes, he could be vulnerable to prosecution.

Maybe this was why he hadn't been able to get a pro-and-con list down on paper. There were too many cons no matter how hard he looked at the situation.

CHAPTER ELEVEN

THE NEXT DAY, Rob's car pulled to the curb a block from the Hollands' house.

Kay fought her reaction to Rob's smile and "good morning" with an accusatory. "You're early. I haven't finished walking Chester."

"You could've let her out in the yard. It's fenced for the Hollands' dogs."

"I know that." That was a lie. It hadn't occurred to her. When dogs had to go out, they were walked, usually by hired dog-walkers. And she had a new appreciation for them after concentrating on holding the leash exactly the way the book said, not letting Chester strain ahead or lag. "Chester wanted to go for a walk."

She'd hoped that in addition to serving Chester's needs, the walk would wake her up. She'd barely slept last night.

First, she'd watched Chester explore her new surroundings, and reveled in the fact that she sat in this homey kitchen, with this homey dog—her, Kay Aaronson, whose experience of homey wouldn't fill the head of a pin.

She'd made up a flyer about Chester, because she'd said she would, but then she'd spent hours flipping from one book to another for advice on dog care. Even after she went to bed, she'd twice gotten up to check that Chester had enough water. She'd dozed, then jolted to awareness every time the dog moved on the floor beside the bed. When Chester didn't move, she strained to hear proof the dog was breathing.

Finally, she gave up, got up, and looked up sites on the Internet about crafts and historical sites, with Chester curled up at her feet.

Rob turned off his car and got out. "Where are you headed?"

"Bliss House."

"Morning, Miss." A man with a semicircle of white hair around a bald pate passed them on the sidewalk. "Morning, Rob."

"Morning, Tom."

Kay paused, but Rob kept walking. She stutter-stepped to catch up and called out a quick, "Morning" after the man.

She was starting to get the hang of this. In Tobias, whether you knew the person or not, you didn't pass without saying hello.

"That's Tom Dunwoody Sr.," Rob said when they were out of earshot. "He'll sell his carved duck decoys when Bliss House opens. He does great work."

Rob waved to a young couple with a toddler in a small front yard of a neat, square house. As they walked on, he exchanged greetings with another half dozen people.

At Bliss House, they found construction at full volume and Miss Trudi and Fran giving a tour of the nascent gardens to a gaggle of gray-haired ladies.

"Garden Club," Rob said. "They've volunteered to help plant."

She eyed the women, who all appeared to have passed the Social Security starting line years ago.

"I know," Rob said, obviously reading her reaction. "Fran's going to have them handle the small plants. It's the trees and bushes she's ordered that concern me. Steve and Max are up to their eyeballs in work, there's no one else on our volunteer roster suited to the job, and the budget doesn't have much room for labor."

"What about you?"

He looked away. "I'll be in Chicago by then."

The undercurrent in that simple statement could have carried her across Long Island Sound in a second.

But before she could examine it, she heard Miss Trudi call out, "Oh, here is our dear Kay Aaronson." In an instant, she was surrounded by gray-haired ladies and Rob had disappeared, the rat.

Kay nearly sank under a wave of introductions to Miss Trudi's fellow garden club members, but did grasp one element. Muriel Henderson and Miriam Jenkins would be among those selling their wares at Bliss House. It gave her an idea.

"Miss Trudi, can you arrange for me to meet with people who will be selling their crafts?"

"An excellent idea, my dear. I will most certainly do that."

After that, conversational eddies tossed Kay this way and that until her head swam. She was grateful when Fran guided the gaggle away.

She found Rob leaning against the newly refurbished front gate.

"I hope that's wet paint," she grumbled. "You deserted me."

"Yup." He grinned. "It only would have been worse with the two of us together to cluck over. Much worse."

Their gazes met, held, then went their separate ways.

He certainly knew better than she if those women might misconstrue seeing the two of them together. She should be grateful, she decided as they began the return trip, that he tried to avoid such misunderstandings. All part of that do-the-right-thing mentality of his.

"Are you late for an appointment?" Rob asked suddenly.

"No. Oh." She recognized what he was getting at. "I was at New York speed again. Sorry."

"No problem. It's good to get my cardio work in early in the day."

She chuckled, and slowed her steps. Simply because adapting this relaxed pace put her in tune with Tobias.

He picked up where he'd left off yesterday, talking about how the town had grown, with timeouts to fill her in on people they met. How this one was related to that one or worked with the other or volunteered with another.

It was easy here in Tobias to see how people interconnected, how they needed each other. People everywhere wove a web of relationships—business or personal. New York offered so many possible threads to follow that sometimes it was hard to recognize an overall pattern, and to know you were part of it. But in Tobias everyone knew the interconnections, and celebrated them.

She glanced at Rob.

"What?"

Her *glance* had stuck. She'd been staring at him, and he'd caught her.

"Tell me about your childhood," she blurted. It hadn't been the track her mind had been following—that track could have earned her a ticket for indecency on a public sidewalk if Tobias had thought police—but once she said the words, she realized she was interested. "What was it like growing up here? That'll help me understand Tobias."

He looked unconvinced, but asked, "What do you want to know?"

"For starters, what did you do during summers as a kid?"

"Swam, sailed, rode bikes, built forts, played baseball, tennis, soccer—about every sport. But my parents also believed in kids having time to entertain themselves." He looked into the distance.

"Miss Trudi told me they were great people. It must have been so hard to lose them so young."

"It was." He cleared his throat. "We used to ride our bikes to the far side of the lake and poke around old cabins in the woods over there."

"Who's *we*?"

"Steve and me, Steve's kid brother, Zach, too."

"Why poke around old cabins?"

"Mostly because it was forbidden." He grinned, and she could see him as a tousle-haired ten-year-old. "I suppose it could have been dangerous, with those things rotting away. But the worst that happened were bumps and bruises and scratches from the raspberry bushes."

"Raspberry bushes?"

"They were on the way back if we did the whole circuit. Other side of the country club, around where the old highway bridge crosses the river. That made it more daring, because we ran the risk of being spotted and word could get back to our parents." He laughed. "But when we got home, they knew anyway. Especially when they spotted Zach."

"Why especially him?"

"Because he always looked the worst. Steve and I would tell him he had to pick raspberries for us or he couldn't come, because he was younger. He'd go charging in there like a maniac. He never passed up a challenge. And he never passed up a chance to make his mother furious."

"Over eating raspberries?"

"Wait until you meet Lana Corbett. You'll understand. And let me tell you, she's mellowed. *Corbetts do not indulge in such low behavior*—that pretty much covered anything a kid would consider fun."

He obviously was mimicking Lana Corbett, but Kay also caught an echo of her mother. Strange that Steve, so relaxed and kind, might have had an upbringing with similarities to hers.

"What about your parents?" she asked.

"Oh, they had rules, but no delusions about social prestige. Looking back I see the rules were about keeping us safe, and teaching us to be responsible. At the time I thought they were killjoys and strict beyond belief."

They were negotiating a tilted patch of sidewalk where a huge tree root had erupted. He let her and Chester go ahead and their hands brushed. For an instant she thought he might take her hand.

He stepped back to allow a cushion of space.

Kay wanted to slap her head—of course he stepped back. Hadn't she gotten that into her skull yet?

"What about you?" he asked. "What was your childhood like?"

Lonely. "The usual—school, lessons, camp in the summer."

"Lessons?"

"Riding, tennis, piano, ballet."

He chuckled. "So you tormented your parents with tournaments and recitals."

"My parents had—have—very busy social calendars."

"Ouch."

"Don't feel sorry for me—it's so poor-little-rich-girl to whine even though you lived at increasingly better addresses, went to the best schools, had playdates in the Hamptons. I am *not* a poor-little-rich-girl."

"But people give you grief about being rich—people like that actor."

She'd forgotten Brice's cracks. She shrugged. "I'm used to it."

He studied her face. "What was your favorite thing to do as a kid?"

The answer came immediately. "Go to Dora's studio."

"Did you paint?"

"Sure. If you wanted to be around Dora, that's what you did. Are you familiar with her style?" He nodded. "Then you know how exacting it is. I remember many canvases that looked amazing to me but didn't meet her standards, so she painted over them. But she let me just be a kid, experiment, play."

"Did you keep it up?"

"No. You could say I outgrew it."

Or you could say her family imploded, she'd never returned to the studio and, until a few months ago, she hadn't talked to her grandmother for sixteen years.

She picked up the pace even as she dug into her tote bag.

"Hold Chester's leash, will you?" Without looking at Rob, she practically flung it at him.

What was she thinking? Walking her dog down a small-town street with a nice guy beside her—all fantasy. The dog wasn't hers, she didn't belong in the town, and the guy had no intention of pursuing the sparks between them. He'd said it—different worlds. She sure didn't belong in his.

She didn't have to turn around to know man and dog watched her. She fumbled the paper against a telephone pole and attached it with the stapler.

"What's that?" he asked.

"Flyer about the dog. I made them last night. Someone will recognize her from the description and she can go back to her true home."

"I thought you liked her."

"I do." She cleared her throat. "I'm being practical. Even if the previous owner doesn't claim her, someone will see the flyers and want to adopt Chester, so she won't be without a home when I leave."

CHAPTER TWELVE

ROB ADJUSTED HIS hold on Chester's leash, wondering why Kay's mood had taken a downturn that made the Stock Market Crash of '29 look like an easy glide. She attacked that flyer like it was an enemy.

Kay Aaronson was a most interesting woman.

She was putting up flyers inviting someone to claim this dog, which spoke of someone determined to remain unencumbered, to keep her life streamlined to allow for maximum maneuverability.

Yet, if he'd been a betting man, he would put money down that she was hoping with every staple that no one would claim Chester.

As she marched on to the next pole, he paused to read:

Found:

Who: One female dog. (No name on collar, but phone number 262-555-2891 imprinted on tag. Number no longer in service.)

Where: In the vicinity of Bliss House.

Description: Golden and white fur. Beautiful markings. Sunny disposition. Well-trained. Knows sit, stay, come, lie down, learning shake. Very affectionate. Tall enough to pet without bending down.

Contact: Kay Aaronson, 262-555-3874, 3 to 4 p.m.

That description sounded more like a besotted owner's list of charming traits than a wanted poster's vital statistics.

"Why between 3 and 4? Will you be around then?"

"The machine can get any calls if I'm not," she said indifferently.

"You could list your cell phone."

"I'm not going to post my cell phone number all over Tobias. It could tie up my phone for emergencies."

He would have laughed if she hadn't been so entirely clueless that she was making it difficult for anyone to claim Chester. She had no idea how her eyes brightened when the dog nosed at her hand for petting or how her face softened when Chester curled up at her feet. Yet she couldn't seem to trust that this animal was at least as smitten as she was.

Why couldn't she believe it?

Kay was a fascinating combination of self-assurance and insecurity.

When he'd tried to apologize for exposing all the flaws in her ideas for the Bliss House opening and she'd said there was no need since he was right, he'd been bowled over. He couldn't imagine anyone else being that non-defensive. And, after a brief setback, her belief that she could do this job—maybe that she could do *any* job, considering the variety in her resume—had rebounded to full strength.

Yet, she'd said Chester *must be desperate* to want to be with her.

And she'd seemed so wistful when he'd talked about his growing up, about his family.

My parents had—have—very busy social calendars.

Miss Trudi had said something similar about the Aaronsons. What could Miss Trudi have been hinting at when she'd talked about strains in Kay's family? Kay's parents sure hadn't supported her when she called off the wedding. Maybe she hadn't treated the guy great, but family should stick by you.

With all urge to laugh long gone, he jerked his thoughts to the present, watching Kay staple another flyer to a pole.

"Today," he said, "we'll cover the official aspects of Tobias—Town Hall, the hospital and—"

"No. I can't leave Chester. It's too soon."

This from the woman posting flyers inviting people to take the dog.

"Okay," he said slowly, mentally adjusting the schedule he'd made.

"We can explore Lake Tobias, starting with a drive around it."

"But Chester—"

"We'll take her. In fact, we can stop at animal welfare for—"

"I told you, I'm not taking her to the pound."

"I meant to get her a county tag."

"Are you some sort of law and order junkie?"

"It's the right thing to do."

Her response was the *whack, whack* of another flyer stapled to a pole. "There. That should get attention."

"Right."

ROB SHOWED HER around the piers and parks of the town's revitalized waterfront before they stopped for lunch at the Tastee-Treat Ice Cream Shoppe, near the community pool. Both were doing good business.

Sitting at a small table under a faded sun umbrella, where no one seemed to object to Chester lying at their feet, Kay had a salad to his hamburger and fries, so she felt plenty virtuous enough to go for the two-scoop ice cream cone he offered. Besides, it was hot.

"Here we are, Pralines and Cream on top of Rocky Road for you." He let the change slide from his hand onto the table so he could hand the cone to her. "Those seem appropriate—you look like you'd be Pralines and Cream, but you lead people down a Rocky Road."

"Hah!" That was all she said as she swept her tongue around the pile of ice cream to make sure no melting driblets escaped. "And what about you?"

"What about me?" He was eating his cone with such a look of deep attention that his thick lashes nearly masked his eyes.

"Strawberry and chocolate? Could you get any more basic? With tastes like that I'm surprised you ever wanted to go to the big city of Chicago."

"Couldn't get what I thought I wanted here."

"Ah," she said wisely. "Back to the financial analyst stuff. So you always knew you wanted to be a financial analyst?"

"I knew I liked dealing with numbers, and helping people with money appealed, but I didn't narrow it down until I decided to get an MBA."

She whistled—not her best, since her lips were cold.

"You can't be impressed," he said. "MBAs litter the ground in Manhattan."

"True, but I rarely eat ice cream with them."

"Got something against MBAs?"

"I'm an open-minded sort, but they're so *scheduled*. You'd have to get an appointment in February to have ice cream in August."

"Must be the Manhattan MBAs, since we didn't know each other in February."

"But you're on a leave of absence. Someone who could take a leave of absence can't be as strictly scheduled as other MBAs."

"Not so. I not only follow a schedule, I had a master plan for my life."

Had. There he went talking in the past tense again.

"By college I had my whole life mapped out. Get good grades, get into the MBA program, find the right woman, finish the MBA, land the right job, marry, move to the city, get established, move up and up. Make our fortunes—" His slight, dry smile tightened her throat. "—then step back, slow down, and have our family."

"Sounds—" She looked at him from under her lashes as she selected the word. "—reasonable."

He crunched into his cone. "I hit a few potholes. You might notice—no wife, no kids."

She dismissed that with a wave. "You've got your fortune, the wife and kids will follow."

"No confidence that I could win a wife without money, huh?"

"Why take the risk?"

He laughed.

It shouldn't feel this good to make someone laugh.

She devoted herself to another neatening-up foray around the cone, making sure she caught every soft slide of ice cream. With the Pralines and Cream long gone, a Rocky Road miniature marshmallow detached from the rest of the concoction, and she caught it with the tip of her tongue before curling it into her mouth.

That was when she met Rob's look.

She stopped, with her tongue tucked inside her top lip with its sweet load. She didn't move, she didn't speak. Under other circumstance she might have even said she froze. But not with that look aimed at her.

It could have melted her ice cream. The earth's crust had to be getting mushy, too. And her personal environment had leapt about six hundred degrees.

Rob jerked back as if escaping a flame.

"Well." That was all he said for a good half a minute. He wrapped his last bite of cone in its paper holder, put a stack of napkins in front of her and threw his garbage out. "You about ready?"

She swallowed, found the sweetness of melting marshmallow in her mouth and had to swallow again before she could say, "Just about."

Rob scooped up the change he'd put on the table.

"Wait a minute," he said. He returned to the window, getting on line behind a mother with four children. He'd decided one cone wasn't enough?

The mother handed cones one by one to her children, a squawk arose, she switched two of the cones, restoring peace, and paid. Rob stepped to the counter, said a few words and handed over money. But he left the window without a cone and headed back to her.

"What was that about, Rob?"

He gestured for her to go ahead, at the same time saying hello to a gray-haired couple eating banana splits.

"I just noticed she'd given me too much change," he said. "What?"

She looked away immediately. "Nothing."

But it wasn't nothing. Barry not only hadn't returned the money when a cashier at a theater had given him an extra five dollars, he had chortled about it. Even if it had occurred to him to do the right thing, he definitely wouldn't have stood on line to do it.

Rob stepped ahead of her to open first the back door for Chester, then the front passenger door for her. She paused, an urge to kiss him—on the cheek, she'd just kiss him on the cheek—nearly overwhelming. But she held back. She patted him on the arm.

He looked from where her hand rested on his forearm to her face. A quizzical expression, along with a renewed lick of flame in his eyes almost had her reconsidering her restraint. Almost.

"What was that for?"

"That was for your being a very nice man, Rob Dalton."

Who knew nice could be so darned sexy. Or was it just her that his decency turned on?

His quizzical expression deepened. "Because I didn't cheat the ice cream shop?"

"Among other things." She sank into the car seat so she didn't grab him and show him exactly what those other things were whether he liked it or not.

CHAPTER THIRTEEN

S HE'D BEEN GIVING him a lot of questioning looks.
At least that's what Rob told himself they were. Much better
for his self-control if they were.

What the hell had gotten into him? As if he'd never seen a woman
eating an ice cream cone before.

"So, picking up our tour around the lake," he said to break the
silence, "we see another landmark—the famous raspberry bushes on
the banks of the mighty Tobias River."

He kept up the commentary, pointing out the country club, a resort Steve had been instrumental in getting reopened, the site of the
rundown cabins he and the Corbett brothers had explored as kids.

They pulled off the road into a tree-lined drive and stopped in
front of a neat one-story frame house.

"What's this?"

"Max and Suz's house."

Kay reached for her phone, clicking on the video recorder as they
got out of the car. She'd had it going during most of the drive. It
provided a buffer between them, so he had no right to object, since
he'd made the rules about keeping their distance.

He hated the damned thing.

"Leave it for now. I promise to bring you out again to record it if
you want, but for now look."

She didn't reply, but she left the phone on the car seat. "Aren't
Max and Suz working at Bliss House?"

"Yup. We're here to use the pier. You can't know this town without sailing Lake Tobias."

"But Chester—"

"That's why we're sailing from here instead of the town pier—shade and quiet so she'll be comfortable. I called while you walked Chester before lunch and had one of Max's guys sail my boat over at lunch, then Max gave him a ride back. We'll tie up Chester in the shade and leave her plenty of water and toys, and we'll be able to see her and she'll be able to see us—you—the whole time."

Chester appeared perfectly content with the plan. It took more coaxing to get Kay to leave the dog and get in the boat. But once they were on the water, and she could see Chester had settled down under a tree, she relaxed.

Out in the sun, she took off the black shirt she'd worn knotted at the waist of her black shorts and revealed a black sleeveless T. No, less than sleeveless. The armholes were cut so high they left narrow straps to bridge the front and back, baring her shoulders. Beautiful shoulders. Creamy white over the strong line of bone. He wanted to taste them.

He jerked his thoughts away from contemplating her taste and tossed her sunscreen from the plastic ready bag kept in the boat.

"This is wonderful." She spread on the lotion.

He tried not to watch, and failed. "Haven't you sailed?"

"Not like this." She swung an arm out in a broad gesture and people on the two boats in sight waved. She grinned and converted the gesture to a true wave.

He looked at her, sitting in his small boat as if she belonged. The sun glinted in her hair and squinted her eyes into an even deeper smile. How the hell had she become this unaffected person, given what her parents were, based on what she'd said and what Miss Trudi had said?

Still looking at the water, she continued, "Some of Mother and Father's crowd sail competitively. Actually they all do it competitively one way or another. You know, whose boat's bigger, fancier. But definitely not like this. This … this is sailing just for the wind and the water."

She sighed such deep satisfaction, he thought the sail would fill with it.

Something in his chest sure as hell did.

His hand on the tiller clenched, starting the boat in a turn without a conscious decision. Following the motion, he warned, "Coming about," swung the boom once he was sure she had ducked, and adjusted his position so he wasn't looking at her directly.

"Now, aren't you glad we haven't spent this day at Town Hall and the hospital?" she asked.

"Yeah, I am."

"Do you sail on Lake Michigan?"

"Not much. Never seemed to have the time."

"Because you were working so hard on your map to success. If you want to talk about how your schedule went wrong or the divorce or—"

"Not particularly."

He was still looking at her. He'd just made it more difficult by coming about. Great.

"It's not good to bottle it up. Eventually the lid pops off and it can happen at the worst time."

"Like walking out on your groom twelve days before your wedding? Bottling things up so the guy had no idea what was happening until you hit him out of the blue?" They stared at each other. He recovered first. "Sorry. I had no right to say that."

"At least you weren't bottling it up." They exchanged small smiles.

"It's none of my business what happened with you and your ex-fiancé," he said. Why the hell couldn't he remember that before he opened his mouth?

"No, it isn't," Kay agreed. "Just like it's none of my business what happened with you and your ex-wife. Not that I don't want you to share…"

Her teasing drew another smile from him, this one real. She smiled back.

She got serious first. "I'll tell you, Rob. After knowing you, I'm more certain than ever that ending it twelve days before the wedding was infinitely better than ending it twelve minutes after, or twelve days after or twelve months after."

What did she mean *after knowing you*?

Because they never would have met if she'd gone through with marrying Barry? Or did she mean seeing the effects of his divorce?

He didn't ask. Maybe he didn't want to know the answer. He caught the wind for a good run, sending the boat scooting across the water. When the wind shifted slightly, he settled for the tamer broad reach.

"That was great!" Kay's eyes sparkled, her cheeks were flushed.

"My mom used to say that in sailing, you always think there's a way you could have made better use of the wind, but that shouldn't stop you from appreciating the motion and balance and breeze you've enjoyed."

"So, your mother was the sailor in the family?"

"Both my parents sailed, but Mom was more willing to give up the tiller enough to let others learn."

"So you take after you father."

"Are you implying I'm controlling?"

She tipped her head, the breeze caught the feathery ends of her hair setting them to dancing, almost as wildly as the devilment in her eyes. "Implying? More like saying it outright."

"Hey, I don't try to make all the decisions. Look at the committee, I go along with the flow and—"

"Until anyone steps on the budget's bottom line and then you come down like a hammer."

"Someone's got to watch for red ink."

"Hah! You don't even let it get pale gray. And what about this showing me around Tobias—you probably have a printed agenda for each day."

"That you'll keep changing."

"It's good for you."

"Maybe."

She gave him that look again. That same one as yesterday in front of the library, when she'd looked inside him.

He cleared his throat. "So, did you learn sketching from your grandmother?"

She raised one eyebrow at the subject change, then said in a humoring-you tone, "Yes, but I don't do it anymore."

"I saw you sketching the gardens as Fran described them."

"Oh those." The humoring was gone. "Those were doodles."

He'd asked the question to gain distance from that look, but now she had him curious. "Looked like more than doodles."

"You know the interesting thing," she said, ignoring his comment, "is that we have so many choices for expression. Take film. That's the medium for contemporary times." And she was off.

Years in business had developed Rob's bull-detector to a fine instrument.

He partially owed his quick rise to it. With one exception, he'd had an unerring sense of when executives were on the level and when they were trying to dazzle him with bull. And with that exception, loyalty and gratitude had clouded his judgment. Granted, his bull-detector was a little out of tune after this summer, but he knew when the stuff was being shoveled. And Kay Aaronson was shoveling for all she was worth, running on about rotoscoping and narrative and POV shots.

He cut across the rambling with a direct question. "Did you stop painting because your grandmother's a famous artist and that can be hard to live up to?"

"I'm not trying to live up to her."

That had a ring of truth to it. "The way you talked about going to her studio as a kid, but then you told Nell you don't go there anymore, and what you said about not sketching, when it's clear you love it ... It adds up to something."

That pane-of-glass face of hers showed her debating whether to keep silent.

"There was a ... a family situation a long time ago. Dora—my grandmother—has been estranged from my parents and me since I was thirteen."

"But she was behind your doing the shoot here."

"Yes, she was. We ... ran into each other. Talked some. I don't know what's going to happen now."

"What do you want to happen?"

"I don't know."

And wasn't that what he'd been thinking all along? That she was a woman who didn't know what she wanted.

THE SUN WAS dropping when they brought the boat in. Max and Suz arrived as Rob was securing it. Annette, Steve, and Nell followed almost immediately. They brought a medium-sized reddish-brown puppy with white markings of indeterminate breed by the name of Pansy. Nell and Pansy made a beeline for Chester. Wagging tails set Kay's worries to rest about the dogs.

"How was the lake?" Suz asked.

"Fabulous. You must be out on the water all the time."

"We mostly look at it from the porch swing." Max put an arm around Suz's shoulders. "Hope you're hungry. We're starting dinner."

"That's so nice of you. Thank you, but—"

"Great. It's all set," Suz interrupted. "Annette brought salad, and there'll be steaks and baked potato—nothing fancy—and I made brownies last night for dessert."

"But I didn't bring anything."

"That's the idea. With all the work we're getting out of you, the least we can do is feed you now and then."

Kay joined the general laughter. "Thank you, that would be great, if you let me bring something the next time. Oh—I could bring Miriam Jenkins's potato surprise. She told me about it at the meeting and she's going to give me the recipe."

"Oh, my God. I thought that recipe would die with her."

"Some of us hoped." Max said, drawing chuckles.

Kay looked around in surprise. "I thought it sounded wonderful. Like scalloped potatoes gone wild."

"It's a matter of over-familiarity." Annette exchanged a look with her brother. "We've had it at every function for decades—including breakfasts."

"She must really have taken to you, to give you the potato surprise recipe," Steve said.

"I'm going to teach her to make mobiles." Kay deliberately did not look at Rob. "I like teaching even more than doing, and she's excited to learn."

"Ah, that explains it. Miriam's pride wouldn't let her ask as a favor, but she's feeling the pinch since her retirement fund lost money by investing in one of those companies with crooked execs."

Annette nodded. "Poor Miriam, wanting to learn but with money so tight—what a dilemma. I'm glad you two worked out an exchange."

"Who's dull Emma?" Nell asked as she ran up, the dogs following.

Annette got it first. "Not dull Emma. Dilemma. D-i-l-e-m-m-a," she spelled out for Nell. "It means needing to make a choice between two things when you don't like either one. Remember, we talked about the expression, *between a rock and a hard place*?" Nell nodded. "That's a dilemma."

"Oh." Apparently satisfied, Nell darted off with the dogs.

Annette said to Kay, "Nell sometimes has interesting takes on words. We're trying to spell words and clarify any confusion."

"When she was little, I told her I was going to a conference in Miami, and she interpreted that as meaning it was *mine*," Steve said. "She told everyone that I was going to Daddy's-ami."

"My favorite was when she lit into Lana about the dip," Max said.

Steve burst out laughing. "That's right. My mother mentioned clam dip being on the menu for an event, and Nell thought it was *lamb* dip—and she gave her grandmother hell." Still smiling, he called, "C'mon, Nell. Time to wash up for dinner."

The girl sprinted past the strolling adults, then spun around to Kay. "Don't forget, we're finger-painting tomorrow."

Steve sighed. "I hope Nell didn't corner you into this, Kay."

"I really should work on ideas for the opening."

"Oh, no you don't," Rob said. "Nell made me responsible for getting you there tomorrow, and I'm not taking the rap if you don't show up."

"Hiding behind a woman to protect you from a kid?" Steve teased.

"Damn straight."

"On second thought, it's an excellent strategy," Nell's father said.

They all laughed.

Kay was glad to see Rob laugh. There'd been something … A look, a shadow she'd caught a couple of times while they were out on the lake.

He'd been so at home there, moving with the boat the way she'd seen excellent riders move with a horse. When she'd sailed with any of her parents' friends they'd seemed to view the event as a three-way wrestling match involving themselves, the boat, and nature, and they were grimly determined to beat the hell out of their two opponents. Rob had an alliance with his boat, and together, they drew what they needed from nature, seeking the wind, skimming the water.

"C'mon, let's get dinner." Max led the way.

Rob put his hand to the small of her back as they walked. A companionable gesture only. That's all.

CHAPTER FOURTEEN

K AY'S PHONE RANG as she put Chester's food bowl down.
Her heart lurched. Wait. It couldn't be about Chester, because she hadn't put her cell number on the flyers. It rang again, and her heart bucked at a new possibility.

"Hello." Did she sound as breathless as she felt?

"Kay? Kay Aaronson? It's Serge."

The air came out of her in a whoosh. Serge. The producer who'd given her the job to shoot an 1899 wedding. It seemed far away already. "Hi, Serge. How are you?"

"Fine, fine. I just looked over what you sent me."

She tried to listen as he discussed the framing and structure of shot sequences. But it was hard to listen while she was telling herself how stupid she was to have thought it might be Rob. He'd just left, for heaven's sake.

"I won't know for sure until I start working with the footage next month," Serge said, "but it looks good."

Those words cut through her distraction.

"Thank you."

"I'll be in from the coast in the next month, so we'll do lunch and—"

"Sorry, Serge. I won't be in New York until after mid-October."

"Oh? Off to Europe with Mommy and Daddy?"

She heard the slice of scorn in that reference. She heard it a lot when people alluded to her family. Almost as much as the patina of envy.

"No, still in Tobias, Wisconsin."

"Wisconsin? Why? Another shoot?"

Suspicion colored his questions. Suspicion, and the sound of a bargain hunter who feared another shopper had spotted *his* great deal.

Kay switched the phone to her other ear.

Her work had been good enough that Serge didn't want someone else to scoop her up until he'd gotten more work at bargain basement rates.

"Not a music video," she said, purposely elusive. "Another job."

"Ah. Well, I suppose you've got to eat." He laughed heartily at his joke that Kay Aaronson would have to worry about money. Something about that plucked at her thoughts, but she didn't have time to pin it down before he continued. "But with guidance and a lot of hard work you might make it. Got to pay your dues, you know."

"If there's no other choice," she tossed off.

He chuckled. "I like your attitude, kid. And if this footage works out, I might have another assignment for you down the road. No promises. And you'd have to be in New York, or here on the coast."

"Of course."

"Good, good. I'll be in touch."

She held the cell phone a long time after the call ended.

She'd finally captured what had nagged at her when he displayed his attitude about her family money—nobody in Tobias had shown any interest in it, much less envy or scorn.

But mostly she considered the odd fact that if Serge had dangled a lunch a month ago she would have met him anywhere, anytime. Yet just now, she'd never given a thought to going to New York to be available for a potential lunch. Because it would mean dropping everything in Tobias.

AT THE DALTON house the next morning, Fran met Kay and Rob as they crossed the lawn from the drive.

"This is a great house." Kay looked at the two-story frame house that managed to be both solid and graceful. A family home. Was it possible to be made to feel inadequate by a house? She produced a sly smile. "The kind of house that should have a dog in it."

"Oh, no you don't," Rob said. "Besides, it's not my house. It's Fran's."

"It's as much yours as mine," his sister said.

"We've settled this, Fran. The house is yours."

Fran grimaced, and Kay knew that issue wasn't settled at all.

From the porch, Nell called. "We're gonna have easels, right, Fran?"

"Yes. Rob needs to get them down, though. They're in the attic room. Rob knows where they are."

He looked from Fran to Kay and back. Almost as if he were worried about leaving her alone with his sister. "I'll be right back."

The porch door smacked closed behind him.

"Have you spent time in a town like Tobias before, Kay?" Fran asked as they strolled toward the porch.

"*Is* there another town like Tobias?"

"It's just a small town," Rob's sister said in her calm way. But under the calm, Kay heard concern. "A nice one, but still, a small town. You've always lived in the city, is that right?"

"Yes. A life-long New Yorker."

"Ah."

Kay thought she knew what was behind the syllable. She would allay Fran's fear. "I know Ro—the committee wasn't happy with my first suggestions, but I *am* teachable, and if I still haven't got it with my next round of ideas, I'm sure the committee will show me where I went wrong."

That won the tiniest of smiles. "We should have given you a crash course in Tobias first. It wasn't fair to throw you in. I'm not worried at all about your ideas for the opening."

"What are you worried about then?"

Fran glanced away. "That's direct."

"Saves time."

"I suppose that's something you've learned living in New York."

"That's what's bothering you? That I'm from New York?"

Was it so obvious to Rob's sister that Kay didn't fit in in a place where everyone said hello, took you in like they knew you, and counted family and friends most important?

"Not that you're from New York. That you're going back there. Soon. But maybe not soon enough."

Kay opened her mouth, closed it, then tried again. All that came out was, "Oh."

"I'm trying not to butt in, I really am. And I like you. It's just … Rob's been through a rough time this past year and half. Janice—that's his ex-wife. Ah, I see you know that. Anyway, she didn't give him a clue. Sprung it on him that she'd made a one-hundred-and-eighty-degree turn. And only when he raised the issue of starting a family. My brother likes to think his head rules all his decisions, but I can see that this divorce is still hurting him deeply."

"Fran, it's not … It's not going to be a big deal for Rob when I leave. He's going to be relieved—believe me."

"I suspect Rob would tell me the same thing. And I don't have that much experience with relationships, but I've seen your faces."

Kay produced a laugh. "Probably indigestion. Seriously, Fran, I swear Rob's more attached to Chester than to me. He thinks I'm a flake. We barely have enough in common to talk about Tobias and Chester and how he used to be a financial analyst and—"

"Used to be?" Fran's forehead wrinkled. "Oh, you mean because he's here this summer? He's on a leave of absence. He's supposed to be having a long, lazy summer, though you wouldn't know it from the way he works at Bliss House and here. He needed a break. Especially after the divorce."

"But I thought…"

"I know, I know. He still has that white band where his wedding ring was. That was self-defense. Because he was still wearing the ring when word seeped out about the divorce not even Tobias's nosiest had the nerve to ask to his face. By the time he took it off, it was old news."

"Thanks for clearing that up. I guess I misunderstood."

But she hadn't.

Rob had definitely put his days of being a financial analyst in the past tense. Yet Fran said he still held that job and she seemed to attribute everything gnawing at Rob to the divorce. Kay knew down to her bones that there was something besides the divorce, the "big thing" she'd asked him about and he'd sidestepped.

Rob wasn't telling her. Okay. That made sense. They'd just met, so who could blame him? But keeping secrets from his sister? Why?

FROM A SPOT beyond the open window in the family room and out of their line of sight, Rob watched Kay clip paper to a well-used wooden easel he'd set up in the side yard.

"You know how to do this," Nell said with approval.

"Yes, I do," Kay said. "It's one of the things I learned in my grandmother's art studio."

"But you don't do it anymore."

"No." And if Rob could distill all the emotions in those two letters he might know Kay Aaronson right down to her soul.

Nell nodded. "Because of your grandmother."

"Why do you say that?"

"Grandmothers don't like messes. And no matter how careful you are, there's mess when you paint."

Kay shook her head. "My grandmother didn't mind my mess, as long as I tried."

"Humph. Then why don't you go to her studio anymore?"

"We grew apart."

Nell tipped her head. "I don't mind being apart from my grand-mother. But Annette says I should look for good things in her. So I try. She has a good cook. Mrs. Grier makes great waffles and brownies. Oh, I like red," Nell added, dipping her fingers into the pot and swirling it onto the paper.

Kay tilted her head at her blank paper, took a healthy load of yellow onto her fingers, and the two worked in companionable silence.

"Now this makes sense," Nell said with satisfaction.

"What does?"

"Finger-painting."

"Ah, because you paint with your fingers and it's called finger-painting?"

Rob was impressed. He often spotted the logic of Nell's comments in retrospect, but Kay had gotten it immediately.

Nell nodded. "And because you paint your fingers."

Kay looked at her hands and laughed. "True."

"It's not like when I told Dad and Annette that I want a sister."

"Oh?" Kay made a curve of brown through the yellow and the shape of a familiar head was born.

"Yeah. That didn't make sense. I said I wanted a sister, but I'd take a brother, as long as there's a baby fast, and they started talking about syllables."

"Syllables?"

"Yeah, they said I had to wait and see if I got a syllable."

Kay half-stifled a snort. "Could your parents have said you'd have to wait to see if you got a sibling? A sibling is a brother or sister."

"Huh." Nell scalloped green across her paper. "I better tell Dad and Annette that I didn't know that because I don't have any."

Nell stepped back and gave Kay's sheet a critical assessment, her head tipped, her eyes narrowed. "That's Chester."

"Yes, it is."

"You're pretty good at this."

"Thank you," Kay responded in an equally grave tone. "So are you."

"I like a lot of colors. Some kids at school only use one color. Like they're afraid of getting more on their hands."

Kay shook her head in sympathetic disbelief. "They're missing out."

"Yeah. Like my grandmother. Have you been to her house? It's all *white*."

<

"Well that *is* a style."

"That's what Miss Trudi said."

"Miss Trudi's pretty smart."

"Yeah, even if she does like opera." The girl shook her head. "All that singing."

Kay coughed this time. Recovered, she said, "Miss Trudi's been helping kids for a long time. Did you know she taught my grandmother art and helped her the way she helps you—finding books, exploring new interests. Even when Dora moved away, they stayed friends."

"People shouldn't go away," Nell said darkly.

"Sometimes they have to."

"Why?"

"Uh, well, for college for instance."

"Uncle Max isn't going away, but he's going back to college."

"That doesn't work for everybody. And adults' jobs can take them away. Or there can be problems between people. Or responsibilities someplace else can make a person leave. Or they might have been only visiting."

Interesting that she hadn't suggested that one first.

"Those things shouldn't make somebody go away," Nell said. "That stinks."

"You're right. Sometimes it does stink."

"You did very well," Rob said.

"You like it?" Kay looked at her finger-painted rendition of Chester's head. "It's been a long time, and I'm not sure I got the ears right."

"You got them right. It's amazing. But I was referring to your conversation with Nell."

"Eavesdropping?"

"You bet."

"Did you catch that part about syllables?" Kay chuckled. "She's amazing, and terrifying."

"Because she's got her eye on the Oscar *and* the Nobel Prize?"

"No, I understand a varied resume." She slanted him a look, then sobered. "Mostly because she's a kid. The responsibility for what you put into her head is awesome. I admire Annette for raising a step-daughter—and especially for how she's doing it."

"Annette is a great mom. You would be, too."

"I'm not sure I make a decent adult yet." She shook off wistfulness and rallied. "Besides, who says I'm ready to settle down? My biological clock hasn't even been wound yet. Oh, gosh, look at the time, Rob. I need to get to Bliss House to meet with people who'll be selling crafts."

"I'll give you a ride."

"You don't need to—"

"I thought I'd take you to the library later. There's an archive of old photographs that—"

"Thanks, Rob. But I'm going to spend the afternoon working on ideas. After I make calls to check on apartments in Manhattan."

"Okay. Get your painting and we'll be on our way."

CHAPTER FIFTEEN

O N THEIR WAY to what?
Nowhere. That was the only sane answer.

And why was she thinking about Rob when she should be working on new, brilliant schemes to promote the opening of Bliss House?

Especially after meeting all those lovely people who hoped to supplement their incomes by selling crafts. Among a dozen crafters, she'd talked with Miriam Jenkins and Muriel Henderson from the Garden Club, officially met Tom Dunwoody and seen some of his amazing decoys. She'd plied them with questions and solicited their opinions to get a better grasp of what Bliss House would be.

By the time she'd returned to the Hollands' it had hardly seemed worth the effort to make calls to start looking for an apartment in New York, what with the time difference. But she had placed a dozen calls to track resources for the opening in Chicago, Milwaukee, and Madison. She'd sort out what she'd gathered and dig up more on the Internet as soon as she took Chester for her walk.

Tomorrow, she would shop for supplies to create a presentation. Maybe she'd get some clothes, too; she hadn't packed with the idea of staying this long. Maybe she'd buy colors, just to show Rob her closet wasn't a black hole.

No! Stop thinking about Rob. Focus on what's in front of you, Kay.

She'd taken a different route for this walk, heading away from the lake, watching the spaces between the houses grow. At the top of a rise the sidewalk ended and a cornfield began. Beyond the corn she saw another field, a rich, sap green, and in the distance, a curving line of trees.

She tipped her head back to a sky so cerulean blue that Nell could have painted it. Clouds like someone had loaded a brush—or fingers—with titanium white and made one bold zag. A solitary airplane bisected the zag.

How many times had she flown over such land? She'd looked down and seen crisp, neat patterns. But on the ground, where the trees met the fields was a flow, a movement, a swoosh you could almost hear. What appeared as hard, straight lines from the air were curves and connections. Like … like a child pretending his hand was an airplane or bird, banking, dipping, rising, curving. That was it. That was what this land made her feel like—almost floating. That freedom, that movement.

She loved New York with a native's pride. Yet there was something about *this* place.

On impulse, she flung her arms wide to the openness. The expansiveness not only of the sky above, but of the air around her and the earth below. As if she'd spent her life with her shoulders hunched and now she could stretch, relax…

… if it weren't for the nagging image of Rob Dalton.

They were like two people face to face in a narrow hall, not sure how to get around each other. First one dodged one way, but the other person dodged the same way. Then you tried the opposite way, but so did the other person and there you were again, only closer, because you'd each taken a step forward. So you paused, and smiled those aren't-we-silly smiles. And then you did the whole dance again.

Finally, one of you has the good sense—probably him, because good sense was clearly one of his strengths and, considering her gene pool, she was lucky to have a standard ration—to step aside to let the other pass. Ah, but that was when you discovered just how narrow the passageway was.

No way to get past without brushing the other person, even if he turned totally sideways. But *was* he totally sideways? Or was he slanted, so when she tried to slide by, she *had* to brush against him. And that meant she felt his warmth, breathed in an awareness of the strength that gave rise to it. If she put her hands on his shoulders and leaned against the strength, the warmth would envelop her and…

And you began to wonder if you were going opposite directions after all, or if the reason you couldn't get past each other was that you were headed the same way. And that brought you right back to the first question. *Headed where?*

ROB HAD LEFT Kay alone the rest of the afternoon and evening, then all the next day.

But she hadn't left him alone.

He'd heard that the crafts people at the meeting adored her. He'd heard that she'd walked Chester out to Petersons' farm. He'd heard that she'd been in town shopping.

Even when he wasn't hearing reports of her, she stepped into his thoughts. So he might as well see her for real. Besides, he'd been neglecting his assignment to acquaint her with life in Tobias.

He parked in the Hollands' driveway as she and Chester came out of the house for their morning walk. He joined them, automatically walking on her right side, closer to the street.

She pulled out her phone and tapped on the video app, then looked at him. "Why are you making a face at my camcorder? What have you got against it?"

"You hide behind the thing."

"I don't hide behind it. It's necessary. It's training my eye for directing. The human eye looking at a scene automatically sorts out what's important and what's not. In film you have to frame the shot, so there's no extraneous material for the viewer to sort through. It's almost impossible for most people to look at a view and know how the shot will look without checking in the viewfinder. Or in this case screen."

"How do you know if the extraneous material isn't more interesting than what you see on the screen if you don't look around first?"

"It's a matter of framing the shot. It's technical—"

"Fine. You're the expert. I thought we'd go to a baseball game tonight."

She blinked at the change of subject. "I thought we were going to the library tonight."

"It's going to be a nice night, why spend it inside?"

"Ah, I knew there'd be a logical reason behind changing your mind," she said with a sassy smile.

He ignored the words, but was less successful ignoring the smile. "Do you know anything about baseball?"

"I'm not a complete heathen. I did date a Yankees fan. Actually, Alexi has a box."

He could see she expected that to get a reaction, but all he said as they neared the turn to Bliss House was: "I'll bring the blanket, be ready at six."

Her confusion showed—Yankee fans, especially those with boxes—clearly didn't bring blankets.

Thinking about that, he turned left toward Bliss House. Trouble was, she kept going straight.

They collided.

Rob wrapped his arms around her to keep from knocking her over. Her hands grasped his arms. The leash somehow crossed over, then under his arm. And to complete the package, Chester walked around them.

She fit against him with softness and warmth and firmness that made his arms tighten. His nose pressed against the fragrant softness of her hair. His hands opened, one across the curve below her waist, the other past her shoulder blade so that if he held her a little tighter, slid it a little farther, his fingertips would…

"Rob…"

She tipped her head back enough for him to see her eyes. Her mouth.

He knew what that mouth tasted like, felt like.

He wanted it again.

He wanted more.

The kiss during the shoot had been intense, but a kiss alone, not a meeting of body against body, not like this … This was how she would feel under him in his bed. This was how they would fit. This was…

"Rob."

She wriggled. He closed his eyes. He knew she meant to gain space between them, but it sure didn't make his body want to let go.

A car horn tooted gaily.

"People are staring, Rob." Her voice reminded him of a dead leaf found in a corner of the garage in February. Touch it, and it crumbles.

"Chester—" He cleared his throat and started again. "You'll have to get Chester to unwind first."

It was a torture the Inquisition could have added to its repertoire, but with commands to the dog that sometimes went astray and would-be helpful moves that nearly made his head—and areas farther south—explode, they finally untangled.

"Sorry," he said gruffly as they resumed the walk straight ahead. "I thought you were taking Chester to Bliss House. That's the most direct way."

"I, uh, change our route."

"Tired of the scenery already?" He tried for light. "I suppose a Manhattanite would be bored by Tobias. There's variety, but you must look for it—and spot change that's as gradual as the continental drift."

She smiled, but not one of her whole-face smiles. "Oh, I love that walk. Seeing the yards and the people. It's not for me we're going this way."

He questioned her with a look.

"It's for Chester," she added, as if that should be obvious. "I read in a book that sniffing is like reading a newspaper for a dog. It's how they find out who's been doing what."

"So to speak," he murmured.

"Don't laugh." Her mouth turned down, but he knew it was to fight back a grin. "It's their way of discovering the world and keeping up with the neighborhood. Chester needs more than updates of the same news every day, so I'm giving her variety."

"Like trading off between the *New York Times* and *New York Post*."

"Chester's interested in local events. More like the *Tobias Record* and the *Milwaukee Journal Sentinel*." Her frown cleared. "Now you may laugh."

He did.

CHAPTER SIXTEEN

K AY CONTEMPLATED THE seating at the baseball game. Bleachers.
Metal bleachers. She wished she'd worn her cross-trainers instead of these contraptions that made each step an adventure and clanged like a Chinese gong.

And she definitely should have worn jeans instead of this new gauzy skirt. Yes, it moved beautifully, and showed off her legs, but it moved a little too much in the sputtering breeze. It would give spectators beneath her a real eyeful if she didn't keep a vigilant hand pressing it down.

"Steady," Rob said, beside her, cupping her elbow.

"How far up are we going?"

"Better view at the top."

"Rob! Kay! Over here!"

She looked in the direction of the voice and felt herself teeter. Rob's hold tightened. Suz stood waving from the top row of seats. Max sat beside her and Annette and Steve beyond her. Leaving it to Rob to wave back, Kay put her head down and climbed. Gingerly.

She was so grateful to reach the last row she hurried ahead of Rob. Amid the greetings she started to sink down.

"Don't sit!" a chorus advised her. Too late.

Sun-soaked metal. Bare legs beneath a gauzy skirt.

Hot seat. No longer a proverb. The real thing.

So breath-robbing hot that for an instant she couldn't move. Rob's hand under her elbow came to the rescue again, tugging her up.

"Why didn't you wait for me to put the blanket down?"

Oh, that's what the blanket was for.

When he had it in place, he gestured for her to sit, and it turned out the first try hadn't blistered her behind beyond repair. The folded over material provided surprising padding.

Rob sat next to her.

How odd. She knew the seat was metal covered by blanket, yet she had the sense the bench was made of something soft, so that when he sat it compressed and made her tilt toward him.

Something soft … like a mattress? *No, don't think about mattresses.*

And, as long as she was giving orders, she added one for her heart: *Stop that ba-BAM-ing.*

The players took the field to sustained cheering. She joined with desperate gusto. She would concentrate on this game like the World Series.

"They're awfully small."

Max handed over a pair of binoculars. "Try these."

She thanked Max. But, no, they were still small. And young.

She handed them back to Max. Only then did she become aware of Rob's speculative look. "You do know this is American Legion ball," he said in a low voice. "High school-age kids."

"Sure."

Actually, she hadn't thought about it. She'd heard baseball and she'd dressed like the crowd in Alexi's luxury sky box. She'd wanted to look good. Jeans and cotton shirts like Suz and Annette wore would have been better.

"Double play! Great double play!" Rob cheered.

Unlike Alexi and his friends, these people watched the game.

The next inning, a great running, shoe-top catch in the outfield brought her to her feet along with the rest of the home crowd. As she settled back on her blanket cushion, she spotted a vendor.

"Oh, hot dogs. I love hot dogs."

"I'll be happy to get you one of those," Rob said. That slant of his mouth was back. But why she had no idea.

Back in under two minutes, Rob held out the hot dog wrapped in white paper. "Here you go."

She opened it, abruptly famished. Without taking her eyes from the field, she took a big bite. Just before her teeth found roll and what it covered, a spicy aroma surrounded her. In that instant flavor exploded in her mouth.

As she chewed, she became aware of Rob and faces beyond him watching her. "Do you like it?" Suz asked.

She chewed thoroughly, swallowing the last bit. "What *is* it?"

"A brat." The way Rob said it, it would be spelled *brahwt.*

"Brahwt," she repeated. "I've heard of that. I love it."

"Bratwurst," he said. "Consider it a Wisconsin hot dog."

"It can be a little strong," Annette said.

"Not your mother's hot dog." Rob grinned as he bit into his.

"My mother's hot dog would be made out of caviar," Kay agreed.

"But it *is* your grandmother's hot dog." Suz said.

After a couple innings Kay had the rhythm of it. Baseball and non-baseball conversation wove together in an informal pas de deux. All talk stopped mid-sentence to follow the action on the field then resumed when the game calmed down. She couldn't talk the baseball talk with the detail and knowledge that Suz, Max, and Rob did—who could possibly tell from here whether Mickey had his change-up working?—but she knew the rudiments of the game, and she was holding her own.

By the bottom of the eighth inning she was living every pitch with the home team, which trailed, 1-0.

When the umpire called the next pitch a ball—the fourth one, allowing the batter to walk with no outs—she jumped to her feet, hollering. In a few succinct phrases, she conveyed that any idiot could see that was a strike, unless his vision was blocked as the result of a certain contortionist move.

She became aware of an abrupt silence around her. She looked down into stair-steps of surprised faces turned to her. She was the only one in their set of bleachers standing. And certainly the only one shouting.

"She's from New York," Max said to someone in the row in front of them. She thought a chuckle lurked under his words.

And she knew there was suppressed laughter in Rob's voice as he added to no one in particular, "And she dated a Yankees fan."

A mutter of understanding spread, and she spotted heads nodding sagely as she meekly sat.

"You don't yell at umpires in Wisconsin?"

"That's not entirely true," Rob said. "But we might not be as, uh, vehement here in Tobias. And seldom at American Legion games."

Suz patted her hand, "Especially not when the umpire's Max's foreman, Lenny. And if he did have his head where you suggested, work on Bliss House would come to a standstill."

"WHAT A GREAT game! That throw to the plate in the seventh—wow!"

"The outfielder who made that throw is Max's assistant's husband's little brother," Suz said as they climbed down the bleachers. "He's a star of the high school team."

Annette laughed. "Suz knows the intricacies of Tobias relationships better than most natives."

"Only ones connected to people I know and who have great throwing arms."

"He does have a great throwing—Oh! The concession stand." Kay scooted ahead to a folding table loaded with team paraphernalia.

Rob chuckled as he slowed to wait for her.

Annette matched his pace. "It's nice to have that back."

"What back?"

"Your laugh."

"I laugh."

"Not much this summer, and it's gotten worse as the summer's gone on. I was a little concerned that … Well, when Suz and Max got together…"

"That I was pining after Suz? No, we sorted that out at the start. As much as I like and respect Suz, there's none of that feeling between us."

"I was certain of that when I saw you with Kay."

Whoa! Talk about blindsided.

"Don't get any ideas, Annette. I'm showing her around Tobias because that's what the committee wants."

Her smile spread to dazzling proportions. She patted him on the arm as she said, "That's okay, Rob. You go on pretending that."

Kay's arrival spared him from answering. She carried two t-shirts— one black and one orange. "I got you one, Rob. As thanks for bringing me to the game and introducing me to brats."

Rob reached for the orange one. "Black. What a surprise."

"Actually, the black one's for you." She held it out to him, arm extended. Her other hand clutched the orange shirt to her chest. "I've never liked orange. But I've decided this is burnt sienna. And it's mine, all mine."

Ten minutes later, he opened her car door in front of Tastee-Treat, and asked, "Are you sure you want ice cream?"

"Absolutely," she declared, emerging from the car with grace despite having the blanket wrapped around her. "This is all part of really getting to know Tobias, right?"

When the sun dropped below the horizon, the stands had cooled rapidly. Sweaters and light jackets popped out all over. Kay sat in that filmy skirt and lethally simple top with goose bumps showing all along her arms.

It had been an act of supreme self-sacrifice to get off the blanket and wrapped it around her. He didn't mind giving up the cushion, it was losing sight of those beautiful shoulders that made him feel like a martyr.

If she had ice cream, she'd probably never let the blanket slide away.

She practically danced with delight through the packed parking lot toward the ordering windows.

"We beat 'em. Pummeled 'em. Sent 'em home crying to their mamas."

"Blood-thirsty little thing, aren't you?"

"You bet. There are winners and there are…"

Alerted by her fadeout voice, he followed the direction she was looking and saw players, still in the sweat- and grass- and dirt-stained uniforms of a hard-played game. "Something wrong, Kay?"

"Both teams? Both teams come to the same place?"

"Sure. They all know each other. Some of these kids play together on the high school team." He jerked his head toward two dark-haired teens sitting side by side, their uniforms showing they'd played for opposite teams. "Luke scored the winning run for Tobias. The other kid's the pitcher who gave up the game-winning hit. They're cousins."

He returned with the cones and found her still watching Luke and his cousin.

"It's hard to be gleefully bloodthirsty about beating a team when you know the other players, isn't it?" she said with a gusty sigh. "When they're your friends. When they're your relatives."

"Yeah. And sometimes it's fun to have that we-won-and-we-don't-care-you-lost attitude," he admitted. "But this way has its compensations."

She smiled. "Life often offers compensations like that, doesn't it?"

"Life definitely has its compensations," he murmured as he watched her eat another ice cream cone.

"ONE MORE STOP if you're up for it," Rob said, once they were back in the car. "I have something I want you to see. Something I want to show you."

How could she resist? Rob's "tour" stops so far had stirred dozens of ideas for promoting Bliss House's opening—none like her original concept—and more never hurt. Plus, she was having fun.

"Of course. Remember me? I'm the one from the city that never sleeps."

He leaned forward, pointedly looking out the windshield at the dark street. "Tobias, on the other hand, gets its full eight hours of beauty sleep."

Was it just a comment, or a way to point out their differences?

He pulled into the driveway of his family home, where one light showed, a second-story bedroom that she guessed was Fran's.

He didn't look at her, but took her hand, drawing her inside. Her pulse picked up and oxygen suddenly became an endangered commodity when he headed for the stairs. He didn't slow and he didn't release her.

Instead of stopping at the second-floor hallway, he made the turn and headed up the next flight with her in tow. She looked once over her shoulder at the hallway, then concentrated on what was ahead.

At a small landing he opened a door, and she followed him onto a roof deck where the night sky blossomed above.

From this vantage, Tobias sloped down to the lake in a patchwork of gray silken streets, velvet green lawns, and scattered sequins of lights. The waters of Lake Tobias shone like rumpled satin under a nearly full moon.

He carried two deck chairs to the railing, opening the first for her.

"Tobias's version of bright lights," he said.

She turned to him, smiling. "This is … magnificent."

"You have the most amazing smile."

His words—so unexpected, so deep with warmth—would have been enough, but that intent look was in his eyes. She gulped in more air.

He seemed to catch himself, grinned ruefully, and she knew before he spoke that his next words would change the mood again. "Guess you're told that a lot. Probably everyone comments on the Aaronson women's smiles."

"No. No one's told me that. And that isn't what people comment about when they mention the Aaronsons. They'd much rather talk about the scandals."

Why on earth had she said that? As if she wanted to discuss any of this.

"Not aware of any scandal."

Committed now, she offered him the lesser Aaronson tale.

"I thought you'd know, since Dora came from here. Not that I really knew until I was thirteen and…" All hell broke loose. But he didn't need to hear that. "Dora never married my grandfather. He was a Pelten, an old New York society family. He died before my father was born, and his family didn't acknowledge Dora or my father. My father felt that unjustly denied him opportunities. It didn't matter to Dora. She worked like crazy, building her art, building her career. But he … resents what he didn't have."

I was shoveled off to public schools among those common, dull urchins. She waited until I was nearly in high school to send me to an acceptable school. Any longer and it would have been too late. As it was, it took years of inching up to earn acceptance.

"Dora had a solo show when my father was in middle school, and she was an amazing hit. Suddenly they had money. I'm not sure they ever saw eye to eye, but they certainly didn't after that. My father's life changed drastically, while Dora's changed hardly at all, because her life was inside the studio. He was determined I would have what he felt he'd missed. You know the drill, enrolling me in the hot pre-school so I'd get into the right college."

He gave a faint nod.

But she shook her head. "You don't know, do you?"

"Not first-hand. I saw that attitude next door. Lana Corbett had big plans for Steve and Zach. But my parents were comfortable. Comfortable financially. Comfortable with who they were. Comfortable with each other. Comfortable with Fran and me. I was lucky, and most of the time I knew it.

"Dad was our rock. Mom … Mom made us laugh, but she also knew when a laugh wouldn't work. When I was a kid, she'd hold me and hum this tuneless little thing, and just be there. But with Fran I used to hear singing. Both of them. Signing as loud as they could to some rock song. I know—hard to believe that of Fran now. If Mom had lived longer I think Fran … Well, Mom brought everyone out of their shells. When I was older she had a way of being quiet that could bring the words out—even out of a difficult teen-ager."

Kay blinked back tears. "You? Difficult? Who'd believe that?"

"Ouch. That was a hit, a direct hit. Yeah, I could be a difficult kid." Only when he dropped his hand onto her wrist, stilling it, did she realize she'd been tapping her fingers on the chair arm. "Not that I was a big rebel. But I had my plan, and I was impatient to grow up, have my independence."

"I never knew what I want to do, what I want to be—who I am."

She would have taken that back if she could. If not the words, certainly the tone. It sounded too poor-little rich girl.

"You'll—"

"No—don't, Rob. You don't understand. You've always known. You played football, didn't you?" She saw it in his face and laughed. "Quarterback, right?" And laughed again. "Quarterback because you wanted to make the plan and pull it off. In fact, I bet you liked to take the ball and run it in yourself. Bet you drove the coach crazy."

"You've been talking to Coach Callahan? Or are you a witch? And yes, I hated giving the ball to anyone else when I had that goal line in sight." The start of a smile faded. "I was so certain my plans would get me to my goals. I thought that for a long time. I was wrong."

"Until your divorce."

"Yeah." He said it a little too quickly, a little too willingly. But before she could probe for that other problem she sensed, he'd continued.

"Janice and I met at college. It seemed easy to go from dating to planning our futures together. We wanted the same things, agreed on how to get them and the timeline. We had it mapped out—finish our educations, get good jobs in the city, advance to better jobs, put aside money, then trim back on career, start a family, have a real home out of the city and enjoy our lives and family.

"We started out hitting each point on our timeline like clockwork. Pretty heady stuff. Neither of us brought it up when we slid right past the point our timeline called for pulling back. Instead we bought a condo near the lake. Not exactly kid-friendly, but convenient for people who weren't home much.

"Then my dad died. Nothing like the death of a parent to make you take stock of your life. Janice and I had plenty of career success, but not the life we'd planned. I wanted to get back on track to that. To get back to our plan,"

He gave a humorless laugh.

"I had to call Janice's office to schedule time to talk about it. That should have told me something. And I sure as hell should have heard alarms clanging away when she said she wanted to talk to me, too.

"But if there were alarms I was deaf to them. And blind. I drove full-speed at that cliff. Got a reservation at a top restaurant, arranged for the best champagne. I held her hand, and said I felt as if we'd gotten into a rut. That I wanted to get out of it, and get back to what we had always dreamed of, to what we'd been working to establish—a real home, children, and a life that revolved around that instead of work. She said no."

"That's it? She said no?" Outrage kicked Kay's voice higher.

"No. She agreed we were in a rut, and needed to get out of it. Our solutions, though, were not compatible. She said she didn't want children, and she didn't want a husband—not me anyway. I fumbled out something about our plan, and she said, *Plans change.*"

"Oh, Rob."

"The champagne wasn't even poured yet. I hope someone drank that champagne."

"And now you feel like you failed."

He snapped his head around toward her. "Failed," he repeated. "Yes, I suppose I do."

"Failing isn't such a big deal, Rob. You're letting it bother you because you have so little practice at it. But you can learn a lot from failing. I have. All the jobs I've held, all the careers I thought I wanted…"

"How many of those changes were because you failed and how many because you wanted to move on?"

"Does it matter? Because that's a kind of failure, too. Not finding where you belong, not finding the right fit in life—in a job, I mean."

"So if it is a failure, what have you learned from it?"

"I suppose," she said slowly, "that what I value more than anything else is loyalty. People who would never betray me."

He removed his hand from where it had rested atop her wrist. Her skin felt cold, vacant when she dropped her hand into her lap.

"Betray." His voice grated on the word. "You said that about Brice."

"It's a sore spot. My family ... well, it wasn't a marriage breaking up, but there was a break up of a kind. I told you my father and grandmother never saw eye to eye, but then there was a ... an incident when I was thirteen. He and Dora haven't spoken since."

"And they made you pick sides. But you were a kid, a—"

"There was no being neutral about this, Rob. I ... It's complicated."

"Complicated." He nodded. "That's what people say when they don't want to tell you."

"Or can't." She shivered as if a wind had kicked up, but the air was still. "What about you?"

"Me?"

"I know there's something more than the divorce—in addition to," she clarified before he could protest. "Something weighing on you."

He looked out at Tobias. "It's like you said. It's complicated."

She returned his words to him. "That's what people say when they don't want to tell you."

"Or can't."

CHAPTER SEVENTEEN

R OB SAT ON the screened porch and considered his future.
Not a word from Mitchell Gordon. And no move to make
changes. It's what he'd expected after the call from Janice.

That put the decisions in Rob's court.

He'd known his decision on the big question from the start, even
though it would end his career as he'd known it.

Now the smaller decisions followed—how and when and where.
And then the personal ones—what to do after.

He should organize his thoughts on paper. Prioritize. Plan.

He knew how a legal pad and a good pen felt in his hand. Knew
the sense of purpose. He just couldn't imagine what he would write
with that pen on that pad. Not a thought came to mind.

"What are you doing?" Fran asked from the doorway.

"Thinking," he lied.

"About Kay?"

"No." He'd been consciously *not* thinking about her.

They had neared a brink on the roof after the baseball game, then
backed away. Whether she had backed away or he had wasn't totally
clear. What was important was that it was the smart thing to do.

Because Janice had been right, his career would be over, his options limited. No responsible man facing those uncertainties in his life
should go over a brink.

Yet the backing away ticked him off, for no reason he could think
of, which ticked him off more.

He looked at Fran and saw her concern. "It's okay, kid. I have my
eyes open. I'm not fooling myself that Kay Aaronson wants what I

want. You know me. I think things through, plan and—"

"Yeah, and look where that got you with Janice."

"What does that mean?"

"That I've been thinking that perhaps a different approach could produce a different result."

He stood, propelled by his kid sister's bluntness. "I'm going for a drive."

She gave him a sharp look. But he was just going for a drive.

In fact, when he happened to see Kay, walking with Chester four blocks from the Hollands', he turned a block short, turned off the engine and sat. So she wouldn't spot the car.

She walked slower than her first days here. She looked toward the treetops, not monitoring where she put her feet. No phone recording video in sight. She smiled and waved to Mrs. Yee, who was watering marigolds.

When Mrs. Yee went inside, Kay looked around, as if checking for anyone watching, and stepped to the telephone pole with one of the "Found Dog" notices he'd watched her put up.

In one quick movement, she tore it down and stuffed it into her tote. She crossed the street and repeated the action. Now that she was closer, he saw the tote was stuffed with what had to be other flyers.

Kay Aaronson, the woman who didn't know what she wanted, knew that she wanted to keep the dog named Chester.

"WOULD YOU LIKE to go sailing after the meeting?" Rob took the loaded tote bag from Kay as they walked to his car in the Hollands' driveway.

He was giving her a ride to Bliss House to present her second round of ideas for the opening.

He would have taken the poster boards, too, but she clutched them. The white poster board showed stark against a bright blue tank top he hadn't seen her wear before. "We'll leave from the town-side pier. Give you a different angle on Tobias."

"I can't. I'm going to pick up Chester at the vet." Suz had given Kay a lift this morning while he and Fran met with the bank about their father's estate. Other than showing her Town Hall and the hospital, he hadn't seen much of Kay the past several days as she'd devoted most of her time to preparing for this presentation.

"What time do you get Chester?"

"Five."

"Kay, that's more than four hours. That's plenty of time—" He backed the car out of the shade of the oak in the Hollands' yard and sunlight highlighted her face. "Hey, is something wrong with Chester?"

"No. Yes. I don't know. They said no. But maybe there is."

They said no was the important answer, but she didn't seem to know that. "You covered every possible response, Kay."

"It's not funny." She meant that.

"Tell me what they said."

"The woman who called said they want to make sure I have time to talk with the vet. She wouldn't say about what. She *swore* Chester's healthy—but there's something the vet wants to discuss with me."

"That's Allison Maclaine's office you're talking about? She wouldn't lie about something like that. She wouldn't let her staff lie, either."

"Really?" Hope pushed back the worry in her eyes for an instant, then worry surged forward again. "She might know the owner or—"

"I'll go with you. In the meantime, we'll go to the meeting, then sailing."

"You'd do that? Go with me?"

"Sure. Now, are you ready for this meeting?"

"Absolutely." Her fingers tapped at the webbing of her seatbelt and her foot bounced against the bottom of the glove compartment, both at double-time. Apparently easing her worry about Chester had allowed her nerves to take over.

"You'll do great."

She cut him a sharp look. "You didn't think so last time."

"That was before you had the benefit of my expert tour-guiding."

She gave a sour, "Humpf." But the tapping and bouncing slowed.

"Be gentle. Remember, these are simple folk from Wisconsin, not hardened New Yorkers."

She snorted as they unloaded her supplies at Bliss House.

"Simple folk. Right. Like Annette and Suz aren't brilliant. Like Steve and Max couldn't hold their own anywhere. Like Miss Trudi couldn't out-talk a New York politician."

That was better, though she was still wound tight about the presentation. What he needed was something to take her mind off it.

She held up her hand to forestall any comment from him. "All right, all right, so I should watch my mouth."

"You don't need to worry about that." He held the door into Bliss House open. "I watch your mouth enough for both of us."

She stopped dead for a second, looking over her shoulder at him. Then she marched inside with her old sidewalks-of-New-York quick-time.

He supposed he should congratulate himself that he had taken her mind off the presentation. Now he could use something to take his mind—and body—off the track he'd substituted. Especially since his duty as a committee member called for him to pay close attention to her throughout this meeting.

Fran helped her set the poster boards on the easel he'd dropped off at the same time he'd set up a screen as she'd asked.

Barely waiting for them to be seated, Kay revealed the first poster board with a headline above photos and drawings of a refurbished Bliss House.

"The theme I worked with—" She paused, then swallowed. "—was *Come Home to Tobias ... Even if It's Your First Trip.* The *first trip* phrase is to instill the idea that they'll return frequently. If you like the slogan, you can use it throughout the year—*Come Home to Tobias ... for Christmas* or *Come Home to Tobias ... for Spring.* For the opening, the idea is to make this the kind of homecoming everyone dreams of."

She launched into specifics. How the high school band would play, how Miss Trudi or a crafter would give each visitor a personal welcome, how there would be homemade food, chances to try hands-on crafts, singalongs, and story-telling. She had arranged special rates at the closest motels plus two B&Bs. She'd wrangled discounts with tour bus companies from Chicago, Milwaukee, and Madison.

"Wow, you've been busy," Suz said.

"Eventually you can offer special sessions for people interested in learning crafts. But at the start it's important to hit with a splash. Without an advertising budget—" Her eyes cut toward Rob for the first time, but didn't make contact. "—we need the media to incite people to come. To get the media to do that we have to do two things. First, make it easy for them."

The next two poster boards had sample feature article layouts and ad layouts. She passed out sheets with pitches for newspapers and magazines. She showed them a video she'd made to give regional TV stations ideas of potential feature articles.

"This is terrific, Kay," Steve said. "We can—"

"There's something more. Maybe the most important."

Rob couldn't look away from her. Her eyes sparkled, her cheeks had pinkened. Along with the blue tank top she wore a red and blue scarf through the waistband of deep red slacks, as if she'd discovered all the colors in the paint box for the first time.

"Every visitor will receive a packet of seeds so they can take a bit of the Bliss House gardens home. Because the gardens are going to be spectacular, and the greatest draw for Bliss House."

"Oh, my," Fran said under her breath. "But they won't be blooming at the opening."

"I know. But we need to make the gardens Bliss House's trademark, a year-round feature. I propose a mural celebrating them. A mural, right here—" She swept her arm across the white expanse of the back kitchen wall. "It can't be simply a painting of the gardens. That would be redundant during the summer and second-best during the winter. It needs to give viewers a deeper appreciation of the gardens in summer and bring them to life in the winter. The way a whiff of a scent can put you totally in a moment from the past."

"Like the smell of cookies can give you a full sensory memory of home," Suz said.

"Count on Suz to connect with baking," Max murmured.

Everyone laughed except Rob. He'd seen a longing in Kay's eyes, the same longing he'd seen when he'd talked about his parents and his childhood. He wanted to know what that was about—But how could he fault her for keeping her pain to herself when he wasn't telling her about the complication in his life?

"I have painters in mind to ask for proposals, and I hope whoever we select will waive at least a portion of the fee."

With color in her face deepening, Kay selected two sheets and handed them to Fran to pass around. Rob recognized her sketches from his white legal pad.

"These are amazing, Kay. Amazing."

"They're rough, but they'll give artists an idea of what might work. I'll keep it as inexpensive as possible. But we can't afford to take the lowest bid. We need someone special to paint this. Someone with the right vision. Then it'll be worth the money, Rob. I know it will," she said, as if he'd disagreed. "To make the most of it, we need to have it finished before the opening. We can preview it for the media to build excitement. If you give me the okay, I'll line up painters to consider—"

"No."

She went stiff at Rob's single word. "No? But it's perfect. It—"

"It's almost perfect, Kay. It will be perfect if we use your sketches for the design and if your grandmother does the painting. Think about it. Famous artist donates a mural to her hometown. Dora Aaronson comes home to Tobias—it fits your theme perfectly."

Exclamations of "What a terrific idea!" came from around the table. He didn't take his eyes off Kay.

"No." Her mouth formed the word, but no sound came out.

"Yes." Miss Trudi said. "That is a wonderful idea. The sketches will serve admirably as a base for the mural design."

"And if you ask your grandmother, Kay," Annette started, then looked more closely at Kay and stopped. "Unless that's a problem, of course."

"Problem?" Kay's voice skidded. "Why should it be a problem?"

"We can discuss the details later," Miss Trudi said firmly. "For now, are we agreed to pursue this vision?"

"Absolutely," said Suz. In quick order the committee made it official.

Kay remained silent, offering only nods and tight smiles. She quickly packed her tote bag, grabbed the poster boards, and exited.

He caught up with her just past the patio. "Kay."

She kept going. Three construction workers by a bench saw at the far corner of Bliss House turned to watch as he reached her and took her arm.

"Okay, what was that about?"

She didn't resist but didn't look at him. "The decision to ask Dora Aaronson to come here? You know. You led the discussion."

Two people walking past on the sidewalk craned their necks to look at them. "Yeah, I did. We can't talk here. We're going out on the lake. Let's go."

"The lake? Sailing? I do *not* want—"

"On the lake you can yell at me as much as you want without anyone overhearing."

The appeal of that made her hesitate just long enough for him to hustle her into the car. She said nothing on the short drive or as they took the boat out. But her fingers tapped, her foot jiggled.

In a calm cove, he dropped the sail, and turned to her. "Say it."

"You knew. I told you there was a break with my grandmother. How could you suggest bringing her here? How could you betr—"

"Because we can't afford not to." He talked over her. He could not hear that accusation from her. "Because Bliss House can't afford another artist. Because *you* can't afford not to."

She said nothing.

He wasn't letting this go. "Okay, there's tension in your family, yet she's the reason you're here. But you go white at the idea of her coming, and even whiter at the idea of you asking her. That makes no sense."

"My New York pallor."

"Kay, tell me to go to hell, but don't give me that crap."

He saw her teetering on the edge, wanting to tell him to go to hell, and more. And then she sighed and slumped, retreating from that edge, and whether that was good or bad he had no idea.

"I didn't ... I don't know if I want her ... here." Her voice barely had sound behind it.

"Why?"

Her gaze went to his forehead. He was rubbing it. He dropped his hand.

"You're right—Dora is the reason we came here for the shoot. When I told her about needing a location, she said she knew the perfect place. I could have found somewhere closer to New York eventually, but ... It was the first time we'd talked in years."

He waited.

"I ... I was making conversation. That's the only reason I mentioned the shoot. To fill the silence."

"How'd you come to talk at all after all those years?"

"We ran into each other." Her mouth twisted. "I was standing in line at the Second Avenue Deli. She turned around with her sandwich. Hard salami, extra tomato, lettuce, and mayo. That was always her choice. She stood there. Neither of us said anything. I couldn't walk away. Then it was my turn to order, and she said to me, *I could wait.*

"I didn't say yes, I didn't say no. She was at a table by the windows. I didn't know if I would walk out or sit down until I found myself in the chair. It was ... strange. When I was a girl, no matter how absorbed she was when I arrived at the studio, she would stretch out one hand to me, just to touch, you know? But that day, she never touched me."

"But at least you started talking. About the past?"

"Not in my family. We talked about how she'd spent a month in France and was returning this fall. How I'd gotten the Donna Ravelle video job. How she'd been in touch with her first art teacher, the person who'd started her on her career. How I hadn't married Barry. She … she liked my haircut."

That had some sort of significance, but he didn't get it.

"And when we hit this huge, yawning silence, I started babbling about the shoot, and how every location I found looked like an antique, but I needed it to look new, because in 1899 it would have been new."

"And she came up with Bliss House."

She nodded. "I found myself going along."

"Because you didn't want the connection to end."

She stared beyond him, toward the shoreline where Max and Suz's house sat.

"I guess."

"Kay. It's obvious you love her. It sounds like she loves you, too. What could have been so terrible that caused a break between you two?"

"You don't know? There must have been talk here, gossip…"

"I don't know." And he needed her to tell him.

She lifted her head. The shine of tears brightened the surface of her eyes, but pain dulled their deeper life.

"She sent my father—her son—to prison."

CHAPTER EIGHTEEN

R OB SWORE COMPREHENSIVELY, but under his breath.

"That about covers my father's view of the situation, too." She tried for a smile, but didn't succeed.

"They wouldn't have sent him to prison on your grandmother's word. He must have done something."

"It's complicated. My father always felt he belonged in the top echelon of society, and Mother had grown up in that life and expected it." Kay expelled a breath. The best thing to do was to stick to the facts. "Dora saw to it that Father had income from a trust. He wanted more income, but an ordinary job wouldn't do. When I was about eight, Dora helped Father buy a gallery and, to help him out, gave him exclusive rights to sell her work. That started the gallery off with a bang. Owning the gallery was acceptable in his circle and lucrative.

"I should have said it was lucrative *at first*. I don't know the ins and outs, but apparently he made bad business decisions." She shook her head. "It wasn't just bad decisions. He was a bad businessman. After five years under my father the gallery was in deep financial trouble, despite all Dora's help. In an effort to recover the losses, he handled paintings that weren't..." No, she would give Rob the truth, uncluttered with euphemisms. "Forgeries. He was charged with selling forgeries."

She saw grim shock in Rob's eyes.

"Forgeries of paintings long lost or stolen—he had nothing to do with stealing them. But he would drop a word to certain clients. You understand? They were people who didn't care if the painting they had hanging in a private room was stolen from a museum or a rightful owner. Maybe it added a thrill.

"And if these people, these buyers, discovered they had a forgery, what could they do? Certainly not sue him or raise a stink, because they would be revealed as having bought a painting they thought was stolen along with being stupid enough to be duped. But none of them did discover it, because the forgeries were very, very good. The man who did them had worked similar schemes all over Europe. Interpol is still looking for him from what I hear."

"But your grandmother recognized the forgeries."

"Yes, but she knew her son. She'd heard about the gallery's financial situation, yet Father hadn't come to her for money, so she wondered. One day she delivered one of her new canvases to the gallery, and she saw a painting in back that she wasn't supposed to have seen, a small Rembrandt lost during World War II. She became suspicious. So suspicious that she walked out with that supposed Rembrandt and took it directly to an expert who owed her a favor. In a few days she had her answer. And then she went to the police."

"Your father must have known the painting was gone. Did he know who took it?"

"He pieced it together. He tried to talk to her. He told her he hadn't done anything wrong. He never stole a painting, never accepted a stolen painting. Just gave greedy people what they wanted."

"And you?" Rob's voice seemed to come from a distance. "Did you think he'd done anything wrong?"

"All I thought was that he was my father, and he was going to jail."

And that Dora had sent him there.

"They told you all this at the time?"

"No. I knew something was wrong, but the specifics—those I found out from the tabloid reporters. A hot story, they called it when I asked them to leave me alone that first day. A Thursday. Odd that I remember that."

"They came after you? You were a kid."

"Thirteen." She laughed, a dry, harsh sound. "But, oh, yeah, they came after me. They followed me to school, taking pictures, shouting questions. About my father, about my grandmother, why she would turn him in, if we all knew he was a crook in league with forgers. That's how I found out."

He reached toward her, but she shifted away. He needed to hear this if there was any hope for ... She shut off the thought.

"After that first time," she continued, "I got better at getting out of our building without the reporters knowing."

Even when she'd succeeded in avoiding them, though, she hadn't avoided how they'd made her feel. She'd thrown up every day. The good days were when she only got sick at home, not at school.

"It was easier to get away from them after school because there were so many of us dressed alike. I figured out they were spotting me because of my hair—I had long, long hair then—so I cut about a foot off. In the end it didn't matter, because the tabloids kept using pictures from when my hair was long. They'd run stupid stories, calling me Rapunzel and saying if I let down my long hair my father could climb it to escape."

"What the hell does that mean?"

"It meant asking my grandmother to help my father."

"Did you?"

"Not then. Because I already had, and she'd said no."

I already had, and she'd said no. How could so few words cover what had happened in those days?

She remembered her father crying—oh, God, crying—and begging her to talk to Dora. And Mother talking, talking...

You're the only one she cares for. If she cared for your father or the family name she wouldn't be doing this. If she cares anything for you or your prospects, she won't pursue it. You have to make her see that. Make her understand. You have to save us, Kay. You have to.

But she hadn't.

Oh, she'd asked her grandmother—begged her. And Dora Aaronson had looked straight at her and said, so very, very softly. *I have no choice, Kay.*

That statement, more than anything else ended Kay's childhood adoration of her grandmother. No choice? Of course she'd had a choice.

"She said no? That's all?" Rob said.

She blinked at him, resurfacing from memories. "She said she could not be a party to diminishing the purity of art. What it came down to was she valued paint on canvas more than her son. More than…" *Me.* "My father was convicted and went to prison. Twenty-three months. His share of the gallery went to fines and legal fees. The irony is that he was forced to put our finances in the hands of a manager who got Father into tech stocks when they were low, so he and Mother have far more money now than they ever would have had with the gallery.

"But he and Dora haven't spoken since. Mother pretends she doesn't exist. I failed to save my family—"

"Kay, you were a kid. It wasn't your job to save anybody."

He reached for her, and she went into his arms, accepting the strength and comfort now. And there she sobbed. Gulping gasps of sorrow and pain that seemed to have been inside forever.

"Kay … Kay…"

Rob murmured her name, not urging her to regain control, but letting her know she was safe to release it. He shifted, and she followed. Down to the bottom of the boat, cradled between his body and the sloped side. She felt the damp. She felt it, knew it, but didn't care. She held onto Rob and let free decades' worth of sorrow and loneliness and loss, until her ribs ached and her body went limp.

"Rob…"

She sucked in a deep breath, exhaled slowly and gradually. How did she even start to explain this? To apologize? To thank him?

He made a sound deep in his throat that she felt more than heard. A hushing, calming sound.

He kissed her hair, her temple. She wiped her fingers across her cheeks and he kissed where she had just removed the tears. Once, twice. She lifted her face, needing. And he kissed her lips.

A gentle kiss of comfort and compassion.

Neither moved, a breath separating them, a balance holding them.

And then he brought his mouth down on hers again. The solid, satisfying slide of lips to lips. His tongue pressed at her mouth, and she opened to him, meeting his tongue with hers.

Their first kiss hadn't lied.

She touched his face. Then lower, her fingers and palm caressing the cords and column of his neck.

Heat flared through her, less an explosion now than an infusion. A cleansing heat, searing a thousand small never-healed cuts on her spirit. A heat where she had been cold, so cold for too long. In her bones, deeper than her bones.

And he did this all with his lips and his touch. Ah, his touch.

She was not alone in exploration. He kissed down her throat and across her shoulders, all the way to the end, then trailed back, lower, finding the ridge of her collarbone.

He drew the strap of the tank top down over her shoulder, carrying her bra with it. She shrugged to further lower the new angle of the neckline. He palmed the point of her shoulder, followed it with a kiss. Ah, yes ... His hand slid lower, fingers creating a delicious friction on her skin.

She shifted, not caring her leg scraped against the other seat, caring only to open herself to his caress.

Oh, the feel of his hand on her...

He cupped her breast, stroked the pad of his thumb across the nipple in a rhythm that matched her pulse, or set it.

He kissed her mouth. Then she kissed his, sliding her tongue across his lips, inside, delving into him, this amazing man who kissed her, tasted her like there was no one better in the world.

This is what people mean about losing themselves in a kiss.

Only she hadn't lost all of herself. Parts of her remained, enjoying—more than that—*joying.*

With no warning, he pulled away, leaving the coolness of loss like a slap across her lips and breast.

"This isn't going to work." She felt his words as a rumble in his chest, as if they had been wrenched out by force.

"Seems to be working fine." Her voice sounded husky, unused.

She had the internal evidence of the way her body churned and tingled. She had the external evidence of his reactions, his heart banging against his ribs under her hand, his uneven breathing. Not to mention the hard, hot evidence against her hip. If this *wasn't working* by his standards, the mind—and body—boggled at what constituted *working*.

A stream of air crossed her face as he let out a breath. "Yeah. *That* part is working fine. More than fine."

"You mean I shouldn't have dumped on you."

He swore, kissed her hard and fast, holding her head between his hands. He raised his head, looked directly into her eyes. "That is bull, Kay. Don't you ever think that. That's not the problem."

As if the word *problem* reminded him of their positions, he shifted so they no longer touched anywhere except his hand on her shoulder.

"You can't say we're not compatible in this area." She hitched herself to a sitting position, accidentally brushing her hip against his lap, and feeling the immediate reaction.

"More than compatible." He sounded strangled, and she found satisfaction in that. Maybe the brush hadn't been entirely accidental if she dug down to the subconscious level. "Easy. Don't rock the boat."

"*I'm* not rocking it."

If he'd meant it metaphorically, he was the one who had jump-cut this scene from one mood to another. If he meant it literally, she had simply used her hold on the edge to lever herself upright, and if the boat swayed a little in the water, tough.

"Kay, listen. It wouldn't be fair—not to either of us—to let this … this other aspect get out of hand. I'm staying here in Tobias. I want kids and a family. You're going back to New York for a career in film."

She could have given the exact same speech herself. It made total sense. Not only that, he was a gentleman. A good person. Looking out for her.

And she felt like shit.

"Are you all right, Kay?"

She whipped her head around, hoping her smile would blind him.

"Absolutely. But look at the time—I have to pick up Chester."

A heartbeat passed. A long, painful heartbeat, while the sun spot-lighted his face and she saw intelligence and caring, all trained on her.

If he didn't look away—*now*—she was going to crack. Scream. Cry. Jump overboard.

"I'll get you back right away."

He raised the sail, and she turned her face into the puff of breeze, grateful it would dry a solitary tear.

IF THE SUN hadn't been behind her head, what would he have seen in Kay's face in that moment?

Her story had explained a hundred things. When Dora Aaronson became estranged from her son's family it had meant the end of normalcy for Kay. She had become the poor-little-rich-girl locked in the tower of her parents' social ambitions.

What a mess.

He hadn't known what to expect when he asked about the rift in her family. But it sure hadn't been that her grandmother had turned her father in to serve a prison term. This is what she'd meant whenever she'd talked about betrayal, about snitches, about loyalty. He thought of her words: *The law? The law has no heart ... People come first. People and animals.*

And here he was about to join her grandmother in the ranks of whistleblowers.

Not only was he about to crash his career into the rocks, but being around him could draw Kay into a rerun of her childhood nightmare.

It wouldn't be as sexy a story as her family's situation had been, but he didn't fool himself that it could be kept quiet, either. The firm was too well-known. The media was going to swoop down on him, and anyone in his vicinity could be caught as well.

Just what Kay needed.

No. He'd been right to stop before they made love. It was the only thing he could do.

And then another thought hit him—what Kay hadn't said, the question she hadn't answered. Her father didn't seem to think he'd done anything wrong, her grandmother did.

But what about Kay? Did she recognize that her father was wrong, that he deserved to be punished? How would she view the effect Rob's whistleblowing would have beyond the wrongdoers?

All I thought was that he was my father, and he was going to jail.

"ROB, I TOLD you, you don't need to stay, you didn't need to bring me here."

"We're here, and I'm staying."

Kay opened her mouth, no doubt to tell him again to get lost. In the politest terms possible, but the message was the same.

And maybe he should get lost. But not yet. She'd been nervous about this vet appointment from the start and after these past few hours ... He wasn't going anywhere until he was sure she and her dog were okay.

He was spared another get-lost message because the office assistant, speaking into a phone receiver, drew every bit of Kay's attention.

"Dr. Maclaine, Ms. Aaronson is here. Chester's owner. ... Okay." The assistant hung up, smiling. "You can go in now. Chester's in with the doctor. That's an unusual name for a female."

Kay wasn't interested in chit-chat. She was headed for the exam room. Rob said, "She's an usual dog," then caught up with Kay.

He put a hand to the small of her back as he reached around her to open the door.

Inside, Kay knelt by Chester, who beat the wall with her tail. Rob faced Allison Maclaine. "Hi, Allison. I'm a friend of Kay's and thought I'd come along in case—"

"Please, Doctor," Kay interrupted, looking up, "if there's something wrong with Chester, please—"

"Nothing is wrong with Chester," Allison said firmly. So firmly that the worry cleared from Kay's face, and Rob felt something expand in his chest. "But it's still good to see you, Rob."

She cleared her throat, and her manner became entirely professional. "Ms. Aaronson, am I correct that you don't have much experience with dogs?"

"I don't have *any* experience. But Chester was all on her own, and I couldn't leave her to starve. I checked about the right food and a leash and—"

"Ms. Aaronson, I'm not questioning if you're a fit mother for Chester. What I'm trying to tell you is you're going to be a grandmother, so to speak. Chester is going to have puppies."

Kay sat back on her heels. Hard. After a beat, her heels parted and her little behind dropped to the floor.

Rob laughed, but his gut also tightened. And that wasn't all that tightened. God, all it took was for her to sit on the floor?

"Puppies? She's going to have *puppies?*" Kay's face had gone pale. "Oh, my God, puppies! Are they going to be okay? Is *she* okay?"

"All fine. And don't worry, dogs do this all the time," the vet said.

"But I don't." It was a very quiet wail, but a wail it was. "Puppies! Oh my God. What am I going to do?"

"You can start by reading the pamphlets I'm going to give you."

"But … but puppies. Puppies!" She sounded overwhelmed, awed, scared, and ecstatic.

"You'll do great." Rob said. He knew the next words were coming, knew they shouldn't, yet couldn't stop them. "I'll help you."

CHAPTER NINETEEN

"WHAT DOES THAT one say about pre-natal nutrition?" Kay asked Rob without looking up from the book she was reading. Doughnuts and cheeseburgers—what had she been thinking?

Rob occupied the extra-wide recliner across the Hollands' sun porch from where she sat on the floor with her back against the sofa. Chester had curled up beside her, resting her head on Kay's thigh with a contented sigh. Kay's leg was now asleep, but she wasn't about to move.

"Relax. We've got the food Allison recommended. And remember she said the first half of the pregnancy isn't as vital for nutrition as the last half, so what matters is from here on out."

"Here on out isn't very damned long. Three more weeks!" She checked the ebook on her laptop sitting on the floor on the other side of her against the book in her lap.

"Or four," Rob said. "Allison can only guess that she's about five weeks along."

Gestation's sixty-three days, the vet had said. *That's give or take. But about twenty-four hours before the puppies start coming Chester's temperature should drop, so that will give you warning.*

Some warning. A measly day.

"They should have classes or something," Kay grumbled.

"Like Lamaze?" He laughed. "Quick worrying. Allison told you, it's a natural process and Chester's in fine shape."

"Yeah, well, you and Dr. Maclaine can be casual about this, but Chester and I have never had puppies before and this *is* a big deal.

The vet had given her a brochure on dogs giving birth—whelping as the brochure called it—and had answered questions. But more questions kept hitting Kay, so she'd asked Rob to stop at the bookstore to add any books she didn't already have. He'd been a good sport about staying in the car so Chester wouldn't be alone.

And when they got back she found more books online that the bookstore hadn't had.

Kay considered changing Chester's name in the face of impending motherhood, but by the time she'd emerged from the bookstore she'd decided Chester would remain Chester. Heaven knows the dog seemed secure in her sexuality.

"This one says pre-natal nutrition is vital," Rob said. He traced a passage in the dog care encyclopedia with his long index finger.

"It's got to be, Especially for a dog like Chester who's been on her own for who knows how long."

"Yes, pre-natal nutrition is vital," Rob pursued. "Also says here that letting an owner and her friend die of starvation is not good for the expectant dog."

That was the second time today he'd referred to himself as her friend.

She had not felt the least bit friendly toward him today.

Too happy to see him when he arrived this morning, wanting to strangle him when he proposed Dora do the mural, relieved to tell her family story, right—so very right—in his arms, hurt when he withdrew, angry he wouldn't leave her alone, grateful for his help.

All that and more. But not friendly.

Since they'd returned to the Hollands' they'd both pursued this fiction that they were a couple of buddies reading up on dogs having puppies.

It had to be as much a strain for him as her. Plus, there'd been that expression at the vet's after he'd said he would help her. A decidedly Sydney Carton-ish expression as he went to the guillotine in *A Tale of Two Cities*. "It is a far, far better thing I do…"

Just what a girl wanted. To have a guy—the guy—feel like being with her resembled having his head cut off.

"Rob, you've been great." She talked fast, not letting worry about her inadequacies in caring for Chester tempt her. "Above and beyond the call of duty. So I'm not holding you to your generous offer to help me with Chester when she—" No, better not to contemplate what she was turning down. "To help me later. I know you have a lot of other things to do, and I can't ask you to do this."

"You didn't ask. I volunteered."

"It was very kind, but—"

"I don't renege. So you've got an assistant canine midwife whether you want me or not. Unless you starve me before the big day arrives."

"Rob, will you—"

"I'm not going anywhere, Kay."

That intent look was in his eyes again. No, not again, because this one was different. There was the heat of desire in it—she'd always recognized that—but there was something else there, too. Something that made her feel more sure, yet terrified.

And the strange thing was, she didn't know what she was sure of, or what she was terrified of.

"What I was going to say," she lied, "was will you order pizza to be delivered? I hate to disturb the mother-to-be."

HUNGER PANGS SATISFIED by pizza, they plotted out the remainder of Chester's pregnancy on calendar grids Rob had printed out from her computer. She'd had no idea her software included calendars.

Rob, who had moved to sit beside her on the floor, wrote in the steps the vet had described, feeding Chester more frequent meals, keeping up the exercise, another vet visit, and the due date.

But it wasn't only Chester's changes that Kay saw in those calendar boxes.

There it was, the weeks sliding away to Bliss House's opening in mid-October … and Kay's departure date.

"October sure is coming fast," she said, fighting to keep the words light.

"I'll be gone before then." He tapped a calendar box less than two weeks after Chester's due date.

"Oh, your leave will be over. Of course." She'd known it was only for the summer, but she couldn't imagine Tobias without Rob.

Could she imagine anything without Rob?

His silence finally penetrated her thoughts. She looked up and found him watching her intently.

"It's not the leave that will be over, it's my career, Kay. I'll go back to Chicago, but not for good. I have to get some things started and then ... The career I've had, the income, the position, the title—they'll all be gone."

She waited, but that seemed to be the end of his speech. "Okay."

"Okay? That's all you're going to say?"

"Yeah."

He had to know she wasn't a material girl. So what was this about? Did he think she wanted him only if he was a high-flying successful financial whiz?

And then she knew.

This was the big thing, the thing that was bothering him beyond the divorce. He'd worked hard to reach his goal, and now he was losing it.

"Do you understand what I'm saying? I've had this career, a successful career, and it's about to go up in smoke. Other than knowing I won't be working in a major financial firm, I can't see any farther than a few weeks. I have no future. So I can't offer you a future."

Questions about what was happening in his career evaporated. Her heart rapped against her ribs. "Do you want to offer me a future?"

"Whether I want to or not, I can't. So there's no future between us."

She stroked the back of her fingers down his cheek. "There's the present, Rob."

Still he held back.

"Kay, I can't offer you anything like you're used to having, the life you've led."

She tipped her head, making sure he could see her eyes. "You are so much better than anything I've had in my life."

Cupping his jaw, she stretched up to glide her lips across his. Praying he didn't draw back this time.

One, slow, gentle kiss.

"Kay, there's more—"

God, she hoped so.

She kissed him hard this time. Hard and hot. Sliding her tongue past his lips, pressing against him. Throwing herself at him as she had that first evening on the patio. But this time with a kiss instead of words.

This time … This time, please…

Yes. His arms came around her, his mouth captivated. Kiss after kiss. Long and fast and deep.

He raised his head, breath rasping. "No stopping."

Ah, her do-right Rob was issuing one last caution. A warning that if she wanted to try to escape this, she better do it now.

"No stopping," she agreed.

ROB NEVER REMEMBERED all of how they got upstairs. He did remember the stop on the stairs.

His shirt was gone … somewhere. Her tank top came off over her head. He stroked across the swell of her breast to the tip already pointed and stiff. They slid, down, down in slow-motion, together. He dragged down the strap of her bra, unwilling to take the time with hooks to free her, and took her nipple into his mouth. The pebbled smoothness, the warmth. Her taste.

She was the catalyst that sparked this reaction that burned through him, seeking more and more of him as fuel for its combustion. His skin, his muscles, his blood, his bones, they all burned for her, with her.

Chester's whimper from the bottom of the stairs was the only reason they didn't make love right there on the landing.

Kay's sound was half frustration, half concern. She struggled to sit up. He was already on his feet, mentally cursing the dog, but also thanking her. Protection. He'd almost forgotten.

Chester gave him a final warning stare before he closed the door to Kay's bedroom behind them. He stepped out of shoes, socks, and jeans, pausing only to secure the condoms from his pocket and slap them on the night table.

Kay, standing still beside the bed, followed his motion with her eyes. He expected a comment about his confidence in bringing them—in fact, it had been his lack of confidence in his self-control.

But she looked back at him, smiled completely, as only Kay could, and inexplicably murmured, "Boxers."

She slid her hands inside them at either side of his waist, then down, down, down. When she traveled back up, with a pause to hold and stroke him, he knew a temptation, but not one that threatened his need to be inside her.

That need clawed at him. It was a most unreasonable need. And it would answer only to her.

They tumbled diagonally on the bed, tangled together. He found the hook at the back of her bra, bared her. He cupped and kissed her breasts, brushing the tight points with his thumb, then his tongue.

Tugs, whispers, moans. Her shorts and panties gone. The condom on. He opened her legs with his knees, found the heated welcome.

Urging him forward with her hands, she tilted her hips. "Yes."

He entered her. Pushing into her warmth, holding back the gathering thrust of need. She tilted more. "Yes."

He braced himself on his elbows, so he could watch her. He drew back, then slid deep into her again. Slow. Then again. And again.

"Rob." One soft word. The final spark.

A tremor passed from her to him, then through them together.

No plan, no thought.

The rhythm no longer belonged to him or her. It was them.

He heard her cry, reaching higher. Heard it shatter into shimmers of sound and satisfaction. Then the roaring in his head, the convulsing flash of pleasure, pain, joy, need.

All Kay.

SHE HEARD HIM get up. Pretended to be asleep when he went from the bathroom to the hall door and downstairs. She heard the back door open and close.

She couldn't react, couldn't feel. She floated in some limbo outside of time. Still rocked in the torpor.

Then the back door opened and closed again. She heard slight sounds of movement, clicks of lights and locks, then footsteps on the stairs.

The mattress depressed, tipping her toward him and she went with it, smiling as she buried her face against his shoulder and his arms came around her.

SHE STRETCHED, STILL half asleep, and found a lovely soreness in uncommon muscles.

They'd made love, slow and sustained after he'd let Chester out and closed up downstairs.

Sometime in the first lightening toward day he had awakened her by kissing her shoulder, and they made love again.

Now he sat up in bed beside her, scrubbing his hands through his hair and yawning.

"Your back…"

He twisted, trying to look over his shoulder, giving it up, and grinning at her. "What about it?"

"It's magnificent."

He chuckled. "I thought you were going to say it had scratch marks."

"Well that, too," she admitted, peering at pink semicircular marks. "But it's still magnificent."

She kissed a semicircle near his shoulder. She remembered when she had made the marks. The ones on his shoulders, and the other set, lower. She crammed a pillow behind her to sit up.

She was remembering other things, too. Pieces clicked into place.

"So, will you finally admit that I was right all along?"

"About us?" He kissed her nose. "Oh, yeah. Definite rocket fuel."

"Rocket fuel?" She chuckled. "I didn't say anything about rocket fuel."

"Story from my childhood." He dismissed it, pursuing her original thread, not distracted by tangents. "Is that what you want me to admit?"

"Only for starters. The real one is that I was right about there being something bothering you beyond the divorce—the big thing bothering you. What you said last night about your career being over— you've known about this since we met, haven't you. That's why you said to me *I was a financial analyst* that first day."

"Yeah. Kay—"

"I knew it! You kept telling me all that WYSIWYG stuff, but I knew it. But why all the secrecy? Since you're not going back to Chicago for your career, you could stay here in Tobias for good, right? Everyone here will be thrilled"

He dropped his head back and cursed the ceiling, then straightened.

"Kay, we have to talk about why my career's going in the toilet. We should have talked about it last night. I should have told you before—" He muttered another grim curse, this one at himself. "You're right. I'll be in Tobias for good. Maybe start a small business as a tax and investment adviser—that's the good news."

Which meant there was bad news, and his body language said it was big bad news.

"A change can be good, Rob. A chance to look at things from a new angle."

He turned, met her eyes.

"It's not like that. The whole story, it's long…" He let out a breath. "Mostly I worked outside the firm, investigating potential investments and consulting with only a few top individual clients. One of those clients, one of our best, ran into complications as a result of a nasty divorce and asked me to check over his investments, taxes, fees, everything."

He shook his head. "It was a fluke. A one in a million chance. But when I ran other figures for comparison, I saw a pattern. At first I thought I had to be wrong … I wasn't. At best there's conflict of interest … and it would need a very generous interpretation to get there. God, it's our job to spot crap like this in other companies, to protect our clients from it. And here we're doing it to them ourselves. I was sick."

Pressure settled on Kay's chest. A thick, smothering pressure.

"Is it illegal?" Her voice sounded small and distant.

"Yeah. And it's damn-sure unethical. And that's what the firm's been built on. The whole foundation will … I've seen—we've all seen—what happens to companies when they get busted. They die. A lot of people, a lot of good people who've only ever done their jobs or done business with the company in good faith, lose their shirts. Shirts, hell, they lose their futures. All because a few people in a position to twist things around get greedy. But I thought if it was caught from the inside, maybe that wouldn't have to happen." He levered himself up on one elbow, facing her. "People would take a hit, but not be wiped out. The firm could survive. And so could our employees and clients."

"What did you do?"

"I went to Mitchell Gordon, the man who recruited me into the firm. The man who gave me chances when other senior partners said I was too young. The man I respected more than anyone else. The man I trusted the most. I told him everything I knew and most of what I suspected. I expected him to grab the chance I was giving him. Shake things up, knock heads together, clean house. Instead, he asked for time to look into things."

"That's why you took the leave?"

He nodded. "He asked me not to be there. Asked me to give him room to maneuver—that's what he said. Room to maneuver."

She drew her knees up under the sheet. "That's great, Rob. He's probably getting things in order, using the time to—"

"Cover his ass—that's what he's using the time for. The first few weeks, I told myself he was making things right. But as time went on I had to accept that Mitchell wasn't putting the house in order. I would have heard. And then I had a call from my ex on Mitchell's behalf, reminding me what a great mentor he'd been, reminding me my career was on the line." He gave a sardonic snort. "Also reminding me that my own ass might need some covering."

"Why? You haven't done anything wrong."

He smiled briefly at her indignation. "Not the things they're doing, no. But the authorities will have every right to ask why I didn't come to them earlier."

"You tell them the truth—you gave your mentor time to make it right."

"Make it right? Or cover it up? It all depends on how you look at it. Because I've got to believe Mitchell is part of it, as much as I don't want to, with the way he's reacting. But even aside from what the authorities do, my career's over." He smoothed his hand over the crown of her head, lowered his mouth to kiss below her ear. "If we'd met a year ago, I could have transferred to New York and maybe—"

She dropped her knees, sat up straight. "Don't do it, Rob."

He lifted his head, questioning her.

"Don't do it. Not any of it. Leave it behind you. You don't have to go back to that company. Come to New York. Get a job with another company."

He shook his head. "Firms might talk a good game, but in the end they don't want whistleblowers. Besides—"

"That's what I'm saying. Don't be a whistleblower."

"Kay, you don't understand—"

"No, *you* don't understand. You haven't lived through this. I know what happens when someone blows the whistle. I've seen the toll." She looked away, unfocused. "Including the toll on the whistleblower. Don't do it, Rob. Don't do it to this man you liked, respected, and above all don't do it to yourself. You have no idea what it's going to be like."

"I have some idea. I've read accounts of what people have gone through. Losing their jobs, losing friends, losing spouses. There's a support organization and I contacted them anonymously. They told me to expect the news crews outside my door for a while, calls at all hours, slams by the firm in the media, the whole thing."

"Then how can you do this?"

"Kay, this involves a lot of people's money."

She swung back to face him. "Screw the money. What about the people? Mitchell, your co-workers, you." And her, too, she hoped. But she couldn't put that on him now. "And all their families."

"I'm thinking about people—the people who could lose their life savings. It's about them, too. People living off the pensions the firm handles—people like Miriam Jenkins, getting less money while some VP gets a private plane. And it's about all the people who work at other companies like ours. It'll come out someday, somehow. The longer this goes on, the less the public will trust. Having the problems exposed by an outsider only makes it worse. Then it's not only my company, it's a whole lot of companies going down."

"You said it'll come out someday—let it. You don't have to be the one, Rob. You don't have to do this. You have a choice."

"No, I don't. I can't leave it to someone else."

"You're putting abstract principle before anyone you lo— anything." Tears choked off her words.

He reached for her. "Kay—"

She jumped up, grabbed a towel. "I told you, I told you what happened when Dora—I can't talk … Please leave now. I have to…"

She ran.

CHAPTER TWENTY

THE ACADEMY AWARDS needed a new category.

Best Performance of Normalcy When Your Insides Are Whirling Like a Blender.

Kay figured she and Rob would share that Oscar.

Then they'd stand at the lectern side by side, just the way they were walking now on the sidewalk beside the brick wall surrounding Bliss House.

They'd met at the corner of the grounds, both heading for an emergency meeting that Miss Trudi had called. "It is not bad news," she'd said, and that's all either of them had been able to get out of her on the phone.

Kay had stopped when she saw Rob, but he came right up to her. He extended a hand as if to touch her face, then dropped it.

"Are you okay?"

"I'm fine," she lied, hoping he hadn't heard her throwing up before he left.

"Kay—"

She shook her head.

"We have to talk."

"Not now."

"Sometime."

"Sometime," she agreed. "Not now."

He'd looked at her a long time, then gestured for her to continue walking toward the entrance to Bliss House's grounds.

She couldn't talk about what he was going to do, but she couldn't stand the silence, either.

"I need a whelping box," she said abruptly, "Actually, Chester does. Is there a store that—"

"I've got my doubts even Manhattan would have a whelping box store." He looked grim, but his voice sounded almost normal. Almost. "There's definitely no whelping box store in Tobias."

"The book does say it's not that hard for you to build a whelping box."

"Who's *you*? Compost bins are the extent of my carpentry skills." They reached the drive to Bliss House in time to see Max enter the gate to Miss Trudi's quarters. "I'll ask one of Max's guys."

"Which one?" she asked doubtfully.

"Kay, if these guys are good enough to put Bliss House back together, they're good enough to build a box for Chester to have puppies in."

"It's not the same thing, but if you're sure he'll do a good job, okay."

Rob started to respond, then looked beyond her and said, "Something's going on at Miss Trudi's."

Looking through the gateway to Miss Trudi's domain, Kay saw the open front door and people milling inside. She and Rob picked up their pace.

Miss Trudi stood in her front hall, urging people there to go on in. At their approach she came outside and met them on the front steps.

"Miss Trudi, what's wrong?" Kay asked. "You said an emergency—"

"A good emergency. Kay, dear." Miss Trudi took her hands. "Your grandmother is here."

Kay's stomach rolled again. It was too much. All of it.

"But … how?"

"I believe a hired car brought her." Then, as if that answered Kay's question, she sailed on. "When I called yesterday to ask for her assistance, she immediately made arrangements. She arrived on an early flight and was driven right here. A few people have gathered to welcome her."

Miss Trudi must have called Dora as soon as yesterday's meeting ended. And Dora must have caught a *very* early flight.

Kay recognized that figuring out flight schedules—with Rob beside her and her grandmother a few yards away—was avoidance.

She wasn't ready to see Dora. Not now. Not with her emotions raw. Over her outburst on the boat, over Chester's pregnancy, over making love with Rob, and over what he intended to do. If she didn't keep the lid on tight, that powerful blender churning inside her would have her emotions splattering all over the place.

Miss Trudi spoke as serenely as ever. "As hopeful as I am that she will provide excellent assistance to us in preparing for Bliss House's opening, I am equally hopeful that you will be able to help her."

"She doesn't need help from anyone," Kay said, "least of all me."

"She has not accepted assistance easily her entire life," Miss Trudi acknowledged. "However, she has never faced this situation before."

"What? Painting this mural? It'll be a snap for her."

Miss Trudi went oddly still. "Surely you knew that Dora hasn't painted for nearly five years."

Through this new shock, Kay felt the warmth of Rob's hand at the small of her back, a gesture of support.

"That can't be right. Dora lives to paint. Always has."

"And yet the fact remains that she does not paint any longer." Miss Trudi's eyes were soft with sorrow, but her voice was firm. "Her arthritis has denied her the ability to control the brush with the exactitude she maintained all those years."

"I know she was diagnosed years ago, but it can't be that bad." Memory washed over her ... Dora at the deli, the long wide sleeves of her jacket covering her hands. Never touching her. No ... It couldn't be. Dora unable to paint was like the world unable to spin. "She would have said something or..."

"When?" Miss Trudi's solitary word spoke eloquently of the estrangement.

Kay shook her head. "You can't be right. New Dora Aaronson paintings have come out."

"After her diagnosis she worked intensely for years without increasing the number of paintings sold or displayed, creating an inventory to mete out when she could no longer paint to her standards, so that no one would know."

"No, of course not. Dora Aaronson couldn't let her reputation in the art world suffer. That was always her priority."

Miss Trudi didn't blink at Kay's harsh tone. "I should say that she could not bear to have anyone who understood her loss feel sorry for her."

For all the serenity of the older woman's tone, Kay recognized it as a rebuke for not understanding—for not trying to understand—Dora's loss.

A memory of the last time she'd been in her grandmother's studio rose. Dora had stood before a newly finished painting, her left hand slightly cupped, absently sliding over the back of her right hand, wrist to fingers, fingers to wrist.

Until minutes ago Kay would have described it as a gesture of tending to that talented right hand. But it could have been checking the inroads of arthritis. Or a way to soothe pain. Or an attempt to accept her diminishing abilities at the same time her only child disregarded his own honor and the integrity of the art world she had devoted her life to.

"She could still paint," Miss Trudi, was saying, "if she were willing to explore new techniques."

Kay gave Miss Trudi a look. Oh, yes, Dora's old teacher knew as well as Kay did that Dora would never compromise her precise style or her exacting standards.

And then Kay read another message in those wise eyes.

"But if her hands...? How's she going to do the mural?" Kay blurted.

"That's something we need to discuss."

That's what Miss Trudi said, but was that what she meant? Or was this a plot—a double plot—to get Dora Aaronson painting again and to heal the rift between granddaughter and grandmother?

Kay swung around to Rob to see if he'd been involved in arranging this, but she instantly recognized his concern for her. Somehow, despite the strain between them, Rob's concern made an impossible situation less so. Maybe it was the sense that she had someone in her corner.

"Yes. We *do* need to discuss this," she said to Miss Trudi. "Because we need that mural for the sake of Bliss House and Tobias."

There. She'd put the older woman on notice that her machinations hadn't escaped notice, and that whatever Kay did, it would be for the good of the project, not because she'd been manipulated.

"Yes, indeed, we do need it. Shall we join the others and your grandmother?"

THE TOBIAS GRAPEVINE had drawn enough residents eager to see the town's famous native to pack the room.

If Rob could have banished them all or whisked Kay away he would have done it in a second. But she was walking in beside Miss Trudi, with her head high and her back straight.

After the past twenty-four hours he wouldn't blame her if she'd curled up in a ball in a corner … the way he imagined she must have after being sick in the bathroom this morning.

What an ass he'd been.

He'd known she was reeling, and what did he do? Dump the fact that he was ending his career and opening himself up to the kind of public scrutiny that had torn her apart as a kid—just after they'd made love.

The bed had been rumpled and warm with the earthy scent of their lovemaking. Lovemaking unlike any he'd known.

He'd expected the rockets, yet hadn't been fully prepared for them. And he'd never known he could feel such overwhelming tenderness at the same time.

God, he couldn't think about that now. That was the last thing Kay needed from him as she was about to encounter her grandmother again, and so publicly.

At a guess, Dora was in the middle of the knot by the windows that included Steve's mother, Lana Corbett. Lana, newly returned from Europe, considered herself the leader of what society Tobias had and would view it as her position to greet a famous visitor.

"Kay," said a husky voice.

Some of the crowd stepped back as Dora approached her granddaughter. Miss Trudi performed an efficient block to turn Lana and other eager visitors aside, leaving Kay, her grandmother, and him in a pocket of relative privacy, at least momentarily.

Dora wore her gray and silver hair turned under at her chin, and was dressed in a pair of finely tailored navy slacks and a lighter blue sweater set. She could have been one of Lana's fellow Tobias matrons heading to the country club. Her long face reminded him of Kay. But where Kay's chin was short and pointed, her grandmother had an elongated jaw.

"Hello, Dora. Hope you had a good trip." Kay smiled.

This woman would smile if her heart were breaking.

Dora's expression didn't change—so different from her granddaughter—yet Rob thought Dora was going to reach for Kay. But in the end neither woman touched the other.

Nell arrived in their small circle in a rush, intent on her own agenda. "Kay, may I have one of Chester's puppies?"

Kay appeared unsurprised that word was out about the puppies, or that the privacy had been so fleeting. Maybe she was getting used to Tobias.

"Nell…" Steve, following his daughter, made her name a warning.

"We have lots of room. Pansy could have a sibling," she said.

"You already have a dog, Nell," Steve said. "You need to be sure you give Pansy all the attention she needs while she's still growing up."

"You wouldn't want her to feel neglected, would you?" Kay received a grateful look from Steve. Before the girl could argue, Kay's resorted to a blatant attempt to distract her. "Nell, I'd like you to meet my grandmother, Dora Aaronson. Dora, Nell is Steve and Annette's daughter, and a talented finger-painter."

"I might be a famous artist someday," the girl told Dora.

"Is Trudi giving you lessons?"

Nell shook her head. "Not painting. Miss Trudi shows me other things. But I'll take lessons when I decide."

"Decide?" Dora blinked quickly.

Kay suppressed a chuckle, and tension eased from Rob's shoulders.

"I suspect," Kay said, "Nell means when she decides where being a famous artist fits into her agenda. She has a lot of goals to accomplish."

"Ah," Dora's face was solemn as she bent to the girl, but her eyes were alight. "I am honored to meet a young lady of such ambition."

"It's nice to meet you, too. You're pretty nice for a grandmother."

Dora flicked a look at Kay.

"Nell feels her grandmother doesn't meet the standard," Kay explained.

Dora only had time to nod before Lana sailed up in full Grand Dame of Tobias mode. "As I was saying before we were interrupted, Dora," she announced, "I am Lana Corbett."

"That's *my* grandmother," Nell said to Kay, her tone adding *See what I mean about grandmothers?*, then peeled away from the group.

"We are gratified that you have forgone the civilization of New York to visit Tobias," Lana said to Dora, either not attuned to the emotions swirling around her or not caring. "But, really, to ask Dora Aaronson to execute a mural in such a pitiful—"

"Bliss House looks magnificent." Dora cut across Lana's words like a scalpel. "And I'm happy to be involved. Although my contribution won't—"

"Now, now, no details, Dora," Miss Trudi interrupted equally effectively. "For any discussion in detail, we need to call an official committee meeting, isn't that right, Steve?"

"I suppose, although—"

"You are absolutely correct, Steve. Our guests must depart now so that we can conduct committee business. There will be a reception for Dora later, allowing everyone to say hello at leisure. Lana, you said you might consider doing something to help Bliss House now that you have returned from your travels. A gathering at Corbett House next week for Dora would be a wonderful contribution."

"A select group would be best, so as not to overwhelm Dora."

In other words, so as not to let the riff-raff into Corbett House, Rob thought.

"Nonsense." Miss Trudi brushed aside Lana's objection. "Everyone will want to come. Saturday about seven. That should suit."

Before Lana could protest, multiple voices were agreeing as they headed out the door. Miss Trudi cleared the room of everyone except the committee and the two Aaronsons in less time than Rob could have believed. No wonder he hadn't stood a chance with his first strategy of staying away from Kay. Pitted against Miss Trudi's stealth efficiency it was no contest.

"Now that we're down to the committee…" Steve started.

But Miss Trudi wasn't done. "Delay calling the meeting to order for a moment, Steve. The artistic sub-committee requires a brief time to meet and view the mural site. Dora, Kay, please come with me."

She herded them out. Into the silence left in their wake, Max asked, "Do we *have* an artistic sub-committee?"

"Not that I know of," Steve said.

"So what was that all about?" Suz asked.

They all looked at him.

Rob had a damned good idea, but he wasn't going to share Kay's family strains. "You think I'm in on Miss Trudi's Machiavellian twists and turns?"

"If anyone knows what's going on it would be you," Steve said. "Whatever Miss Trudi's up to, it has to do with Kay. And you two have been joined at the hip since … well, since you joined at the lips that first day."

Rob had no inclination to join his friends' laughter.

"And now you're going to help her with the puppies when they come," Annette said. "I'm glad you're together. You're a good fit."

"We're not together. And we don't fit."

Sliding into her slick, tight heat ... Her legs wrapped around him. Later, her head tucked against his neck, his arm around her shoulder. The peace, the rightness...

He jerked his mind back to this moment. "Kay's—Emotions push her decisions one way or the other. I don't operate that way."

"No, you've always had a lot of common sense," Annette said. Somehow it didn't sound complimentary.

"Right. You've got the sense," Suz said—and he was *sure* that wasn't entirely complimentary. "And Kay has the feelings, the emotions, the—"

"Sensibility," Annette supplied. She and Suz exchanged a look.

"Sense and sensibility," Suz said with triumph.

Rob rubbed at his forehead. "What the hell are you talking about?"

"Chick flick," Max said.

Steve was nodding. "Oh, yeah. I had to watch that one when I lost the coin toss for movie night. *Sense and Sensibility.*"

"It's a wonderful movie based on a Jane Austen book," Annette said. "And it perfectly describes you and Kay."

Before Rob could refute that, Steve hooted. "Hey, I've got a better movie—forget *Sense and Sensibility.* Their movie should be *Clash of the Titans.*"

Rob was saved from responding when Miss Trudi's front door opened.

"It's all settled," Miss Trudi announced, leading Dora Aaronson in. "Kay's going to assist her grandmother with the mural. It's going to be magnificent. Now, Fran, Dora would like to hear more about the gardens."

Everyone except Rob clustered around Dora. He waited, but Kay didn't return. So he went in search of her.

She wasn't anywhere in the small garden around Miss Trudi's quarters. He walked across to Bliss House.

Inside the empty tearoom Kay stood staring at the blank wall she'd selected for the mural.

"Are you okay?"

"I ... I agreed to fill in any painting Dora can't do."

One good thing about Dora's arrival, it had pushed them past the worst of the awkwardness this morning.

"I heard."

"I showed Dora the wall, and she said it was a good choice because none of the windows give a view of it, which means no sunlight can hit it. And then ... and then..." She shook her head. He wished Kay's wide eyes and pale face weren't so zombie-like. "One minute I was talking about capturing an impression of the gardens rather than strict representation, the next Miss Trudi was showing Dora a copy of the sketches I'd done."

"That sounds like Miss Trudi. She has her ways and nobody knows what they are."

Kay nodded absently. "We were discussing the surface, and how one more base coat added now would allow work to start as soon as tomorrow. And then I heard myself agreeing that after Dora paints as much as her hands allow, I'll layer in details."

"That'll be good—great for Bliss House."

"I suppose so."

"And it could be good for you, too. It'll give you a chance to be with your grandmother, work things out. That's good."

She brought her gaze to his face. "I don't know if it is or not."

She looked so lost that he naturally took her into his arms. And naturally didn't stop there.

He smoothed her hair, knowing it was an invitation, a request, when he shouldn't be asking. He should be giving her time and space...

She accepted, tipping her head back. He kissed her.

Her taste had something he couldn't define. Some chemical that invaded his blood stream and exploded through it.

She was holding onto him, not trying to gain space but to eliminate it.

Closer, he needed her closer.

Two steps and she was against the wall, freeing his hands to touch and explore. Those hands of hers, those quick, clever hands of hers, had his shirt open to his waist and stroked across his chest, trailing those electrical sensations.

He caught her hip in one hand, wadding the cotton material of her skirt in his fingers. And he felt her cool, smooth skin. Her thigh, then a lace-trimmed edge of panties.

The heat beyond that lace.

He bent, got his knees between hers and straightened, urging her legs apart, his hand now gripping her hip under the panties. She expanded the motion, wrapping her legs around him, shifting to welcome him.

He would fit in her, as she fit so wonderfully around him.

She felt like heaven and sin and home.

He edged his fingers around, seeking her heat.

"Rob." Her breath fanned his ear, accelerant on the flame.

Beyond the soft yielding of her breasts, he felt the tightened points against his flesh, responding to him as she had in the boat, as she had last night.

The jolt of his own thought sucked away the oxygen.

As she had in the boat, as she had last night.

Not half an hour ago he'd been thinking how vulnerable she was after all the emotional turmoil of these past twenty-four hours. What sort of ass added to that this way?

They hadn't settled anything. Everything that had made her cry, made her sick this morning still rested between them.

He dropped his forehead against hers, searching for control.

"Kay, We can't…"

"We could go to the Hollands'…"

He closed his eyes. A little longer, a little more, and he would have taken her—here, at the Hollands', on the steps of Town Hall.

"That's not a good idea. The committee's going to meet and—"

"You can skip one meeting. They'll never even miss us."

Yes, they would, and they would draw their own conclusions. But, hell, they'd probably approve. That wasn't what stopped him.

Hand on her shoulders, he shifted away from her.

"Your grandmother will miss you. And I ... This doesn't make good sense, Kay."

Abruptly, she stepped to the side, away from his touch.

"Sense." She made it sound far worst than Annette and Suz had.

"Kay, you have got to know how much I—Last night was—" He wouldn't give her platitudes and his brain short-circuited in an effort to find the right description. "But after this morning—"

"Yes. After this morning. It's a good thing you came to your senses."

"Kay—"

But she'd walked out.

And letting her go did make sense, even if it hurt like hell.

CHAPTER TWENTY-ONE

MISS TRUDI CAUGHT him at the compost bin again the next afternoon.

He should have stuck it out longer sitting on the roof with his legal pad and pen. Miss Trudi wouldn't have tracked him down there.

But the damned blank page had annoyed him so much he'd opted for physical labor. Maybe if he wore out his body, his mind would work again.

He had two of the posts in and was working on the third, his brain still completely AWOL, when Annette's car pulled up and Miss Trudi got out of the passenger side.

Annette gave a happy wave after depositing that ticking bomb, and drove off.

Miss Trudi stood, hands clasped before her, surveying the back of his childhood home.

"Your parents were such lovely people. I can almost see them sitting on the porch there. I remember the four of you on the lake in that large sailboat you had then, a lovely family, thoroughly enjoying each other's company."

He gave the post a good whack.

"Yes, indeed, there should be more of that. Having experienced such a life, however, is not the only path to an appreciation of it. Some who have never experienced it still have a great capacity to appreciate, to long for, and most of all to give that sort of love."

Whack. "No way, Miss Trudi."

"I beg your pardon?"

"Begging my pardon is exactly what you should be doing, but I doubt you mean it. I saw your fine hand pulling strings that pushed Steve and Annette, then Max and Suz together. I'm not saying that wasn't right for them—it seems to be working out okay."

"Okay," she repeated in a twinkling murmur. "Oh, yes, they do seem to be working out *okay*, as you say."

"All right, better than okay, but they knew each other. It's great for them. But it's not for me. I can see what you have in mind, and it's not—" He stopped. He wasn't telling anyone, and certainly not Miss Trudi, what was happening between him and Kay. "The timing sucks and even if I were looking for someone, we're all wrong for each other."

"Putting aside why you might be wrong for her, I would be interested to hear why you believe Kay is wrong for you."

Because she couldn't believe in the hardest thing he'd ever had to do in his life.

He didn't blame her, not after what she'd gone through as a kid. But it didn't change what he had to do.

"Because she's all over the place, scattered."

"Consider, Rob, that for all the diversity in her jobs, they are unified by their creativity."

"Look, Miss Trudi, I tried with a woman I thought was on the same page with me and that didn't work. No way is it going to work with Kay. There's no … no logic to it."

She snorted. Miss Trudi Bliss, who had always exhibited a certain kind of elegance—rough elegance maybe, idiosyncratic elegance absolutely, yet still a kind of elegance—snorted most inelegantly.

"Logic has been elevated to a status it does not deserve. It is all very well when it is maintained among a range of tools. It loses its efficacy when it is raised as the sole ruler."

"Logic is all I have to work with, Miss Trudi."

Her bulldog expression softened in a blink. "Oh, Rob, you have so much more, so very much more."

KAY AND DORA worked in an air-conditioned plastic cocoon.

Max's men had finished the major work in the tearoom and kitchen, but continued elsewhere inside. That meant dust, which threatened the mural.

Dora suggested tweaks of the design, all good suggestions.

They used an overhead projector to display Kay's sketch on the wall and Kay traced it lightly with pencil. Kay had made several other copies of the sketches and they experimented with colors, agreeing to a combination of their ideas.

Under Dora's direction, the workmen constructed a two-layer wall of thick plastic sheeting, sealed inside and out with tape, that curved out three feet from the wall. It eliminated most of the dust and let in light. A free-standing air-conditioner and filter kept them from sweltering and captured more dust. The only opening from their plastic room was a sort of enclosed vestibule where they did their best to leave the dust on their way in and the paint on their way out.

These conditions were far from ideal, yet to Kay's surprise, they found a working rhythm almost immediately.

Dora would lay in the forms and colors that would be the backbone of the mural, then, while she moved on to another area, Kay would do the details.

It was strange watching her grandmother's motion. Not the short, meticulous brush strokes Kay remembered watching for hours on end as a child, but a more open movement, awkward and tentative.

What surprised Kay—astonished her—was that Dora began to talk while they worked. She had never known her grandmother to talk while she painted. But she didn't question it. At least it kept some of her mind off Rob.

It started that first afternoon, when Kay began filling in detail at Dora's instruction.

They had chosen a corner likely to be hidden by a table for their first work, but Kay's hand still trembled, its unsteadiness exaggerated by the time it reached the tip of the brush she'd dipped into paint.

"That dark chromium green is a good choice for the leaf veining,"

Dora said. Then, in a subject change Kay suspected was meant to prove she wouldn't micromanage Kay's work, she added, "These young people heading this renovation are an impressive group."

"They are." Kay expelled a breath, and stroked the brush up the center of the leaf, lightening the color as it reached the tip. "They've pulled this Bliss House project together in an amazingly short amount of time."

Kay added feathery strokes out from the center.

"It already looks so much better than I ever remember it."

"Tobias must have changed a lot since you left."

Her grandmother chuckled. "The houses look smaller and the trees bigger. Ah, yes. Deep cobalt green does well for that shadow under the leaf. Very nice. When I lived here the library was in a ramshackle old house…"

And in the neutral subject of Tobias and Bliss House—Dora's memories and Kay's recent education—they found a rhythm to talk, to work, to be together in their plastic cocoon.

ROB ARRANGED TO be outside Bliss House's back door when Kay emerged from her first day of painting with her grandmother.

He arranged it by hanging around out there for the better part of three hours.

He knew all the reasons—solid, *logical* reasons—their relationship shouldn't go anywhere. Shouldn't have gotten this far. But put her in his vicinity, and it was like his experiment with homemade gunpowder—unpredictable and likely to singe.

So the logical answer was to stay away … Yet here he was.

Kay looked pale. She and Dora came down the stairs together, and yet with a hesitation that said they didn't know what came next when they reached the bottom. Kay saw him, then looked away, her expressive face impassive and unreadable.

For a second he thought a brick had landed on his chest. Nope. It was all inside.

Before Rob could move forward, Eric, one of the young men on Max's construction crew, stepped in front of Kay. He'd seemed to come out of nowhere to Rob's way of thinking, but then Rob hadn't seen anything but Kay.

"Hey, I hear your dog is going to have puppies," he said to her. "I'll take one of those puppies."

Kay frowned. "Do you have a house?"

"Apartment."

Her frown deepened. "A fenced yard?"

"No, but I live across from a park where dogs play. So he'd have company."

"You only want a male?"

"Uh." He glanced at Rob, who had joined the group. "No, I used *he* in general, ya know?"

Kay sniffed. The way Rob imagined a dowager empress might sniff. He stifled a chuckle. Not only would Kay not be amused at his chuckling, but if Eric laughed, his chance at a puppy—already on shaky ground—was a goner.

"What about when you're at work?"

"Well, depending on the job, he—or she," Eric added quickly, "could come with."

"To a construction site? With all the ways a dog could get hurt?"

"Be fair, Kay," Rob said. "You found Chester at this construction site. Or, she found you."

Kay's bristles eased slightly. Rob was aware of Dora looking from her granddaughter to him, but he kept his attention on Kay.

"She's an adult dog. And street smart. A puppy wouldn't know all those things." She gave Eric a stern look. "A careful owner wouldn't want his dog to have to learn those things."

"I'd look after the dog real good. I love dogs, and I miss having one."

Kay's attitude softened at that, but Eric left without any promises.

"Planning to call in the FBI to investigate people who want puppies?" Rob asked Kay.

"Not a bad idea," she said with cool politeness. "Do you have any contacts?"

"Sometimes it's hard to find homes for puppies. Especially mixed breed. And you won't be here to—"

"I know." She cut him off. "That's all the more reason to make sure the puppies go to people who won't need to be checked up on after—later."

"I'll check on the puppies after they're settled if you want."

She sucked in a breath, let it out slowly. "Thank you. I'd like that."

She turned away, but he'd seen the sheen in her eyes. So had her grandmother.

"I'd like to invite you—both of you—to dinner at The Toby," he said.

"No thank you, Rob, I'm going to pick up Chester from Miss Trudi, have a sandwich, catch up on projects for the opening and crash," Kay said.

She didn't meet his eyes.

Worse, he realized, he was being watched by Kay's grandmother.

"Thank you for your offer," Dora said with a small smile. "But I will likely follow a similar regimen to Kay's. Although I would like to take you up on your invitation another night."

The smile didn't fool him. The menu that night would be Grilled Rob.

"DID YOU SEE this?" Dora asked Kay the next morning.

How could she have missed it? A bushel basket filled with chocolates sort of stood out in their plastic room. Just the scent could put you on a chocolate high.

"Terrific, isn't it?" Kay enthused. "Card says it's from the committee to help stir our creativity."

"How lovely." The rustle of a wrapper came from behind her. "Trudi tells me that young man who came by yesterday evening, the one you arrived with at Trudi's, has been your tour guide around

Tobias these past weeks. Rob Dalton, is that his name?" Dora asked. As if she didn't know. At least she couldn't know the basket must have come from Rob, since he and Nell were the only ones she'd told about Dora eating chocolate while painting.

Kay didn't look up from adding highlights to golden tulips. "Yes."

"He's a very attractive young man."

"Yes."

"Not at all like Barry."

That did get Kay to look up. "You know Barry?"

"Slightly. He has been part of your parents' set for some time and I ... When your engagement was announced I was particularly interested."

"Oh." She had wondered if Dora might show up at the wedding— a speculation she had banished as soon as it popped up. "Knowing how you feel about keeping commitments, you probably disapproved of my breaking the engagement as much as Mother and Father did."

"To the contrary. I thoroughly approved of your calling off that wedding. You would not have won your parents' love by marrying a man they like, and you would have been miserable."

Kay gawked at her grandmother, but Dora continued to work on a background lilac bush in that awkward, tentative movement she now had.

Finally, Dora spoke again. "I know your parents, and I know you, at least I knew you as a girl." There was such sadness in her voice that Kay blinked at the sting behind her own eyes. "I made it my business to know more about your Barry, too."

"He's a good guy," Kay said automatically.

"He's the best of your parents' set," Dora said. Kay realized that was an entirely different thing from "good."

She couldn't talk about this anymore. Not and keep working.

"Well," she said brightly. "Nothing like their set here in Tobias."

"Oh, I believe Lana Corbett might try her best to qualify."

Their eyes met, and for a moment connected with that sympathy of understanding they'd had all during Kay's childhood.

Kay broke the look first. "It must have been a shock to leave Tobias and go to New York the first time. What was that like?" she asked.

"Amazing, terrifying."

Dora not only accepted Kay's change of subject, she launched into an entertaining account of a starry-eyed girl from Wisconsin stumbling into the art scene of Greenwich Village. And of first finding the studio that Kay had known so well as a child.

"By the time you came along I owned it and it had been renovated—rebuilt, really," Dora said. "But when I first rented it ... oh, my. Paul said it made a foxhole look like five-star accommodations."

"Paul?"

Dora's brush stopped as she turned to Kay. "Your grandfather, dear. Paul Pelten."

"Oh. Of course." Although there was no "of course" about it. Kay had rarely heard Dora refer to the father of her son.

"We had a wonderful time. We lived the most Bohemian existence." Her eyes twinkled. "Now, don't get any ideas about orgies or anything. I was blessed in Paul. What's that song? I was a one-man woman who found my one-woman man. Not that we didn't have opportunities."

She laughed, a sound rich with memory and love.

"I've never heard you tell those stories, Dora."

Her grandmother gave her a considering look. "No, I don't suppose you have. He was gone long before you were thought of."

But the pain hadn't been gone—Kay understood that in Dora's answer. How long did it take to get over losing the man you love?

"What was he like?" she asked simply.

And her grandmother gave Kay her first real introduction to the man Dora Aaronson had loved.

CHAPTER TWENTY-TWO

ROB WAS WAITING at the end of the driveway when Kay brought Chester out for her walk that evening.

Chester wagged her tail and pranced out the length of the leash to greet him. It was the warmest welcome she'd ever given him, the traitor.

"Thank you for the chocolates," Kay said.

"The committee—"

"Rob, aren't you the man who means what he says?"

He expelled a breath, bending to pet Chester. "Actually, I said I think before I speak. You've put a few dents in that, but you're welcome. I'll go if you want, but I've missed our walks."

This was dangerous.

Yet there were things she'd wanted to talk to somebody about. She could call her friends, she supposed. But she knew what they would say before she called them.

The small group in her parents' camp would tell her to get her butt back to New York, stop being an idiot and patch it up with Barry.

The majority would tell her to get her butt back to New York, stop being an idiot, and forget her parents and Barry.

She didn't know what Rob would say, and that was his value. That and when it came to being in a camp, she knew he was in hers. Odd to feel this way when she hadn't sorted out any of her emotions about him.

"You can walk with us with a few conditions. First, no touching." *Because she might disintegrate if he touched her again without following through on it.* He held his hands up in surrender. "Second, I get to ask the questions."

"Okay."

"Okay, then."

She related what Dora had told her about Paul Pelten and the fact that it was the first time Kay had heard about her grandfather.

Then they walked three blocks in silence, the day's warmth cooling quickly toward night. The leaves on the arching branches still green and full overhead, yet with a slight whiff of dryness that spoke of autumn coming. Of weeks passing. Of departures drawing nearer.

It made her think back to the beginning. When Miss Trudi had walked in to the frenzy of the shoot with this broad-shouldered island of calm.

"Do you ever regret not taking me up on my offer to make the most of those thirteen hours that first night?" she asked.

"No, because you would have regretted it. You'd already kissed me and regretted the first time, during the shoot."

"I did *not*." Indignant, she stopped and faced him. "You wasted all that time, and now things are so complicated, but I was willing to explore from the start."

"Bull." He made it a level challenge. A challenge to be as truthful as he'd been.

She drew in a steadying breath then let it out in a stream. "Maybe you're right. You're not like the men I've known." He wanted honest, that's what he was going to get. "You're considerate, solid, responsible, not the least boastful, but sure of yourself. It's unnerving."

"What the hell kind of men have you known?"

She didn't answer directly. "Rob, you've told me about your divorce. I want to tell you about my engagement. About why I broke it off."

"Okay." Under his level tone she heard surprise, and tension.

"When I say why I broke it off, I mean what I've realized recently about why I'd broken it off. At the time it was gut instinct." She smiled slightly. "Literally gut instinct. I kept getting an upset stomach. Dealing with the wedding stuff I was fine, but when Barry showed up, or I thought about him and about living with him, I'd run for the john. I knew I couldn't go through with it. He truly is a decent person. So it had to be me. That's what I've worked out over the past months—*what about me.*"

She stopped to let Chester inspect the post of a stop sign.

"It wasn't Barry's love I was after when we got engaged, it was my parents'. I've spent most of my life trying to get them to love me."

It was why she'd let Barry take over the apartment when he came back from South America. At some level she'd recognized that she'd used him.

Rob reached for her, but she stepped back.

He swore. "Sorry. I know I promised. But ... what the hell is their problem?"

"I get to ask the questions, remember? Besides, I'm working on my problems, not theirs. That is one thing I've learned. And my problem was wanting more than they had to give. Love, attention, time. For a long time Dora filled that gap. But in the month before she found out about the forgeries, she'd been distracted, not herself. I knew she was having medical tests, but it didn't sink in ... It must have been when she received the diagnosis about her hands, had to face that painting in the Dora Aaronson style would become ever more difficult until it became impossible.

"Anyway, when the crisis hit, I already felt adrift. And then my parents came to me—came to *me*—to ask Dora to protect Father. They needed me. I was important to them. I could do something that would gain their attention and gratitude. And Dora would surely say yes, because she'd always been my rock, my shelter.

"But Dora said no."

She bent and stroked Chester's head, finding comfort in the contact.

"I can't even describe how devastated I was. I had failed. I was even less to my parents than before, because I had failed. What good was all the time I'd spent with Dora if I couldn't get her to do what I wanted? That was their viewpoint. And I ... I was so angry at Dora.

Because she'd kept me from winning my parents' love."

"But—"

"Yeah, I know it's not logical. But that's how I felt. Besides, I was a kid. And I hadn't realized any of the underlying stuff. Neither did any of the therapists my parents sent me to." He raised a questioning eyebrow, and she shrugged. "It was the thing to do in my parents' circle."

They'd returned to the Hollands' block. Twilight's shadows had lengthened into night and streetlights popped on like miniature full moons.

She let out a long breath, not entirely steady. Rob faced her, his eyes dark and hidden by the shadows.

She wished she hadn't made that no-touching edict.

"And that brings me back to Barry," she said. "See, he was part of their group. One of their favorites. And somewhere deep down I thought that if I married Barry, it would make them love me, too, so we would turn into a real family. That's what I thought about when I said yes to Barry's proposal. And I kept trying to make it right, to make it work. But my gut told me that even marrying Barry wouldn't make a real family of the Aaronsons. And I finally listened to it."

Silence, along with the shadows, closed around them.

"End of story," she said.

"Do you know what an amazing woman you are, Kay Aaronson?"

"No, I—"

"Amazing." He overrode her. "And all the more amazing because you did it yourself—you raised yourself."

He reached for her then, and she had no strength to remind him of the rules. His palm smoothed her hair, stopping to cup the back of her head. He closed the space between them. He was going to kiss her. He was...

His lips touched her forehead.

Her heart pounded so hard he had to hear it, feel it. If he kissed her now, really kissed her...

He stepped back.

"Good night, Kay."

He got in his car and drove off, and still she stood there, with patient Chester sitting beside her.

"DORA, I WANT to tell you something." Without looking up from her work on peony petals, Kay felt her grandmother's sharp attention.

They had worked silently all morning. Kay's brain felt mushy and foggy, the way it could after a crying jag. But she hadn't cried.

Last night she'd gone inside and worked like a fiend. She'd drafted news releases, written four crafters' profiles, gathered media outlet addresses on the Internet, listed tasks to be done, made up a schedule, pulled together a roster of volunteers, roughed out a brochure layout, and begun a proposal for workshops and classes to be taught at Bliss House. Filmmaking, mobile-making, and even sculpting among others. The sky had started to lighten before she fell asleep with her head on the desk.

At least she hadn't cried.

"I want to tell you about a conversation I had last night."

Before her grandmother could respond, Kay launched into an account of her discussion with Rob. It took quite a while because there were detours to fill in Dora about Rob's background, his idiotic ex, and how Rob and she had worked together these past weeks. The one thing she didn't tell her grandmother was what Rob intended to do when he returned to Chicago.

In all the talking, she kept coming back to her realizations about her family and herself.

"You've become a very wise woman, Kay."

"I'm not so sure about that." Would a wise woman have gotten engaged to Barry in the first place? Would a wise woman have that emotional blender going this hard? "But I have a question for you, Dora. And I hope you'll give me an honest answer."

"I will do my best."

Kay almost smiled. The way Dora said that reminded her of Rob.

That make-a-promise-and-stick-to-it attitude.

"Did you love Father?"

"Oh, Kay, yes, I loved him. I love him now, with all my heart. As you love your parents. It did not—does not—blind me to who he is. Or you to who he and your mother are. The difference is, I bear responsibility for who Ronald is, and you do not." She sighed and put down the brush, using her other hand to gently unbend the fingers that had held it. "Kay, I need to tell you things that perhaps I should have told you a long time ago. So you can understand."

"I do understand. I—"

"You need to listen, Kay."

Kay put down her brush, too.

"I was very much in love with your grandfather. I told you how we met, but not about how Paul courted me. He was a rich, worldly man, and I was a poor, struggling artist barely into womanhood. He knew about my strict upbringing, and he never pressed me. But I loved him." She smiled, and in that moment Kay saw the young woman her grandmother had been, and she understood why Paul had lost his heart to her. "I shocked him and myself when I couldn't take it any longer and threw myself at him. Never has a woman been caught so well."

Her face went misty with reminiscence.

"When I discovered I was pregnant," Dora said, "he asked me to marry him. I first said no. I had my pride after all—the Aaronson pride—and I didn't want him to marry me only because I was carrying his child. I wanted him to marry me for me. He said he was, but…"

She shook her head. "He immediately moved in to my studio—this man whose family owned a half dozen homes, settled in to heating soup on one burner in that ramshackle studio. He said someone had to look out for me, and he kept asking me to marry him. After a month I said yes. But it was too late. He died two days before we were to be married."

Kay had always known Paul Pelten died before her father's birth, but the topic was rarely discussed.

"You know he fought in World War II? He was hit by shrapnel.

But he insisted they patch him up and he went back to his unit. A friend of his told me about that at Paul's funeral. They left a lot of shrapnel in him. And the doctors said it must have traveled to his heart.

"One morning he just didn't wake up. I was five months pregnant."

"Oh, Dora."

"Don't feel sorry for me, Kay. You're the one I feel sorry for. You never had a chance to know him, to be loved by him. And neither did your father. But Paul did his best for us. He made a will, dated the day I told him I was pregnant, with a trust for me and our baby."

She pushed her hair off her face with the back of her hand.

"I don't remember those last months of my pregnancy. I don't remember the birth of my only child. I was drowning in grief. I was letting myself drown in it. Your father wasn't neglected—not then, not ever. Paul had seen to that. And I loved him. How could I not? He was part of Paul. Ronald was given everything I could give him. Everything except rules and the self-respect they bring." She looked straight at Kay as if making a confession. "He had everything except my time and my attention. That I gave to painting. It was my salvation. Those early years of painting like the possessed made my career. But it cost my son. And that is my failure.

"We have never really known each other, Ronald and I. After he married and became so involved in your mother's circle, we rarely saw each other. Until you were born.

"You brought me back to the realm of the human, where I saw Ronald's weakness all the more clearly."

A niggle of the familiarity Kay had felt that last day of the shoot, when Brice had come back and expected to have everything the way he wanted, surfaced. She'd thought Brice's ego was like a blindfold, keeping him from seeing anything else around him. Of course it had been familiar, she'd grown up with a man just like that.

"Oh, Kay, sweetheart," her grandmother said, "I should have fought for you. And that's my shame and my regret."

CHAPTER TWENTY-THREE

FROM EVERY OBJECTIVE standpoint the reception at Corbett House for Dora Aaronson was a roaring success.

Lana Corbett's usual idea of entertaining lacked the basic ingredients of fun and warmth, but there were so many excited people here waiting to meet the famous artist that it boosted the conviviality factor ten-fold from past gatherings. Plus, the guest of honor did a lot to make the atmosphere festive.

Dora dazzled the reporters Kay had tempted here with news releases. She took every opportunity, from what Rob heard, to talk up Bliss House, the mural, and the opening. He knew Kay had hoped for TV, but everyone else was wildly impressed that the *Tobias Record*'s editor was joined by reporters from Milwaukee and Madison papers.

But to Rob all that was peripheral.

He'd arrived early at Corbett House, but Kay was already there, at the far end of the living room, assisting the photographer from the *Record* to get shots of Miss Trudi and Dora. Her head came up and their gazes met for an instant, then she turned away.

He'd stayed away since then. Although he couldn't seem to do anything about the direction of his eyes.

What was that Kay had told him about framing a shot? How the human eye could sort out the extraneous material to focus on the important, but the director had to do it for the camera. Well, either he had an extremely efficient editor focusing his views or everything except Kay was extraneous.

He'd thought that if he gave her time, her first reaction to his decision about his career would ease and they could talk about it. She would see that what he planned to do was right.

When she said she got to ask the questions during their walk the other night, he'd hoped she would ask about his decision. But she hadn't brought it up at all. She wouldn't talk about it, yet it remained there, solid and thick, between them.

"Here, have some punch," Fran ordered, materializing at his elbow. "At least that will get your arms uncrossed while you stand here staring at Kay like a thundercloud."

He looked down at her. "I'm not."

"Yes, you are. I'm worried about you. Rob. I've tried to give you privacy this summer, time to figure out what went wrong with Janice. But that's not what I'm worried about now. You're not going to mess this up with Kay, are you? Just because she's not in lock-step with you like Janice seemed to be doesn't mean you're not good together—in fact, she's just what you need."

Need … Yeah, he needed Kay. That didn't mean he could have her.

Fran was unfazed by his silence.

"I was concerned at the start, concerned you'd get hurt when she went back to New York. But … Do you know Kay doesn't have a place to live in New York?"

He opened his mouth, but had no chance to speak.

"Don't tell me that means she's not organized, doesn't think ahead. It could also mean she's totally organized and thinking ahead beautifully … if she's not interested in returning to New York."

MONEY CAME IN from one of the grants Max and Steve had obtained in the spring. Rob spent the morning on the Bliss House budget. Even with the grant, the numbers weren't great, but they were logical, and the work was familiar, straight-forward, uncomplicated.

Besides, he needed to have the finances up to date for whoever picked up this job when he left, which would be soon.

He transferred money to reimburse Trevetti Building and drove to

Bliss House to deliver the news. Max and Suz had put the business out on a limb for this project and he wanted them to have the money as soon as possible.

He found them and their foreman, Lenny, discussing how much renovation of the turret exterior had to be done now and how much could possibly wait.

After his report, Max and Lenny happily expanded their horizons on repairs to the turret.

Rob went the back way to his car. Through the tearoom window he saw Dora, but not Kay.

"She is not here today," Miss Trudi said.

He jerked around. He hadn't heard her behind him. "Miss Trudi."

"She called Dora this morning to say she was remaining at home because Chester is acting strange and her temperature had dropped yesterday. Apparently, such a drop—"

"I know. The puppies are supposed to come twenty-four hours later. But it's earlier than Allison thought. Did she say ... How's she holding up?"

"I should image Chester is—"

"Kay."

"Oh, you were inquiring about Kay?" The woman's face was prac- tically saintly in its innocence. "I have no idea, my dear. No idea at all. Now, I must get on with my duties."

Without looking at him again, she proceeded into Bliss House.

He'd promised to help with Chester. He wasn't going back on that. Whether Kay wanted him there or not.

KAY OPENED THE door.

"Oh, Rob." She looked relieved, and that eased one knot in his gut. "I was going to call, but I didn't want to leave her."

His arms encircled her without any thinking involved.

"How is she?" He meant, *how are you?*

"I don't know. It seems to be taking forever. I haven't called Dr.

Maclaine yet, but I was about to."

She had turned toward the hallway. With effort, he released her and followed to the sunroom.

The dog wasn't in the whelping box that Max's foreman Lenny had built. Towels were scrunched on the floor with Chester lying stretched full out with her nose between her paws. Rob thought he recognized one of Kay's black t-shirts in the impromptu bedding.

The dog's eyes followed Kay with pathetic confusion. Abruptly she raised her head and started panting.

"She's been doing this for more than an hour. She keeps changing position, then panting, then pacing. And it's so early."

"That date was a guess, Allison told us that. And this is all part of labor. Remember what the book said."

Kay picked up one of the dog encyclopedias lying open on the desk, but didn't look at the pages. "I know, I know. But—God, there's got to be something we can do." She dropped to her knees with the book in her lap and stroked the dog's head.

"What about that raspberry tea you got. You said it's supposed to relieve stress. And—"

"And strengthen contractions and help lactation. That's a great idea. Would you make it?"

"Sure." He could boil water.

Returning with the tea, he told her, "I called Allison, to let her know. She says it sounds like we're doing everything we can do."

Which basically was nothing. Allison had also said they should stand back and let Chester handle it. Rob didn't say that to Kay.

Chester turned away from the tea Kay offered her, got up and circled once, twice, three times. Then settled down again on the towels.

"The book says Chester should be getting into the whelping box." Kay chewed on her lip, her fingers tapping the bowl of cooled tea.

"Maybe Chester didn't read the book."

"Real funny, Dalton. Chester didn't read the ... Oh. Oh!"

Chester got up, stepped delicately into the whelping box, laid down on her side, gave a sort of deep pant, and the birthing started.

Kay flipped forward two pages in the book, made more difficult by the plastic gloves she and Rob had donned. "Here. The book says the placental material should be dark green or purplish and odorless."

"It's odorless. And that's—"

"What does that mean—*dark* green or purplish? How can it be both? Why aren't they specific? Chromium green oxide or hunter hue?"

"I'd call it dark green, Kay."

"You really think it's dark green?"

"Yes. And I'm the guy who thinks before he—"

He stopped. They both did.

"Oh, my God," she breathed. "There's the puppy."

They grinned at each other like fools. She had tears in her eyes and he couldn't swear he didn't.

"And she's doing what the book said she'd do," he said. "She's a great mother."

"Of course she is. The best."

The euphoria didn't last.

With the puppy stumbling through its first steps, more placental material appeared, but no puppy. Chester strained, panted, pushed, and still no puppy.

"Please call Allison again," Kay said, totally calm now.

The vet told them to bring Chester and the new puppy in. Right away.

Rob carried Chester, wrapped in a blanket, to the car. Kay, with the solitary puppy in a clean towel on her lap, sat on a narrow strip of the back seat next to Chester, talking quietly, as he drove and vowed to rip a strip off Steve for letting Tobias have such damned rough streets.

Allison shooed him and Kay out of the treatment area.

"We're going to supplement her calcium to help her deliver, Kay," she said. "It's basically inducing labor with an injection. Give the puppy to Hannah, and we'll let you know as soon as we know anything. Now we need to do our jobs."

Kay walked out with him, but she stopped and faced the door that closed behind them.

"Kay, they're going to take care of her. It'll be okay"

Rob put his arms around her and pulled her to him, wrapping his warmth around her chilled shoulders. He moved chairs directly across the hall from the door. Another assistant suggested they move to the waiting room. He told her it wasn't happening.

Kay's fingers tapped against her thigh. He took her hand, their fingers interlocking, and she calmed. They talked. Disjointed comments about Bliss House, the opening, the mural.

Allison came out. Kay half stood, but Allison gestured for her to sit. "Everything's going fine so far. She's had another puppy and it went well. We're going to give her some privacy and we'll keep checking on her."

She and the assistant went to other examination rooms. One or the other returned to Chester's room every few minutes. Each time Allison passed, she said everything was fine, and Kay nodded numbly.

After more than two hours, Allison opened the door of Chester's room.

"Kay and Rob, Chester has six healthy pups, and everyone seems fine." Rob let out a restrained whoop.

"She's ... she's okay?" Kay asked.

"She's fine. I'm going to keep her overnight for observation, but she and the puppies should be able to go home tomorrow. Do you want to see her before you leave?"

KAY TOOK ANOTHER load of towels out of the dryer and started folding.

Today had been the most peculiar blend of fear, elation, grossness, and beauty.

When she'd seen Chester with the pudgy, stumbling blurs of fur, she'd had the insane urge to burst into song and tears simultaneously. Chester, for the first time in their brief partnership, had largely ignored her. Chester had more important things—six of them—to worry about.

Rob had brought her back to the Hollands' and pitched in helping her clean the sunroom and prepare the whelping box for the next day when Chester and the puppies came home.

Home.

Except this wasn't Chester's home. Or hers. No matter how comfortable she'd come to feel in this old house.

She'd have to think about that eventually. She'd have to think about a lot of things eventually.

With the towels folded, she flopped down on the sunroom sofa next to Rob, but careful not to brush against his side.

"I am dying for a shower. But I can't move yet. Lord, after this, it's going to be easy to be a mother—at least babies usually come one at a time." He rolled his head toward her, and raised his eyebrows. "What?"

"That sounded pretty positive for someone who doesn't want a family."

"I never said I didn't want a family. I said my biological clock hadn't been wound yet."

Questions and comments pinged between them without a word being spoken.

"Look, Kay—"

"Rob, can we…" She'd interrupted, but now she didn't know what she wanted to say. "I don't know how to say this. I just know you're leaving, then I'm leaving, and after that … But until we leave, we're both here. Now."

Heat flared in his eyes at that final word. But his tone was calm. "Why don't you go take a shower and I'll get some food together."

And then we'll talk.

It hung in the air between them, but she wasn't ready to pull it down and examine it. Not yet.

WRAPPED IN A terry cloth robe and turban, Kay came out of the bathroom to find Rob sitting on the bed with a tray of two kinds of cheese and crackers, a cut up apple, two wine glasses and a bottle in ice. The ice was in the Green Bay Packers cookie jar from the top of the refrigerator.

He held out one of the glasses. "If this isn't enough, we'll get delivery."

Trying to calm that *ba-BAM* cadence of her heart, she took the glass. He filled it, then his own. Gingerly, she sat on the edge of the bed.

He raised his glass in a toast. "Until."

She understood. A toast to finding a way to be together for now, to taking this time they had until they left.

"Until." She touched her glass to his.

"White or orange?"

"What?"

"Cheese." He gestured with the knife to the cheese board.

She laughed, releasing nerves and fear, knowing that had been his intention and grateful for it.

They settled more comfortably on opposite sides of the bed, eating the cheese and crackers, drinking the dry white wine and talking about how they would care for the puppies, especially for these first few vital days.

The wine was gone and the tray mostly crumbs when Kay shifted on the bed and her turban tumbled off. She automatically put her hands to her hair, mostly dry now and no doubt sticking out to rival a punk rocker's.

Rob's hand covered hers, smoothing over her hair, down to the back of her neck. Leaning across the bed, he kissed her. His tongue plunged into her mouth, questing without any hint of question.

He eased back, pausing to kiss her again, lightly, then sat straight, looking into her eyes.

She didn't know what he saw there, she didn't know what she felt. Except that she wanted him. She wanted this, their *until*.

He put the tray on the floor, then came back to her. Kissing her the same way from the same angle. She touched his face, and as if that had supplied some power he'd been awaiting, the kiss changed, deepened. He kissed down her neck, spreading the robe open, pushing it back over her shoulders.

She accepted, but only for so long. His clothes got in her way, so she evicted them. Then it was only them.

Her. Rob. Not future. Not past.

She knew what she was getting into this time. She went after it. Inviting the explosions, looking for the heat.

Under her hands, against her skin, inside her body, the contraction and release of his muscles sparked her to life, to lust, to ... No, better not to let that thought in. Not now.

CHAPTER TWENTY-FOUR

THEY BROUGHT CHESTER and the puppies home the next morning.

Rob carried the box with the puppies into the sunroom, while Chester supervised. The dog got right into the whelping box and watched with a seeming frown as he reached for a puppy.

"Maybe you should do this," he said to Kay. "She doesn't look happy, and she didn't look that way when you put the puppies in the box."

"The book did say the fewer people handling the puppies the better the first few days, so they form a strong bond with their mother."

Kay scooped squirming puppies out of the box one by one. Chester greeted each one with licks. When all six—three beige and white, two dark red with white and one light red—were lined up to nurse, she touched each with her nose as if taking inventory, then licked Kay's hand.

"Geez, it's warm in here." Rob wiped his forehead.

"It has to be eighty to ninety degrees for the puppies the first couple weeks. This is only eighty. The heating pad is in the box to improve the temperature there. That way—Where are you going?"

"I'm going to need shorts. Plus, I have some Bliss House duties to attend to. I'll be back in a few hours."

Seeing the questions and doubts in her eyes, he bent to where she was kneeling in front of the whelping box. With his hand curved around her neck, he kissed her, possessive and promising.

By the time he returned—he'd packed toiletries and a few changes of clothes into a gym bag and left a note for Fran—Kay had fallen asleep on the sofa in the sultry sunroom, one arm dangling into the whelping box. Chester could touch her anytime she wanted by lifting her head.

Rob looked at the dog, who paid not the slightest heed to any humans as she nudged one of the darker puppies into position for a tongue-cleaning.

If he moved Kay to the bedroom, out of earshot of the puppies, she'd have his hide.

Rob picked her up. She stirred against him. It shouldn't have turned him on. Shouldn't have made his groin fill and pulse. Her shoulder pushing across his chest for God's sake. How could that have him this close? He closed his eyes, trying for control.

He'd acted without a plan, on impulse. And look what happened.

He could sit on the sofa with her in his lap, but how comfortable was that going to be for either of them. Not comfortable enough to catch up on the sleep they hadn't gotten last night. Not comfortable enough for the long-term togetherness he wasn't willing to forfeit.

No, he had a better idea.

He sat in the wide recliner with her in his arms. Once he was sure Kay hadn't awakened, he levered it as flat as it would go, and stretched out with Kay along his side.

Ah, this was better. Much better.

He slept, and was glad of it. But waking was a lot more fun.

Kay, warm and slightly damp, snuggled beside him. "Mmmm, Rob, you're almost as warm as Chester."

He kissed her forehead. "And you're considerably hotter."

She stretched and twisted into a sinuous curve that traced a line of burgeoning fire wherever it brushed and retreated across his skin. He turned on his side to face her and drew her leg up over his thigh.

"Is that so?" She slid her hand down his chest, burrowing under waistbands to circle a finger around his bellybutton.

"Mmmm. A little lower."

She obliged.

THE NEXT DAY Kay returned to work on the mural. She didn't have any choice if they hoped to be done in time for the previews she'd scheduled.

She worked in bursts while Rob was at the Hollands' house. She dashed to Bliss House, most often taking his car, painted like a fiend, then dashed back.

In between, she fielded calls from the media, wrote emails, made pitches.

Rob helped with all that, plus put together reports and projections on the Bliss House budget, moved money to an account that should earn more interest, and otherwise cleared the decks. He'd also contacted the lawyer he'd talked to in June, and told him to contact the authorities. He did most of that from the Hollands' house so Chester and the puppies had one or both of them within yelping distance at all times.

Neither Rob nor Kay was getting much sleep. That could only partly be blamed on Chester and the puppies.

The sofa had turned out to be less difficult than he'd thought, although the recliner remained their stand-by.

"I'm starting to dream about beds," Kay said on the third morning.

"For sleeping? Or not sleeping?"

"Yes."

He knew just how she felt.

One of the beige and white puppies and the light red one weren't keeping up with their larger siblings, so they held back the others and let those two start nursing first. Chester appeared to approve. She accepted Rob handling the puppies, now, although both he and Kay kept it to a minimum. Chester was totally focused on her litter. And eating.

The third night after bringing the puppies home, Rob returned from a run for Chinese food and placed an unmarked paper bag on the counter.

"What's that?" Kay frowned.

"Kung pao chicken, sweet and sour pork, and a baby monitor, so you can hear whatever's going on in one room, say the sunroom, while you're in another room, say the bedroom." He returned to the food bags and pulled more containers out. "Also shrimp cashew and spring rolls."

"That's brilliant!" she said.

"So you like shrimp cashew?"

"I'll show you what I like."

They used the baby monitor first.

ROB FELL ASLEEP the next afternoon face down across the bed, wearing only his boxers, the baby monitor on the floor at his fingertips. He woke to the sight of Kay's legs, sporting several spots of mural paint, extended from the towel-draped chair she'd pulled up next to the bed.

"Don't move!" she ordered the instant he tensed his muscles to sit up.

"Why? What are you doing?"

"Don't move. If you turn around, I'll be seeing your front, and right now I'm sketching your back."

"Ah-hah. You're sketching."

"Yes, Mr. Know-It-All, I'm sketching and it's my first attempt at anything serious since I was a kid and it's not half bad and I'm enjoying it, so hold still."

"That's all I wanted to hear. Was that so much to ask?"

He kept his torso still, but twisted his head to look at Kay. And Rob Dalton, who thought things through, who weighed risk and reward, who always had a plan, knew that, despite thought, risk, or plan, he loved her.

"HEY KAY, IT'S Serge."

Kay answered the phone in the kitchen, expecting another call about the opening, not one from the video producer.

She glanced toward Rob, who was putting away sandwich-makings in the refrigerator, and went to the sunroom as the voice on the phone continued.

"Where are you? I lost your cell number, but I'm in the city and called your place and got some guy who said you weren't living there any longer. Didn't sound like one of your fans."

"No, I'm not living there anymore." Where she would be living after the middle of next month she didn't know and, right now, didn't particularly care.

"Shooting anything?"

"No."

"Good, good. I might have something for you down the road. No promises, you understand."

Her sketchpad propped against the chair snagged Kay's attention. She had smiled as she'd shaded that narrowing at Rob's waist. The lines of his back were so beautiful it made her eyes sting. "No promises."

"That's right, but I've shown some people your work. How about lunch next week?"

This was it. The opportunity she'd aimed for. The next step in her plan.

Why didn't she care?

"Next week won't be good, Serge." She leaned against the door-jamb to the garage. "Let me call when I know I'll be around."

"Don't tell me it's that guy I saw you making out with on the tape that's keeping you there." He laughed. She'd totally forgotten they'd shot her kiss with Rob. "Well, don't wait too long. I've got people who want to meet you. I think they'll like your work, too."

"Thank you, Serge. That's great to hear." She just wanted to get him off the phone.

"Even Donna liked it," Serge said, "and that's saying something."

"That's great, Serge. Great."

Kay turned and there was Rob, watching her from across the room.

She didn't remember precisely how she wrapped up the conversation—although she knew Serge had to remind her to take his phone number.

"You want something to drink?" she asked as she passed Rob on the way back to the kitchen.

"No thanks. Good news?"

"Uh, yeah. The producer likes the B roll of the wedding in Bliss House."

"That's great. You're going to make us famous in Tobias. They'll shoot movies here like they do in Toronto, huh?"

The twist in her chest was entirely unexpected. But so was the certainty that his *us* had not included her.

She laughed. It sounded forced. "I wouldn't count on it."

"He wants you in New York?"

"Well…"

"Make you a job offer?"

"Just wants me to meet a few people."

"That could be a great opportunity."

She looked at him across the kitchen counter. "Yeah. A great opportunity."

ROB STOOD IN the bedroom he'd occupied throughout his childhood and all but the last few days of this summer.

Until was over.

He'd told Kay he needed to get back to Fran's house. Neither of them had said anything about why. They both knew why.

And they both knew their bubble of time had ended. The phone call from her producer hadn't burst it so much as evaporated it.

He jerked the closet door open and took a briefcase from the back.

He'd already delayed this to have these few days with Kay, these days detached from reality.

On the desk, he carefully laid out the briefcase's contents. He opened his laptop with materials already organized for transmitting. He punched in the phone number he'd spent all summer wishing he would never have to call.

"My name is Rob Dalton, I believe you're expecting a call from me."

He had to do this.

He had to do this now.

ROB PUSHED OPEN the plastic sheeting that cut off their painting room from the world.

Kay felt the instantaneous heat right through to the soles of her feet. She wanted to wrap herself around him, to feel his weight and warmth.

Even though he'd only left this morning, she missed him.

"What do you think?" she asked, gesturing at the mural. "We're almost done."

"It's fantastic. Amazing." He was looking at her. "Kay, can you take a break?"

Kay looked over her shoulder to her grandmother. Dora had been watching him, but now she shifted her eyes to Kay, and her expression softened. "Of course, you go ahead."

Rob had withdrawn after Serge's call almost as surely as she had after asking him not to blow the whistle on his company. Neither retreat had gotten them anywhere.

But she doubted standing there and talking until doomsday would have gotten them anywhere, either.

He was going to report the wrong-doing. He couldn't be Rob and do otherwise. And she couldn't shake this gut-gnawing sensation.

He guided her to the bench set into the patio wall.

"I brought Chester and the puppies over to Miss Trudi's for her to look after while I'm working. You're right—the wagon worked perfectly. I just put the box with the puppies in it, their supplies, and

Chester walked along—"

"Kay. I called the authorities this morning. It won't be known publicly for a few more days, but it's started."

Her stomach took a sickening plunge. *It's started.*

"Oh."

His mouth twisted, not quite a grin. "You usually have more to say than that."

"I don't know what to say, Rob. I know you think you're doing what you have to do."

"It's the only thing I can do."

She blinked at the burn in her eyes, breathed in through her mouth to try to steady her stomach. "I know it is. But…"

"I know." He leaned forward, his forearms slanted across his knees, one hand cupped inside the other. "Maybe down the road when this is over…"

She shook her head numbly.

"You deserve a woman who'll be with you through this." She stood, her knees weak. "I can't, Rob. You deserve someone who can."

KAY CURLED UP on the sofa in the sunroom. She couldn't even look at the recliner.

She'd told Dora she wasn't feeling well, gathered Chester and the puppies, came back home—no, this wasn't her home, it was the Hollands' home—and threw up.

She hadn't been sick this frequently even in the weeks before she called off the wedding to Barry. She hadn't been sick this frequently since … A long time ago.

Chester got out of the whelping box and stood in front of her, her tail wagging tentatively. Kay buried her head in her arms so the dog couldn't see her face.

Chester bumped the crown of her head with her nose and made a question out of a sound that was part cry, part moan, part growl.

"You can't make me feel better, Chester," Kay said. "I'm going to

disappoint you when I go back to New York, just like I'm disappointing Rob because I can't be part of what he has to do. And if you make
me feel better now it will make me feel worse later."

The dog made that sound again, then Kay felt the cushion sink and
rock. She popped her head up. Chester circled with precision in
approximately six square inches of space between Kay's calves and the
back cushion, then laid down, resting her head on Kay's hip, and
looking at her.

Tears slid down Kay's cheeks and fell off her chin. But she did feel
better.

"I love you, Chester."

There, she'd said it out loud. To a dog. But it didn't feel stupid, it
felt good.

"And you love me."

Chester whined in what could only be agreement.

This dog loved her. Unconditionally. She hadn't believed it when
Chester showed up in her life, she'd been afraid to believe it.

She'd come to believe love just wasn't for her.

As much as she'd tried to win it, her parents had never truly given
her love. As much as she'd tried to will it, the man who'd asked her to
marry him certainly hadn't loved her. As much as she'd tried to find it,
her varied jobs had never made her feel loved.

Even Dora ... *Oh, Kay, sweetheart, I should have fought for you. And
that's my shame and my regret.*

But in these few weeks in Tobias, Kay had felt love and she had
loved.

"I love you, Chester, and somehow we're going to be together.
Somehow. I promise."

The tears came harder now.

Why couldn't she have said those words to Rob?

KAY DABBED DARK paint to shade a rosebush cane. Too bad there
wasn't more black to paint on this mural. She should have included a

section of the gardens at night. That would have matched her mood. Swirls of black and gray and brown, tumbling into each other, overlapping, running in circles. Like her thoughts.

"Damn!" Dora dropped her brush, it hit at an angle on the bench, flipped end over end, swiped down her work pants and landed on the plastic-covered floor.

"What's the matter?"

"These damned useless hands. God, look at this mess—" She jabbed her cramped hand at a clump of gold and orange mums. "I don't know how you'll be able to fix this."

"I haven't fixed anything you've done. I haven't had to. I like it the way it is."

Dora snorted. "No one would ever believe those half-formed swirls were Dora Aaronson's work."

"Maybe it's time to stop worrying about Dora Aaronson's work, then."

"What on earth does that mean?"

"That is beautiful work, Dora. Beautiful. Just because it's not how you used to work doesn't change that. Forget what the art world might say. Forget expectations. Forget everything but how it feels."

"Can't you see the shading isn't—"

"Perfect? So what? How could anything be more wrong than you not painting?"

"How can I paint with hands like this?"

"Maybe not in any way you've painted in the past, but—" An idea, brilliant and terrifying exploded across her mind. "Dora, I have something I want you to try," she announced as she pulled out her cell phone and got busy.

Twenty minutes later they pulled into the drive of Annette and Steve Corbett's house in a car borrowed from Suz.

As arranged, Kay led Dora around back, where Annette had easels and paper. Nell waited for them. Dora stopped when she saw the set up.

"What is this?" she demanded.

"This is finger-paint," Kay said more calmly than she felt. She was trying to convince an American treasure artist to finger-paint for heaven's sake. "We're going to finger-paint with Nell."

"This is absurd, I am not going to—"

"Knew she wouldn't," Nell said. "She's a grandmother."

Dora's indignation seemed to evaporate with her quick-drawn breath.

She held up her gnarled hands to Kay. "How can I? I can't hold a brush properly with these hands, how can I paint with them directly?"

"That's what we're here to see. Forget your expectations, forget what you could do before. You can't paint as you did, but that's not the only way to let that urge that's inside you out," Kay said. "If you can't find a style of painting that works, we'll try other media—I have a little experience with trying something new when the previous plan didn't work. But I recommend we start here."

It was like their relationship—they couldn't go back to how they'd been years ago any more than Dora could go back to her controlled brushstrokes. But they could find a new relationship, as Dora could find a new expression for her creativity.

"We?" Dora asked almost meekly.

"We."

"Are we going to paint?" Nell demanded.

Without looking away from Dora, Kay said, "We're going to paint."

She and Nell dug into the pots with gusto. Kay tried her best not to watch Dora, but she knew the moment her grandmother dipped two fingers in the green and smeared it across the white paper.

Nell chattered about school and the mini tablet with a video camera included that she was sure to get for her birthday in November, with an Academy Award soon to follow. Kay felt a pang that she would not get to teach Nell how to capture moments and tell stories with that camera.

Dora stepped back from her easel, staring at Kay's, Kay had barely noticed what she was creating. She'd been concentrating on stealing glances at the broad swaths of greens and blues flowing across her grandmother's page without letting Dora know she was being watched.

But now she focused. Orange dominated her work, an impressionistic image of a man in orange … an orange prison jumpsuit.

"Hey, Dora," Nell said, tearing both women's attention away from Kay's painting.

Nell was peering at Dora's work. "That's neat!"

All three of them looked and saw that Dora's gnarled fingers had added a texture and depth to her painting that the others lacked.

Dora tipped her head and considered it. "Yes, it is. It's neat."

"ROB, WHAT'S GOING on?"

Rob tore off the top sheet of his legal pad, folded it and slid it in his wallet. He'd finally been able to write a pro-and-con sheet. First one this summer.

Fat lot of good it did him.

"Sit down, Fran. I have a long story to tell you."

CHAPTER TWENTY-FIVE

K AY DIDN'T FOOL herself that Dora Aaronson was going to take finger-painting seriously, but she hoped this experiment would open up possibilities for her grandmother.

"It's my responsibility that he is the way he is," Dora said abruptly, nodding toward the backseat, where Kay's painting lay.

Kay turned off the car in the Bliss House driveway. She didn't know what to say. She didn't know what she could say. She felt hollow, the adrenaline of pushing her grandmother into trying finger-painting drained into emptiness.

"I know you don't want to talk about this, Kay." Her grandmother hesitated, as if waiting for Kay to refute that statement. She couldn't. Dora sighed. "Come, let's get back to work. We're so close to finishing, and you and Nell have inspired me."

Kay produced a smile, but as she and Dora pulled on their paint clothes and returned to their plastic room, the hollowness threatened to overwhelm her. After all these years, they couldn't talk about what really happened? *She* couldn't talk about it?

And if she couldn't, would the scars ever truly heal?

Kay dabbed cerulean blue onto the lobelia Dora had painted in the front border, but the image that held her thoughts remained her painting of a man in prison-jumpsuit orange.

She remembered one blustery March day sitting in the prison visitors' room waiting for her father to arrive. She hadn't been listening to the conversation at the next table until familiar words caught her attention.

If I hadn't done it, someone else would. How many times had she heard her father say that? *If they didn't want to buy, I couldn't sell.*

Slowly, she'd turned her head and looked at the speaker. Not her father, but a grizzled stranger in the same prison garb he wore. Saying the same words, making the same excuses.

A criminal. A dishonest man.

That March day, she'd dropped a gate in front of those thoughts, letting them go no farther. But not today. She let them take the final step.

A criminal. A dishonest man. Like her father.

This was the cliff, the precipice she'd avoided since she was thirteen. Now she'd gone over it. Seeing her father as he really was. For the first time.

Even as she'd grown up and accepted on the surface who her parents were, underneath she'd clung fiercely to the dream that they could be different, that their family could be a real family. She'd nearly married Barry in an effort to preserve that fantasy.

She'd long refused to see her father's guilt for the same reason.

It was what had kept her away from Dora, because loving Dora threatened the fantasy.

She couldn't have Dora in her life as long as she maintained the myth that her grandmother had betrayed her father. She'd *had* to believe Dora had betrayed him, because otherwise it meant he'd deserved his punishment. Making him face the consequences of his actions wasn't betrayal, it was justice.

There'd been another threat to the fantasy—those reporters and their questions. Questions she couldn't answer, couldn't even think about, because if she thought about them she would know…

She would have to face her father's guilt.

They'd become her nightmare, those questions. A nightmare that had made her sick every day for months as a thirteen-year-old. They had resurfaced just a few days ago, when Rob had posed the final threat to her fantasy.

Yes, Rob posed the greatest threat.

Because he was a good man, a man determined to do the right

thing. A man offering her love and support and acceptance. All the things her parents had not given her. To see Rob as he really was showed them as they really were and ended the hope that her family would ever be a real family.

"Kay?"

She swung around, startled by her grandmother's voice.

"Are you okay, dear?"

"Wh—Yes. Fine. I'm … fine."

"Do you love him?" Dora asked quietly.

"Yes."

"Then why…?"

"It's complicated." Her throat closed, tears flowed. But her stomach didn't flip.

Dora wordlessly handed her tissues and a glass of water.

After a long pause, her grandmother's voice came softly. "In a life as long as mine, with as many twists and turns as mine has had, I don't know if it's possible to avoid regrets. Certainly I regret not being a better mother to your father, not raising him to be a better man and father. I regret not fighting for you. But in my heart, the largest regret is that I didn't say yes to your grandfather when he asked me to marry him."

Kay turned to her, her eyes burning with unshed tears.

"Not because of the name, or even how your father felt about not having his father's name," Dora said. "Whether we married or not, I wouldn't have this regret if I had told Paul yes right away, so that he knew, not just that I loved him, but that I appreciated how much he loved me.

"Loving someone can be the easiest thing in the world, but sometimes allowing one's self to be well-loved takes a great leap of faith. Some people need to be pushed into that leap. I was one of those people."

Kay stared at the mural.

Her own words of advice to Dora came back to her. *Forget everything but how it feels.*

"What are you thinking, dear?" Dora patted her hand. Kay turned her hand over and gently clasped her grandmother's.

"I'm thinking about a man who needs to allow himself to be well-loved. And about going over cliffs."

She had to talk to Rob.

"I'M SORRY, KAY, Rob's not here. He's out sailing. Said it was his last sail before he goes back to Chicago. He told me what he's going to do—finally. And he told me about your past and—"

"I've got to find him, Fran. I've got to find him now."

There was silence on the other end of the phone for a moment, then Fran said, "Give me your cell number. I'll call around, see where he is on the lake."

"Thank you, Fran."

"And Kay? When you find him, make him show you the pro-and-con list he's carrying around with him."

"I will. Thank you, Fran. Thank you so much."

THE DESULTORY BREEZE wasn't offering much of a sail, but at least he had to keep his mind half on what he was doing. And that meant half his mind wasn't thinking about what happened next, or about how Fran's eyes had filled with tears when she asked, "Why didn't you tell me sooner, Rob?" or about Kay.

Only a little over three weeks until the opening, then Kay would return to New York. She'd be gone when he returned to Tobias for good, though he doubted there was a corner of his hometown that didn't hold some memory of Kay for him now.

"Rob! Rob!"

He twisted around. That sounded like Kay. But…

It was Kay. Standing at the end of Max and Suz's pier, waving and calling.

Without the wind behind him, he tacked the boat toward her, a zig-zag path that seemed to try her patience. She gave a hop, then ran back down the pier to the shore, shed her shoes on the bank and waded in. The water was halfway up her thighs when he reached her.

"What's wrong?"

"Nothing. Help me get in."

He helped her crawl in the boat without either of them getting too much wetter or sinking the boat.

"If you'd waited a couple more minutes, I would have gotten to the pier and you could have gotten in without getting wet."

"I don't mind getting wet. And I couldn't wait, I had to tell you."

"Tell me what?"

She opened her mouth, closed it, then blurted, "Chester taught me about love. How to give it and how to get it. Chester and Dora."

"Kay—?"

"I love you, Rob."

He sat back, feeling as if a wind had just caught him and swirled him around in the air like a leaf.

But that leaf had to come back to earth sometime.

"I love you, too, Kay. But—"

"No buts. I love you and not only do I believe in what you're doing, I'm going with you."

"I don't—"

"I've learned from you, Rob. After all these years of not questioning what happened, I've been thinking. Thinking and talking with Dora. And then something happened today. You could say I painted myself an epiphany. What it comes down to is I understand what you're doing. I support you. I'm proud of you. We'll get through this together. So when do we leave for Chicago? I'll have to find someone to take care of Chester and—"

"Now wait a minute, Kay. You can't just come out here and say you've changed your mind and now you're coming with me—"

"Why not? Although, actually I haven't changed my mind. I just started listening to my heart and not listening to childish fantasies."

"But things haven't changed, Kay. I'm going to be tied up with this investigation for a long time. I might have to testify. And there's still the fact that my career's over. There's no reason for you to go through this. Once things settle down and—"

She leaned forward and kissed him. Lips touching lips. That was all. He kissed her back, capturing her bottom lip between his, taking in her taste.

His hands grasped her shoulders, pulled her to him, brought her onto the seat beside him.

"Oh, Rob, don't you understand? I wouldn't care if you were selling pencils on the street." She grinned. "Although the fact that you're going to live in Tobias is a definite point in your favor."

He shook his head, even as his hand smoothed over the wispy ends of her hair. "Kay, there's going to be media attention. They could dig up the story about your family. I won't let you make that kind of a sacrifice. For what?"

"For you. But I don't think it will be such a horrible sacrifice. I finally figured out the reason those reporters upset me so much was because their questions were pushing me to recognize my father's guilt. But I could take on every reporter in the country now, because you're doing what's right. And I love you."

"I don't want you caught up in something and then be miserable because of me." He shook his head. "This has been too fast, too intense."

"Like something we can't control. Something that's bigger than us." She smiled, yet there were tears in her eyes. "You don't trust it because it's not something you mapped out or worked for, Rob. But that doesn't make it less real. I wish I could make you—" She leaned closer, so he had to look at her, see her. "It's like the wind."

He opened his mouth. She spoke over him.

"Yes, exactly like the wind. And sailing. You don't work for the wind when you sail, Rob. It certainly doesn't appear according to some plan. You take it when it comes and make the most of it and enjoy it. You don't mistrust it. You accept it. And you adjust so it will fill the sails. That's what our feelings for each other are. Something you can't control, can't predict, can't schedule. But you're a talented and patient sailor and if you work with it, you—*we*—can get wherever we want."

"Kay, it's because of how I feel about you that I want you to go back to New York. It's the sensi—"

"It's not sensible or reasonable for us to be apart. It's insane. You have to let me love you."

"When this is over—"

"You listen to me, Rob Dalton. The worst thing I can imagine is not being with you." Abruptly, she sat up straight. "Show me the pro-con list."

"What?"

"The pros versus cons list you wrote up. Fran said you had one and to make you show it to me."

"I don't—"

"Rob, if you show me that list, I'll stop arguing with you."

He reached into his back pocket for his wallet.

Just before he unfolded the list, he wondered if he was doing this because he hoped to win this argument or lose it.

Kay's hands trembled as she read the sheet.

"Oh, Rob … Oh, Rob…"

Clutching the paper in one hand, she put her other arm around his neck and kissed him.

He could do nothing but pull her to him and kiss her back, because that sheet of paper told the whole story.

Under the heading "Propose to Kay" one side carefully listed all the logical cons, from her parents' certain disapproval to his uncertain future to the necessity of waiting until the investigation ended to win her. The other side had a single word: Kay.

And beneath it, he'd written, "Pro wins."

KAY SAT PRESSED against him in the car she'd borrowed from Suz to track him down, wrapped her arms around his neck and prepared to pick up where they'd left off.

They'd brought the boat in only because Rob finally noticed it was nearly dark. If they ever stopped kissing, he was going to take her back to the Hollonds' and up to that bed in the guest room and…

He held her off one second. "I've been thinking—"

She groaned, and he grinned.

"You borrowed me to play a groom in a pretend wedding at Bliss House. How about making it the real thing?"

"Oh, Rob…" Her voice shook and her eyes glistened. "It's not sensible or planned out or reasonable—that's the most wonderful thing you could ever say to me."

"Is that a yes?"

"That's a definite yes."

She stretched up, he bent his head, and their mouths met.

Kaboom!

THE BLISS HOUSE committee and the mural artists, along with a canine guest of honor, stood in front of the mural in Bliss House, toasting its completion.

"We're so sorry you won't be able to be here for the opening, Dora," Fran said.

"I wish I could be, but I've had this trip to France planned for some time and I have commitments there. But I will be back." She smiled at Kay, who stood snug in the curve of Rob's arm. "For the wedding."

They had told only Dora and Fran, but the news didn't appear to come as a big surprise to anyone else, though it did seem to please them all.

After another round of champagne and enthusiastic congratulations and hugs, Annette asked, "So are you going to be okay living here in Tobias, Kay?"

"Are you kidding?" Rob said. "It's one of the conditions of getting married. I don't think she'd take me, otherwise."

Grinning, Kay kissed him. "As long as we stay in Tobias, you'll never have to know."

"But what about your film career?" Steve asked. "I heard the producer was hot on your video."

"I've realized that I'd much rather teach all the skills I've learned than be limited to doing just one of them myself. It turns out my varied resume is the perfect background for one particular job—teaching all kinds of art here at Bliss House. If you'll have me."

"Are you kidding? That's fantastic!"

After a quick discussion of how courses in mobile-making, video-making, sculpting, drawing, and painting in several media would work into Bliss House's offers, Kay wrapped up with, "So we'll go to Chicago first, then after the wedding here—"

"You're getting married here?" Suz asked. "I would have thought New York."

"I wouldn't think of having our wedding anywhere but Tobias. In fact, we're going to have the wedding right here in Bliss House. I thought we'd recreate when we met, with Rob in that old-fashioned suit and—"

"No way. I love you, Kay Aaronson, but I'm not getting married in that suit—and you're not dyeing my hair, either."

While everyone else chuckled, Miss Trudi Bliss sighed with the air of someone who'd completed a difficult but worthwhile task.

"A wedding is exactly what Bliss House needs."

Thank you for reading Rob and Kay's story!

Bad boy Zach returns to Tobias, where relief at knowing he's okay after years of absolute silence is complicated by what his arrival means to those he left behind. A daughter who is still absorbing the news that her beloved Daddy isn't her biological father. The brother obligated to clean up his mess. And Rob's sister Fran, the girl-next-door who watched Zach's rise and fall from afar.

Even when they were kids, Fran saw beyond Zach's bravado to the pain in his sparkling baby blue eyes. Time has changed him. And, unlike when they were young, she's now grabbed his attention. Can Zach and Fran escape the past's hold to make a future? Can his fractured family forgive him?

Baby Blues and Wedding Bells

Annette, Steve, Nell, Miss Trudi, Zach and friends ask if you'll help spread the word about them and the Marry Me series. You have the power to do that in two quick ways:

Recommend the book and the series to your friends and/or the whole wide world on social media. Shouting from rooftops is particularly appreciated.

Review the book. Take a few minutes to write an honest review and it can make a huge difference. As you likely know, it's the single best way for your fellow readers to find books they'll enjoy, too.

To me—as an author and a reader—the goal is always to find a good author-reader match. By sharing your reading experience through recommendations and reviews, you become a vital matchmaker. ☺

For news about upcoming books, as well as other titles and news, join Patricia McLinn's Readers List and receive her twice-monthly free newsletter.
www.patriciamclinn.com/readers-list

Marry Me Series

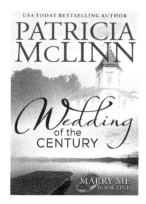

Wedding of the Century

Annette's a working-class bride. Steve's a well-to-do groom. Their botched wedding is only the start of their storybook romance.

The Unexpected Wedding Guest

At his sister's wedding, Max's eyes lock on her best friend, Suz, who years ago had a girlish crush on Max. When the wedding celebration leads to unexpected passion, neither knows what will happen next.

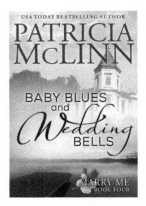

Baby Blues and Wedding Bells

Bad boy Zach returns to Tobias, where he is a stranger in his own town, to his own daughter. But perhaps not to Fran, the woman who really sees the man behind those sparkling blue eyes.

What people are saying about the
MARRY ME series

"Set in a perfectly realized and perfectly charming small town, McLinn has created two beautifully written, richly emotional love stories that are a joy to read."

—*John Charles, American Library Association*

"Gifted Patricia McLinn has written another wonderful series filled with emotion and romance."

—*CataRomance Reviews*

"Once again author Patricia McLinn pens an evocative and powerfully told tale [in *Wedding of the Century*]. The secondary cast also dazzles, especially Steve's precocious daughter. Fans will eagerly anticipate the sequel."

—*C. Penn, Amazon review*

Also by Patricia McLinn

Seasons in a Small Town series
What Are Friends For? (Spring)

The Right Brother (Summer)

Falling for Her (Autumn)

Warm Front (Winter)

The Wedding Series
Prelude to a Wedding

Wedding Party

Grady's Wedding

The Runaway Bride

The Christmas Princess

Hoops (prequel to The Surprise Princess)

The Surprise Princess

Not a Family Man (prequel to The Forgotten Prince)

The Forgotten Prince

Wyoming Wildflowers Series
A Place Called Home Series
Bardville, Wyoming Series

Explore a complete list of all Patricia's books
patriciamclinn.com/patricias-books

Or get a printable booklist
patriciamclinn.com/patricias-books/printable-booklist

Patricia's eBookstore (buy digital books online directly from Patricia)
patriciamclinn.com/patricias-books/ebookstore

About the Author

USA Today bestselling author Patricia McLinn spent more than 20 years as an editor at The Washington Post after stints as a sports writer (Rockford, Ill.) and assistant sports editor (Charlotte, N.C.). She received BA and MSJ degrees from Northwestern University.

McLinn is the author of more than 50 published novels, which are cited by readers and reviewers for wit and vivid characterization. Her books include mysteries, romantic suspense, contemporary romance, historical romance and women's fiction. They have topped bestseller lists and won numerous awards.

She has spoken about writing from Melbourne, Australia, to Washington, D.C., including being a guest speaker at the Smithsonian Institution.

Now living in northern Kentucky, McLinn loves to hear from readers through her website, Facebook and Twitter.

Visit with Patricia:

Website: patriciamclinn.com

Facebook: facebook.com/PatriciaMcLinn

Twitter: @PatriciaMcLinn

Pinterest: pinterest.com/patriciamclinn

Instagram: instagram.com/patriciamclinnauthor

.

Printed in the USA
CPSIA information can be obtained
at www.ICGtesting.com
CBHW031055310824
13969CB00020B/363